The
Skeleton Crew

Andrew Swales

BLACK COCKIE PRESS

The Skeleton Crew

Published by Black Cockie Press

Copyright © Andrew Swales 2024

The moral right of the author has been asserted

Cover design © Natalie Muller 2024

Distributed by IngramSpark

Printed by IngramSpark

ISBN: 9780645489682

About The Author

Andrew Swales was born and raised in the north of England and has been living in Australia since 2011. He has spent more than 20 years working as a journalist for news outlets in the UK and Australia, and writing fiction whenever time allows. He lives in Naarm/Melbourne with his wife, young son and middle-aged cat.

Part 1: The Platform

October 2: Blackout +12 Days

She wakes in darkness. This is new. Before the comms blackout, ersatz sunlight would begin streaming from the ceiling panels at 6am, a false dawn triggered by the room, triggered by the platform, triggered by something else somewhere else, every signal connected and proper. The light would be weak at first, easing her in, then growing in intensity, peaking about 7am. She could appreciate the sense of normalcy this brought. Even before, reality had hung by a thread on the platform. Day following night, a still-turning world – that was one such thread. Now she wakes in darkness, and day arrives only at the flick of a switch.

The powder-blue walls are bare, the carpet tiles worn but warm underfoot. In the cramped bathroom is a porthole. Its plastic pane is milky and opaque, scratched and scorched by decades of salt spray. In the mirror next to it she sees a bag of bones, hard lines showing through flesh and fabric alike. Her back aches, it always does now.

'Everything falls apart so quickly.' She mouths these words, but does not give sound to them.

The platform still has power – light, heat and warm water. Small mercies. She brushes her teeth without paste and showers without soap. These are the day's first small reminders, were they needed, of the new world.

****

She leaves her room and follows a narrow corridor to the eastern stairwell, through a fire door that requires a two-handed heave. The air is colder on the other side. The wind finds gaps in bare steel walls, and whistles through and around the scaffold staircase. She hugs herself, rubs at her shoulders, and quickens her step. On the next floor up, back in stuffy warmth, is the canteen, three rows of Formica-topped trestles. In the serving hatch, Daws has left a pan of porridge, a jug of iced water. Some mornings they have had coffee. Not today, though – not for several days now. Their diet is pinched, stripped of flavour and colour.

The only other person in the room is Seule. He glances up from his meal as she enters. She nods, and the young man returns the gesture. For a moment he holds her eye, as though he is about to speak, to motion her towards him, but instead he returns to the quiet contemplation of his gruel. She takes a bowl, fills it almost halfway, up to a line scratched in the plastic – storeman Daws' carefully calibrated ration marker.

She returns to the stairwell, ascending again and emerging onto the admin deck – the top floor. Her clinic is at the end of another featureless corridor.

The porridge is lukewarm, but she scoops it down eagerly, scraping up every remnant, running a finger around the bowl. When it is done, she sits a while, rocking gently on her chair, staring into the empty container. Her stomach emits a gurgle of protest, a demand for more, but it isn't the hunger that preoccupies her; she has mostly learnt not to dwell on that. It is Seule – something in the wordless exchange, in eyes that seem to suggest this day has laid fresh weight upon him.

She flicks on her desktop console. When the antiquated system has warmed up, she opens the data log, a slew of audio files. The top one is dated four days previous. Her finger hovers over the screen for a second before she thumbs the file. From the speakers comes a click, a muffled scratch. Then a voice, Seule's.

'You're recording?'

'Yes, of course.' Her voice.

'Why?'

'It's normal procedure.'

'Normal?'

'For transparency.'

'Oh. Whatever.'

'It's force of habit, I suppose. That's how they get you. Normalisation: we used to warn each other against it, but –'

'Whatever.'

'That was a long time ago. Or it feels that way. Anyway, this is Kathleen Pardue with Robert Seule, communications operator, employee number …'

An irritable huff, then, '2574629.'

'Okay.'

'This is stupid. I'm not here for a … consultation. I just want some damn painkillers, or whatever you take for migraines.'

'Migraines?'

'Well, you're the doctor. Headaches. Blinding pain right behind my eyeballs.'

'I'm not a doctor.'

'Huh?'

'Medic. There's a difference, legally speaking. Never mind.'

'Right. Whatever.'

'How often do they come on, these headaches?'

'When I've been on comms. Afterwards.'

'Okay. How is that?'

'I don't –'

'On comms. What's it like? What do you hear? Like static?'

'Static? Only on the old kit, obsolete. On the proper channels, it's just silence. Silence and blank screens. Just … waiting.'

'Stressful.'

'I don't know. It's pointless. There's no connection. It's … hey, I'm no mental case.'

'Okay.'

'Can you make me better?'

'Maybe you should stop working on comms.'

'Duh. It makes no difference whether I'm on or not. But Porter won't have it.' Seule mimics the platform manager in pitch and broad, country accent, ' "We have to keep signalling, keep listening." It's stupid. No one's there.'

'I didn't mean we should stop altogether.'

Seule's voice becomes hushed, contemplative. 'No one's coming for us.'

'I do have painkillers. These are … quite strong.'

'Okay.'

'Actually, I'm not really sure …'

'What?'

'It's okay. I'll fetch them.'

There is a scraping sound, a shuffling, a thud, then her voice again, faint at first, gaining in volume.

'Do you have asthma, any other respiratory issues?'

'No.'

'Are you taking any other meds? For depression, or –'

'What!? No!'

'Okay, here. I've only a few left. Take one when you need. Make it a half, even. Take it, then rest. And maybe someone could help with the comms.'

'Porter does help, I suppose.'

There is another soft click as the recording ends.

It is the last file in the data log. Some day, she realises – in weeks, months, years, decades or longer – people will surely come to this place, by chance or design. They may be looking for clues, answers, and this is what they will find: Seule's headaches, abstract fears; the wrong prescription for the former, and no insight on the latter. She deletes Seule's file and thumbs the tile marked Audio Entry. A message appears: 'No connection! Record offline?' She responds in the affirmative, a red dot appears.

'This is Kathleen Pardue, medic. Employee number 24 … uh, 2467218. The dateline on this recording is correct. I will try to explain what has happened out here, as I recall it …'

Her mouth hangs open, ready to deliver. But nothing comes. She closes the data log, rises from her desk chair and crosses to the leatherette treatment bench. She lies there a while, wide awake, staring at the ceiling.

****

A knock at the door. She checks her watch, rolls her eyes. It is dead, disconnected, as it has been for a fortnight. The analogue wall clock, one of the old platform's oldest components, shows 9.30am. She rubs at her eyes, runs fingers through close-cropped, greying hair. When she opens the door, Porter is

9

looking away, down the corridor. He raises a hand to whoever is holding his attention, smiles weakly, then faces her. He seems almost surprised to see her there, as though he has forgotten knocking.

'Oh. Hey, Pardue. Can I come in?'

She gestures him to enter. Porter wheels Pardue's seat back from the desk and plants himself on it, leaving her to perch on the edge of the bench opposite. He eyes her empty bowl, grimaces. 'I hate porridge.'

'It fills a hole.'

'Well, almost. The meals were stingy enough here even before all this …' He frowns, then stands. 'Hey, I'm in your seat.'

'That doesn't matter.'

'No, no – come on now. I'm sorry.'

She is about to protest further, but he is already halfway towards her. She shrugs and swaps places with him.

Sitting on the bench, Porter's feet dangle well short of the floor. He stares into the corner of the room for a moment, removes his heavy-rimmed glasses and begins cleaning them with the hem of his sweater. 'I've lost the knack, I think. The social rules. Well, not rules, but … just, I don't know … not stealing someone's chair.'

'It's really not important.'

'No, well I –'

'How are you feeling, Porter?'

'Ah, tired, you know.'

'Hmm.'

Porter replaces the glasses, meets her eyes. 'But that's not why

I came.'

'No?'

'I wanted to know, have you seen Broz?'

'Not today. Yesterday maybe. Or was it the day before? I think perhaps I saw him in the canteen yesterday.'

'No visits then? He hasn't said … anything?'

'No. What's wrong?'

'Oh.' Porter's eyes fall to the floor again. He gnaws at the nail on his right index finger. Finally, he straightens and says, 'Well, he's gone.'

'Gone? Gone where?'

'Uh, over the side, I'm thinking. He was out on deck yesterday afternoon, I know that. I sent him to check the desal unit. No reason really – just trying to keep him busy. After that, well, now we can't find him. I've looked everywhere.'

'Another one.'

'Yeah. So, I'm really … oh, lord. I'm scared we've hit a tipping point here. I don't want it to go like this, you know?'

'The longer we're stuck here, the harder it's going to be,' she says. 'I suppose each person handles things differently.'

'I know. Is it despair? Have we reached that stage?'

'Everyone has their limit.'

'It's not right though, is it? I mean, it's not right. What can we do? We have to hang on. Don't we?'

'For what?'

Porter smiles ruefully. 'I don't know. It doesn't look so good, hey.'

'So …'

She leaves the word hanging, prompting him to respond, but Porter seems not to have heard. He hops down from the bench and says, 'I'll take another look for him. Staff meeting will be at …' He checks his watch – as dead as Pardue's. 'Oh, sure. Well, it's at 1pm. In the canteen. You'll be there?'

'Yes.'

When Porter has left, she lies down again, arms folded across her chest, an impression of repose. Only the tapping of her fingers betrays her disquiet.

****

At 11.45am, the intercom beeps. She rises, flicks on the mic.

'Hey, Pardue. It's Porter again.'

'Yes.'

'Could you come here, to Control? Broz has … turned up.'

'Turned up?'

'He's been found. I mean … his body, I'm afraid. It's snagged on one of the legs. Saria saw it. She's gone down to fetch him.' There is a crackle, breath rattling through the receiver. 'Have you got another bag, or something we could use?'

'I think so.'

Control has the look and feel of a ship's bridge, its half-dozen work stations arrayed against a grimy window that looks out over the main deck. The smell of grease and detergent clings to everything. When she arrives, Porter and Gill, the hulking, shaven-headed engineering ops leader, are donning fluoro coats. Seule is there too, a slight figure tucked away in the corner, huge headphones slung across grimy brown hair. He is hunched over the desk, back to the room, narrow chin resting in cupped hands.

It is not clear whether he is awake.

'I didn't bring a coat,' Pardue says. 'Is it very cold?'

Gill grunts. Porter crosses to a row of hooks behind Seule and grabs the last of the identical coats, its company branding faded, its waxy surface stained with oil. The collar comes up over Pardue's chin, the sleeves hang below her finger tips.

Gill grumbles, 'Fucking come on then.'

He throws open the external door, allowing an icy gust to tear through the room. He has to duck beneath the frame as he exits. Pardue braces, tries not to flinch as she follows Gill and Porter onto the steel landing and downstairs to the deck. They follow a narrow path beside a block of grey pipes and blank LCDs, then a tall, red silo. At the end they turn left and follow the eastward railing, where the gale swirls stronger still. They pass beneath the candy-striped arm of the crane, descending another set of steps to the cage lift, its cables whirring away. Porter peers over the edge.

'---- they come.' He is shouting, but still the first word is snatched from his lips and whipped away on the wind.

Saria's hooded head, a smooth black dome, heaves into view. The lift climbs level with the deck and settles with a clunk. She slides the gate aside, stoops, grabs Broz under the armpits and drags his body onto the deck. She steps aside without acknowledging her audience, and begins removing her dive gear.

Broz's torso and feet are bare, clothes torn away by the sea. His jeans have clung on, though, plastered tight to thin legs, held up by girlish hips. His skin is white and puckered, his lips violet. The only other colour is found in livid bruises near his neck and forehead.

'Bloody stupid ----- kid.' Gill wheels away, hawks and, working with the wind, gobs over the railing.

Porter winces, crosses himself.

Pardue kneels beside Broz and smooths chin-length blond hair back from his face. He really is a kid, 18 or so. In death he seems somehow younger. She tilts his head to one side, then the other. There are more bruises on the right cheek and behind his ear.

'Pretty sure --- dead.' Gill again. He hangs behind the group, hands in pockets, kicking his heels. '---- wrap this --.'

She ignores him, finishes her check, and rises creakily, pushing her right palm into the small of her back as she straightens. Porter looks concerned, opens his mouth to speak, but decides against it. Gill strides away, back towards Control. Porter watches him leave, then asks Pardue, '---- some help?'

'Yeah, it's ---'

Saria interrupts. 'I'll -- it.' She kneels beside Broz's body and rolls him roughly towards her, allowing Pardue to slide the bag underneath.

'We'll put --- in --- same shed,' Pardue calls to Porter as she works the bag's zippered edges around the young man's form. 'Go inside, I'll see --- back ------.'

****

When the body is stored she returns to Control, but there is no sign of Porter or Gill. She calls to Seule, 'How's your head?' But he is oblivious, ears sealed, eyes fastened on the deck and the sea beyond. She decides against disturbing him.

Back in the clinic, she again takes up her position on the bench. Not ten minutes later there is another knock at the door. It is Saria.

'Another visitor,' says Pardue.

'A bad time is it?'

'No, it's fine. Are you hurt?'

'No.'

'Okay. But you'd like to come in would you?'

'Yes, please.' Saria makes for the treatment bench. She swings her long legs up and lies flat on her back, just as Pardue had. 'Did I disturb you?' she asks.

'No.'

'But you were resting here.'

Pardue eases into her chair, says nothing.

'The bench is warm. It's quite comfortable up here.' Saria pats her palms against the cushion. 'More comfortable than the beds.' She purses her lips, whistles a few fairly tuneless bars. 'Do you sleep in here? Overnight?'

'No.'

'I would. I think it would be better for your back, too.'

'What would you know about my back?'

'I've noticed you struggling. I know what chronic pain looks like.'

'If I slept here, I'd never leave the room,' says Pardue.

'Hmm, you are in here a lot.'

'Are you keeping a check on me?'

'No. I just haven't seen you around much.'

'I've been maintaining the pretence of work as normal, I suppose. It wasn't much different before all this. I just wait here till somebody needs me. Still … that pretence slips a little when you're mostly bagging bodies.'

'Going out to get him – that was my first dive in forever,' says Saria. 'Honestly, I was quite excited. I suppose I really shouldn't have been, but –'

'How did you come to see him?'

'Oh, I was out on the helipad. I like to get outside sometimes, just to see the sky, the horizon. Consider the distance, whatever. It keeps the cabin fever at bay. I'm not sure why I was looking over the edge, though. Maybe I was looking for him, had some sense he was there. That would have been strange. But there he was.'

'You didn't know Broz well, did you?'

'No, not well.'

'You're about the same age. I wondered.'

'Right. I didn't much like him, actually. A bit of a creep, I thought. I suppose I shouldn't say that now. What a mess! I mean, if it was his choice – well, that's something. But ...' Saria clasps her hands and begins to twiddle her thumbs back and forth. 'It's funny how quickly you adjust, isn't it? I mean, one of us has died. I carried him, felt the weight of him. The dead weight. It's sad, I know it's sad. I feel it still. But all the same, I thought – oh, this is so awful – I thought about food.'

'More now for the rest of us.'

Saria hurries on. 'What do you think was up with Gill?'

'I don't know. He's squeamish, perhaps.'

'Hmm. You were annoyed with him, I could tell.' Saria pulls herself upright, shuffles back on her behind and leans against the wall. 'He had bruises.'

'Gill?'

'Broz. So ... he didn't drown?'

'Oh. His skull's fractured, I think. And yes, there are bruises, which might suggest injuries before death. I think. It's not really my field.'

'So …'

'So? You found him right under the platform, yes?'

'His sweater was snagged on the south-east leg.'

'So, he jumps, is swept onto the leg, cracks his skull. Maybe it kills him, maybe it knocks him out and he drowns. The fall alone could break bones. It's a hell of a drop.'

'Okay, but that –'

Pardue arches an eyebrow. 'You're launching an investigation?'

Saria laughs. 'No. I'm interested. This keeps happening. But I'm not there yet. Checking out, you know? Not even close. I wonder how someone could do that.'

'Who can say?'

'Things are going to get a bit wild, don't you think?'

'Wild?'

'Maybe it's already started,' muses Saria.

'What's started?'

'Oh, I don't know. How are you doing? You look quite strung out.'

'I do?' Pardue drags a hand across her hair, catches herself, turns the stroke into a scratch. 'Well, yes … I'm sure I do.'

'Do you smoke?'

'No. I stopped all that some time ago,' says Pardue.

'Porter does. Did. Vapes, I mean. He's out of juice. Yesterday, he was walking around, chomping on that empty stick until it shattered in his mouth. It made me wonder about his … stability.'

'I doubt nicotine withdrawal is his greatest concern,' says Pardue.

'But it's one more thing to contend with.'

'He'll cope, I'm sure. *You* seem in rude health. What's your secret?'

'I don't know. Maybe I'm descending from a greater height.'

'Ah. The arrogance of youth.'

Saria is quiet for a moment, then she replies, curtly, 'I didn't mean to offend or –'

'It's just some old saying. Maybe you were built for this. Cool in a crisis.'

'Do you think?' Saria slides from the bench and makes for the door. 'That's funny. I had thought the same of you.'

'Where are you going?'

'I think you probably want to be alone.'

****

She heads to the staff meeting, the all-hands that has become central to their new routine, its format a carryover from the old one. It used to be the two or three department heads up in Control; now they each attend the canteen with reports from their old or assumed roles, few of which have mattered beyond the word from communications – and each day that word has been "nothing". Nothing coming in, nothing reaching out. Still, the practice and its nod to normality stand as a barrier to the kind of collective breakdown that seems to advance on them with every day. Today, Broz will lead, and their agenda will have additional heft.

'Hey, guys, thanks for coming.' Porter is last to arrive. He flops down at the head of the trestle where Gill, Seule, Daws,

Saria and Pardue are waiting. His round face is flushed; sweat shines in the creases of his brow. He takes them in one by one. 'Uh, Dawsy, you already know about Broz?'

'Hmm.'

'Sorry. It's, um … I don't –'

'Hell of a way to go.' Daws stares impassively into the cradle created by clasped hands, liver-spotted palms. 'So they say.'

Seule rolls his eyes at Gill, but elicits no reaction.

'Yeah.' Porter offers a watery smile, drums his fingers on the table top. 'Should we take a moment, say something? Maybe all that can wait. I guess we can hold his body outside until … ah, anyway. Moving on, we –'

'Moving on?' says Saria. 'Is that it? That's all there is?'

'I don't know what else …' Porter seems to chase some thought or other around his mind, then shrugs. 'There's another pressing issue. The food situation is –'

'The end is nigh,' deadpans Gill.

'Well, yeah.'

'What's our status?' asks Pardue.

'We've about six days' worth, I reckon,' Porter replies. 'We seem to be going through it a bit quicker than expected. I don't know how. There's porridge still, crackers, odds and ends, mostly rice packs. Is that about right, Dawsy?'

'Yeah. But now we're six mouths, not seven. So we can last more than six days.'

'Oh … yeah.'

'And we'll go longer still if you cut it to one meal a day. I've told you before –'

'We'll be eating Broz at this fucking rate,' murmurs Seule.

Daws snarls at the teen. 'Hilarious.'

Seule's cheeks flash red, then he forces a smirk. 'I'm not joking, Pete-o.'

'No? I'll fetch you a cleaver then.'

'Hey, hey,' stutters Porter. 'This isn't helpful, not at all. Anyway, we were thinking … I mean, I was thinking of trying some fishing.'

Daws scoffs. 'What?'

'Yeah. What do you reckon? We'd have to knock some wire lines together somehow, hooks, I don't know, but –'

'These waters are dead,' says Pardue.

'For trawlers, yeah. That doesn't mean they're barren. You'd see poachers out here now and again.'

'Hmm, that's right,' concedes Daws. 'They were desperate, mind; a long way from home.'

'It sounds a bit crazy, I know,' Porter continues, 'But –'

'It's time to act,' interjects Gill. 'There's no question any more. We're up to our necks in shit here.'

'Well, yeah,' says Porter quietly.

'We'll fish, that might work. And we'll get the lifeboat ready.'

'Oh, I knew it.' Daws chuckles. 'Now that is crazy. What in hell makes you think …' He meets Gill's glare, holds it a moment, defers with a bitter smile.

'I think Gill's right,' says Porter. 'With Broz going like that. This is serious … um, it's the reality now. We have to face that or we're just –'

'We're sitting here waiting to die,' says Gill.

'So we just get in the boat and float home do we?' asks Saria.

Gill's cheek twitches. He makes to respond, but Seule beats him to it: 'What do you mean by "get the lifeboat ready"?'

'I don't know,' Gill mutters. 'A sail? Oars on it? Saria out the back paddling? Whatever it takes.'

'Right. It's just, we sail. Me and my father.' Seule shrugs. 'Nothing special, you know. Just dinghies. But I know how to sail.'

'Well, shit! Really?' Gill throws up his hands. 'Thanks for sharing. So, we strip it down, put a sail on it. We can manage that. You can drive it, sail it, whatever the word is. Me and Porter and you,' Gill prods a finger at Saria, 'can get it ready. We have materials here. We've got tools. It can be done. There's nothing to lose now.'

Saria offers a wry smile. 'Okay then!'

'What about the coast guard?' offers Pardue. 'We'd be sailing awfully close to Australian waters. Or KI Defence – they'd be no different. They'll think we're immigrants. They'll hit us –'

'That's not real,' asserts Seule, dropping the diffidence he had shown Gill. 'They don't really do that.'

'What? What do you think –'

'It's real, I've seen it.' Daws raises his hands, flicks out his fingers, mimicking an explosion. 'They light those boats up, kid. No questions asked.'

'KI Defence won't be there,' says Gill. 'If there was still a KI Defence, there would still be KI Energy – shipping and comms.' He shakes his wrist, his dead watch. 'There'd be a data connection. There'd be planes in the sky, choppers and drones coming from the island to find out why one of the last manned platforms has suddenly gone silent. And – hey, just possibly –

they would be looking for the eight people who came out here and were never seen again. We wouldn't be sitting here starving. For fuck's sake, I …' He puffs out his cheeks. 'Something has happened. Something real bad. It's not just us here. It's everyone, it's everywhere.'

'And you want to sail into the middle of it,' says Daws.

Gill bites his bottom lip, shakes his head.

'But what else can we do, Dawsy?' pleads Porter. 'What else can we do?'

No answer. Instead, Pardue asks, 'Will we eat again today?'

All eyes fall on Porter, who in turn looks to Daws.

'Fine,' Daws says, rising. 'I'll split the kid's rations. We can move to a single meal from tomorrow.'

He returns soon enough with a pan and six bowls. More porridge, but no one is complaining. They watch as he ladles it out. When he is satisfied the servings are equal, the pan scraped clean, he meets their eyes, invites comment or protest. There is none.

****

Pardue retreats to the clinic, sets the data log to record audio, and takes up her position on the bench.

'Six of us remain; I will attach staff files. Broz is gone; I'll compile a separate report on fatalities. We have decided our rescue is now … unlikely. So we will leave, take the lifeboat, take our chances.' She pauses, closes her eyes and allows the weight of that to settle. 'I wonder if this is the best course of action.'

She can, however, see a kind of cruel logic to it all.

When she was a girl, she had wanted to live by the sea. More

22

than a want, it was a dream, a fantasy, because from her inner-city block she had deemed it impossible. But then, nearing middle age – with her later, loftier ambitions flattened, and in search of a reset – she had reverted to that childhood wish. She made it come true – but only for a while. Perhaps it had offended her. Perhaps, after everything that had preceded it, her life there was a hollow victory, and undeserved at that. So she trashed it, abandoned it and cut herself adrift. From 'by the sea' then to 'on the sea' now. What next? In the sea, under it? Where else is there to go? In her darker moments, it seems almost inevitable, fated even.

Porter says they have no choice. That's been an old favourite of hers too, an oft-used crutch. I've no choice here: it's what she told herself when they strapped her into the chopper before her first rotation on the platform. Eight passengers across two rows of seats, pinned against each other from shoulder to knee. The others were young mostly, gruff types from ops and maintenance – tech and engineering contractors from Victoria or Tassie. Some nodded her a curt hello; most ignored her as they chatted and joshed and reacquainted after weeks apart. When the blades began to spin, the talk stopped, drowned out. The chopper rose slowly at first, straight up, an orderly ascent, before tilting forwards into its run, a fearsome burst of acceleration that put the modular, prefab city of King Island New Port at their backs, until all around was ocean, the vastness of the KI Energy Exploration Zone.

Some of the contractors slipped into sleep then, chins lolling against chests; hung over perhaps after Sunday-night farewells to friends, lovers. She couldn't comprehend how they slept. Her stomach churned with every drop and wobble along their turbulent path, and after a while she became certain she would vomit. She closed her eyes, tried to focus only on breathing. The thought of throwing up in front of everyone filled her with horror. She wanted to shout, 'This isn't me! I was in a war!'

She must have looked as bad as she felt. A man opposite put a hand on her knee, yelled across, 'Are you okay!?'

She opened her eyes and he offered a sympathetic smile. He was older than the others, and different in other ways. Short, plumpish, with a kind face, a bald crown encircled by dark, wiry hair. He shouted again to say they were almost there, and flicked his head, gesturing towards the front. She didn't understand, but then she saw the platform, little more than a dot in the distance. She nodded her thanks, took another deep breath, and began to think she might make it.

Then she fainted.

When they landed, she came to with the first jolt and almost immediately felt the blood flooding back to all parts – a brief, burning relief tinged with embarrassment. When the engine was cut she swallowed her pride and thanked the man again.

'It's nothing!' he told her. 'The first time I got on this damn thing I puked all over my lap and the two people either side. Imagine that!'

She never knew if that tale was true, but she was grateful for it.

'Are you uh … visiting us?' he asked.

'I'm the new medic here. I'm supposed to find a Mr Porter.'

'I'm a Mr Porter! Didn't anyone tell you? My god. Well, just Porter will do.' He thrust out a podgy hand. 'You must be … um … Parsons, no …'

'Pardue. Kathleen.'

'Uh … I must confess, I had forgotten you were coming, Pardue.'

He led her to Control, dropped his bags, then showed her the clinic, her dorm. Next, the full tour, the induction. They visited the communal areas, all on the middle floor, all painted in the same washed-out blue: the canteen and kitchen; a small rec room with brown couches and a pool table – one cue, no cue ball; the laundry; a gym of sorts. He walked her around the decks, pointing out complex machinery and equipment, the names and functions of which were immediately forgotten and remain lost to her. He tried to explain how the place worked: how oil and gas were pumped, stored, transported; how the facility generated its own power; how seawater was purified for drinking and bathing; so on, and so on, and so on, until she slipped into a waking sleep.

'We're completely self-sufficient,' he had told her, unaware of how quickly he would be proven wrong. 'Still, it's a clunky old thing. Brought down from Perth way during the rush. A retrofit job. There used to be dozens, scores working here. It's a skeleton staff now. We just monitor the machines.' There was no satisfaction in his voice, only sadness. After a moment, he added, 'They'll have this old place fitted up for full automation soon. I'm not sure we'll still be here in a year.'

That didn't worry her.

Later, she sat in the windowless clinic and waited, and wondered again about her decision to come: no choice? At dinner time she was hungry, but she couldn't stomach sitting alone in a communal canteen – or sitting communally in a communal canteen, for that matter. She went to bed hungry, and how that missed meal haunts her now.

She saw little of Porter after that. He would smile as they crossed paths in the corridors or the canteen, and he would stop to ask how she was. Then, before she could really answer, he would hurry away on some apparently urgent task, and she would chide herself for feeling slightly crestfallen. He seemed as overworked as she was under. Her days were spent alone, reading or dozing in the clinic.

That two-week rotation seemed to last forever. On the final day, ascending from the helipad, she peered out the window and watched as the platform grew smaller and smaller below: a cluster of irregular blocks painted in vibrant, clashing colours; thrumming machinery; stacked and striated steel; flashing lights and bursts of flame; steam like hot breath. All this atop four stumpy-looking legs that, in fact, go on forever. She watched the replacement crew, the A-shift, scurrying from a chopper that arrived as hers was departing. People in boots, jeans, jumpers, an unofficial uniform with a hint of prison issue about it.

October 3: Blackout +13 Days

Her morning shower is interrupted by a muffled, increasingly insistent thudding that she fails, at first, to recognise. Eventually, she wraps herself in towels and rushes to the door.

'Oh, Pardue, good.' Porter averts his eyes from her exposed shoulders. 'Um, you weren't answering. Got a bit worried for a minute.'

'Worried?'

'Well, you know –'

'It's fine. I was in the bathroom.'

'Clearly. Well, me and Daws are off fishing. I wondered if you wanted to come?'

'I've never been fishing.'

'We'll show you how it all works. It's just, I guess they might need me to work on the lifeboat too. And Dawsy could use the company, um –'

'I'll see you up there.'

'There's breakfast in the canteen. Eat first.'

She is the last to arrive in Control. Gill, Seule and Saria sit around a desk strewn with yellowing booklets and blueprints, pulled, presumably, from some long-forgotten corner of the office. Seule is sketching something on a tab, eyes narrowed, tongue poking from the corner of his mouth. Porter and Daws stand near the comms console. On the worktop before them are three reels of thin steel wire. Porter waves her over.

'No one on comms?' she whispers.

'Can't spare the manpower now. I guess we're all in on the boat project.'

'Is that a good idea?'

'Um, maybe I'll jump on comms later. Look, here's where we're at.' Porter points to the reels. 'See, we fix these to the railings, then drop the lines straight in, hooks at intervals. Saria can weld the reels on. Dawsy's fashioned the hooks. And these.' He picks up a condom; it is slightly inflated, weighted, tied off and adorned with thin strips of black tape. 'A lure.'

Pardue glances at Daws.

'I know, I know.' He grins, blushes, a rare flash of colour on grey cheeks. 'It's supposed to look like a squid, or a jelly. I don't know. It's an experiment. Or we have …' He produces another prototype, a bright orange bottle cap, bent to look like something vaguely crustaceous. 'These were easier to make.'

'It's got a chance, hey,' says Porter.

'Who knows. I've never used lures. If there's a current, bit of a swirl … I don't know. We could try bait too … but that's our food.'

'You've fished before then, you two?' asks Pardue.

'Heaps of times,' says Porter.

'Really fished?'

'What do you mean?'

'Killing it.'

'Oh! Well, I've never killed one actually. Illegal, eh. They always go straight back. I guess we … chop its head off, bash it in?' Porter swallows hard, scratches at his cheek. 'You know, I hadn't even thought of it. I'm not sure I've killed anything before.'

'I've killed them,' says Daws. 'Sometimes it's been the difference between eating and not. I'll go fetch a knife.'

'Ready then?' Saria is approaching. 'Oh, sexy lures! Nice work, Daws.' She flashes a mischievous grin, a wink, drawing another blush from the old man. She nods to Pardue. 'On the fishing party?'

Pardue offers a thin smile. 'So it seems.'

When Daws returns they wrap up in coats and hats, and take the reels out to the cage lift, Saria lugging the welder. A stillness has settled over the platform. Black clouds sag heavily; the air and ocean are becalmed. Porter and Saria enter the lift, but Daws lays a hand on Pardue's arm to hold her back.

'We'll need something to sit on,' he explains.

The other two nod and begin their descent to the platform's lowest floor.

'Is that what we do?' Pardue asks. 'Just sit and wait?'

'Pretty much. That's fishing.'

'Right.'

'Not your thing then?'

She shrugs.

'Well, that's fair. What is your thing, Doc?'

'I'm not –'

'Not a doctor. Yeah, I know that. Well, I'm not so qualified to cook porridge, but –'

'I like cricket,' she says.

'Cricket? Huh. Do you play it?'

'No, I only watch.'

'Okay … well, that's just sitting too. To each their own, I guess.'

She says, 'There are some old camp chairs in the shed over there.'

'There are?'

'I saw them in there yesterday.'

'Why were you in that place?'

'I put Broz in there.'

'Oh. Is he –'

'It's okay, you can wait here. I'll get them.'

At the shed door, she claps a mitt over nose and mouth. Inside, as the strip-light stutter-strobes into life, she sees Broz where she and Saria left him, against the far wall, wedged in below a shelving unit loaded with machinery parts, cans and plastic tubs. Next to Broz lies another identical black sack.

'How the bodies stack up.'

The fold-up chairs are piled neatly in the nearest corner. She scoops up three – two under one arm, one under the other – and shuffles awkwardly back outside, clattering against the door frame as she goes. She spills the load and drags the door shut behind her, and this final exertion takes its toll. Something spinal seems to loosen, to slide like a needle into the nerve. She drops with a wince to one knee, head bowed, teeth clenched. When the mini-spasm has passed, she rises stiffly, clasping her hands to her hips. She straightens her back, rubs at her tailbone, twists gingerly at the waist, blowing hard as she flexes the vertebrae.

Now Daws is approaching. 'Ah, hey, I'm sorry,' he says, quickening his step. 'I should have come. Are you hurt?'

'No, I'm fine. This is nothing – an old niggle. You can help me now.'

'Sure. I should have come, though.'

'It's fine. It's actually quite cold in there. I'm not sure it really smells. And there's nothing much to see, so –'

'Oh, no. It's not that I'm too soft for that sort of thing. It's just –'

'You weren't friends were you?'

Daws stoops to grab a chair. 'No, not friends. We talked sometimes, that's all. Or I talked. It's always the same with the younger ones – I just want to give them a shake, you know? Knock some sense into them. Pointless probably. I felt for him: second-generation deportee, family kicked out of WA when he was in mum's tum, and this is where he ends up, stuck out here doing odd jobs. I mean, an apprentice! An apprenticeship in what? Mopping? I told him, "You've got your freedom, more or less. Got your KI citizenship, got your youth! Go back to the island. Get an education, do something good, something important." Well, he reckoned he might join KI Defence. That is *not* what I meant. But hey, he was just a boy. Like I say, pointless. Who'd listen to an old screw-up like me?'

'Oh, I don't –'

Daws raises a hand, bats away the platitude. 'He reminded me of myself 40 years ago. They all do. Just dragged along by life. I told him, "Think! Be something. Do something. Do good things. Or you might wind up doing bad things. Bad things will be done to you." I don't know, even now I struggle to explain it. I guess he took control in the end. Not really what I had in mind either. We just let them down, don't we?'

'He wasn't your responsibility.'

'No, I mean all of us … and all of them, the kids. Like, I always thought I must've been born under a dying star or something. Bad times. Now I think, hell, I might be one of the luckier ones. Sure, half this planet isn't fit for living, but at least I was from the safer half. I've had most of my five-score, some of it good. But the younger folks, you know? Broz, Seule, they're innocents, really. And Saria. That girl, hell, she could've been anything. I mean it. But now … ah, anyway.' He snatches up another chair, hugs it tight to his chest. 'Come on.'

****

On the shadowy lower deck, Porter has picked three spots, equally spaced along the railing, for their lines. They settle behind the middle reel, facing ocean and the unseen coastline of King Island. Daws slumps low in his seat, pulls down his woollen hat and allows his chin to sink into his collar. Within minutes he is snoring softly.

Porter leans across to check on him. 'Poor old Dawsy. He doesn't do too well … in the night-times, I mean.'

'It's the hardest time.'

'Yeah. But he never *could* sleep. Not at night. Even before all this.'

'Oh.'

'Sometimes me and him go fishing together. Between rotations. Down at the jetty. Not much in there, mind. All he does is sleep, just like this. That's the thing with fishing though, I guess – no need to talk, no need to be awake even. The only thing that'll get him up is a bite. Then he's like lightning, you'll see. Hunter's instinct or something. Quick and smooth. To watch him, it's really amazing. And the care he takes. Handles them like

32

newborns, he does. Stroking and whispering.' Porter eyes the knife at Daws' feet. 'Um ...'

'I didn't know you two were close.'

'Oh, I don't know. We lodge near each other, both like to drop a line in. It just suits us, I reckon. I used to fish when I was a kid. Stopped when I was married. But after ... I guess I just invited myself along with him at some point. I get lonely, Pardue. And Kenno, well, he's –'

'Kenno?'

Porter frowns, questioning her question.

'I thought he was called Pete.'

Porter tuts, shakes his head. 'That's what Seule called him, is it?'

'Yes, but –'

'Lord, I tried with that boy. I truly did. He should never have been out here, that's the problem.'

'What do you mean?'

'Well, you know. Most people come out here because they have to. Even some of us bloody contractors: we need the work and no one else will have us. And then, well ... for folk like yourself ... um, it's this or a lock-up, hey. But Seule, his father works for the company. I mean, he's an executive, high up, King Island royalty. And daddy, in his wisdom, has packed his boy off for six months of graft before he gets stitched into a suit and tie for life. An internship on comms – easiest job here, not even a job really, because nobody was talking to us much even in the best of times; all the important chat went on between computers ... until they shut up too. Still, here he was, all part of the management pathway, I guess. Oh, it's not the boy's fault, I know that ... god, you can't help what you're born to. But try telling that to the other guys out here. The ops crew – well, they're a type aren't they. Hard to explain … best paid, worst manners. Just a mean bunch. All of them, except for Gill, funnily enough.' Porter casts his eyes around the deck, then leans in conspiratorially. 'He's more mad than mean, I always thought. And Seule, of course, he's another type. When he sat down in the canteen, they'd all get up and move to another table. They laughed at his accent, his clothes, his … body, his hair. And it was Gill who started it. He was calling him His Lordship. You know, old money. And that's all it took. It was like a … a declaration, a signal to the others: he's fair game, I'll wear the consequences, so you can pile on.'

'You tried to stop it?'

'Stop it? Well, I guess I had words with some of them, but what can you do? The ops team, like I said, they look to Gill, not me – old duffer admin guy. No, but I tried to be there for him, be a friendly face, you know? Someone to talk to in Control, to eat with in the canteen. Well, Seule found his own way in the end.' Porter peers under the rim of Daws' hat, ensures his eyes are firmly shut. 'He'd hate me for saying this: they used to pick on Dawsy too. Tried to, anyway. Someone, at some point, decided he was a paedo. Just like that – and it stuck. Crazy! So Seule started calling him Pete-o. At meal times: "Hey, Pete-o, no sausage for you today, Pete-o? Haha." Put-on ocker accent and everything. Dawsy, he just batted it away. He's past caring. I don't know why they picked him. Because he's old, I guess, because they thought him weak. Or he … represented something to them, something they hated. Truth is, it doesn't even matter, just so long as someone's taking the punches. Someone, anyone, soaking it all up. God, this cruelty; it seems ingrained now. Anyway, Seule understood the rules. After that he got to sit with the ops guys and Gill started using his real name.'

'Ridiculous.'

'Uhuh, that's right. I just wanted Seule to get through his time here and clear off, because I knew how fast it could all turn around again. Back on him. Do you know what he said to me the other week, before all this mess? He said, "I could see myself staying here." Reckoned he'd found his niche, I guess. Aiming a bit lower than his father, eh! I told him, "They'll get bored of Dawsy in the end. This place, it's not for you." You know, part of me thinks ... well, I look at this trouble we're in now and I just think, Ha, this is what you get. This is the real world, this is the life you came to see: struggling, then dying. Yeah, here's your life lesson. But I know he shouldn't have been here. I do feel bad for him.' Porter crosses his legs and begins picking at the seam of his jeans, worrying away at the golden thread near his inner knee. He has already created a thumb-sized hole in the stitching. 'Anyway, social cliques, bullying – what does all that mean now? Not a damn thing.'

For a while Daws' unconscious whinnying is the only sound between them, until Porter asks, 'What do you think is happening here?'

'I wish I knew.'

'Yeah. Actually, I'm not so sure I do want to know. When we pulled Broz out yesterday, when I saw his body like that, all I could think was, lord, how bad must it be? How bad must it be to jump? Oh, god. Did he see something I don't? That half-witted kid? It was all I could think about last night: how bad must it be to jump? How does that feel? Hope must endure, I suppose. It's natural enough that we try do something. The survival instinct and all. But if we make it back, then what? What's waiting for us there? I don't have anyone to run to – no wife, no children. And you?'

'No.'

'Thought not – I mean, there's nothing on your profile. What a happy crew we make. And I only learn that about you now! Questions like that – out here, we just don't ask them of each other, hey. Because deep down we know the answers, and it doesn't make for great conversation. Everything here is … surface. Mostly. I used to sit in Control and watch the guys working away on their consoles, or out here checking the machines. And sometimes, when my mind was wandering, when I was really just staring into nothing, I'd catch glimpses – something out the corner of my eye. Like I was seeing double. There was a second shape, an outline around each person: their own ghosts. Or the soul showing through. That's what I liked to think anyway: that there's *something* in each of us. The mind's a funny thing, hey. I don't know … when I look out over the ocean like this, I still think maybe I'm going to see something good. A ship, a chopper, something. But it's not happening, is it?'

'We're off the grid. Forgotten.'

'Or the grid doesn't exist now. Are you religious, Pardue?'

'Not really. I mean, no. I prefer … science.'

'Oh, yeah. In data we trust. That's fine. I was raised with the church. Faith is something else. Not always for the better, I know that, I've got eyes. But, you know, I've realised, there is goodness there. You just have to find it, take the message you want to take. Love thy neighbour, I say. That sort of faith, it makes sense to me. That sort of god. It's been the only thing keeping me half-decent, I reckon. Keeping me centred – alive, not just existing. Because you strike a deal: try to be good, and the pay-off is waiting. You know, Heaven. But there's downside too. Now I think, maybe this is it.'

'This is what?'

'End times. You know ...'

'Ah. But it's a little short on fire and brimstone.'

'Really? I don't know, all I've ever seen is fire and brimstone. Barrel bombs, phosphorous ... and that's just the man-made stuff. All across the world, every flood, famine, outbreak ... every blaze, every windstorm. More each year. All I see is fire and brimstone. What would you expect the end to look like – great fists descending from above? No. It's happening. Sargent knew it.'

'Oh.' Her eyes are drawn upwards, to the floors above them, towards the shed where the bodies are stored. 'Yes ... Sargent.'

****

As hunger weakens body and mind seeks respite, she sleeps too. When Porter rouses her in the late afternoon, they haul in the lines. She watches as the lures wobble jauntily up towards the deck. Daws stares accusingly at the water. He hums and haws, rubs at the silvery bristle on his jaw.

'Maybe tomorrow,' Porter tells him. 'Let's see how the others got on.'

Saria and Gill are in Control. They sit apart, no talking.

'Where's Seule?' asks Pardue.

'Bed,' grunts Gill. 'He's got a poorly head.'

'How did you get on today?'

'We've got a shitload of work to do.' Gill nods at Porter. 'We need you with us tomorrow. Daws can fish alone, I'd say. There's cutting, fixing to do.'

Porter mumbles his assent.

'So ...' she prompts Gill to continue.

'We'll put a mast up through the cabin, a boom comes off that. There's tarp for the sail. We've got the gear together, and that's all.'

'How long?'

'I don't know. We didn't get so far today. Bloody Seule spent most of the time doing sums. I hope his sailing's better than his damn –'

Saria cuts in. 'We can launch the boat tomorrow, bring it up here and fix it on the deck.' A sardonic smile plays at the corner of her mouth. 'Easy.'

'Yeah,' scoffs Gill.

'And the boat's engine, it's out of the question?' ventures Pardue.

'You know it is.'

'Right, I do know that, but I mean –'

'It's sealed in,' Gill continues. 'There's no time to jury-rig it, even if we knew how. And we sure as shit can't afford to break it.'

Pardue glares at Gill, pointed silence forcing him to meet her eyes.

'Please don't interrupt me,' she says finally. 'This is your idea, this is your project. And you seemed very confident yesterday. It would be good to see more of that.'

Gill holds her stare. 'The engine's a non-starter, so to speak.'

This declaration, far from revelatory, seems to hang heavy over the room. Daws sighs and leaves without speaking. Gill's eyes narrow as he watches the old man shuffle away.

'It'll work,' says Saria.

'There's no room for screw-ups.' Gill's chair skitters back

violently as he stands. 'Let's hope the old boy catches us some protein.'

As the door clatters shut behind Gill, Saria flashes a grin at Pardue. 'I don't think he liked that.'

Pardue smiles in spite of herself, then straightens and asks, 'Will this really work? It seems … unlikely.'

'Oh, it'll float. It'll steer. It has a compass, an actual one, magnetic. So … the sail? Who knows? Ask sailor boy. The currents are in our favour, I know that much.'

'If we hit storms, big waves?'

'What is it, mid October?'

'Early.'

'The Dry should start soon. Maybe it already has. It's been a while since it rained. I don't know. All sailors need the weather on their side, I suppose.'

'Like this,' says Porter, with a flick of the hand, a gesture taking them beyond the room, beyond the platform. 'Low and slow. It's all about pressure … in the air.'

Saria says, 'Are you sure that's how it works? Low? I think it's … oh, never mind. Low or high, when the food's almost gone, I suppose we go too.'

****

She stops at the clinic before visiting Seule's room. After a few knocks, he pulls the door open a fraction. His eyes are shot with red, and the acne that dots his face is flaring angrily. His mouth hangs open, snaps shut, as though he is disappointed to see her, had been hoping for someone else.

'I brought you some pills,' she says, handing him two aspirin. 'We're running out of these too, but I thought you could use them.'

'Okay.'

'For your headache.'

'Sure, sure. Are they like the others?'

'No. Those were moxodone, and I shouldn't really have ... I mean, these are probably better.'

'Oh, right. Okay then. The others were good. The moxo ... uh.'

'Moxodone. Yes. Have you taken them all?'

'I took the last one yesterday.'

'How did you go today?'

Seule sniffs hard. 'I didn't do much. What do I know about ... making things?'

'I meant, how did you feel today? Physically.'

'Today – bad.'

'Okay. Look, you shouldn't mind Gill.'

'I don't mind Gill. Why the hell would I mind Gill?'

'Did you eat this morning?'

'Of course. What are you, my mother?'

'No. I'm a doctor. Or I used to be.'

****

She wakes with a start to find Saria standing over her, a blurred figure, edges sharpening into focus. She reaches instinctively for the covers, to pull them up and over her exposed chest, but they are not there – they are under her body, pressed to the narrow bed, and she is fully clothed.

'I didn't hear you knock.' She rubs at her eyes, squints at the clock. It is not yet midnight. 'Why are you –'

'I didn't really knock,' says Saria. She sits on the bed by Pardue's feet, wriggles back to the wall, pulling her legs up flat before her, body forming a perfect L.

Pardue drags herself upright. Pain receptors sound off around her spine; through gritted teeth she asks, 'Why are you here?'

'I suppose … I just wanted to talk to someone.'

'But I'm shattered.'

'Today, I had to dive: down the north-west leg to cut some struts – for the boat project.' Saria shakes her head. 'Much harder than I'd imagined.'

'Hunger.'

'It's getting worse now. We're all spoilt, I suppose. Used to running on full … or near enough. Porter said we could go six more days, Daws said even longer. I think in two, three days, we need to leave. While we still have the strength.'

'Did you tell Gill that?'

'He knows. Oh, he got darker and darker by the hour today. Seule caught it.'

'What happened?'

'Gill bawled him out.' Saria tucks her chin in against her chest and mimics his low rumble. "Sort yourself out, think about what you're saying, bloody idiot. We can't do this, we can't do that, grah, rah, rah." And Seule cried.'

'Oh.'

'He tried to hide it, but I saw.'

'And you? You see the clock ticking, Saria. You lay it all out, matter of fact. But you don't seem afraid.'

'Well, I think I … we can make it back.'

'You do?' Pardue rubs at her eyes again, sighs. 'I've been trying to imagine it. Trying to imagine what it would be like: to get on the boat and to leave here; to be at sea; and then … in the water, waiting to slip under. I can picture it, but I can't feel it. It's just images, like scenes from a movie. It has no weight for me. Maybe, deep down, I don't think it'll really happen – us all sailing away.'

'Waiting to slip under?'

'You came to talk. I'm talking.'

'Sorry.'

Pardue ignores the apology, continues. 'This was only my second rotation here, did you know that? And I almost didn't come.'

'Oh. What would you have done instead?'

'Back to Melbourne. But in the end, I felt compelled to return here. After my first rotation, when I got back to King Island, it was like … ah, I don't know. Like something had changed. The bus left the landing pad, along roads I recognised, past the docks, industry, homes and apartments I'd seen before. But it was changed, like looking through a new lens, a filter that sharpened and dulled, brightened and shaded. And in the town … shuffling crowds and cars, they seemed full of menace. Dumb menace. Ugh. I was angry. Bloody sheep, sleepwalkers. Or worse – criminals, mercenaries. I got to my boarding room, hid under the covers. Next day, that lens had lifted, and the dread and disgust had dissipated.'

'Everyone has days like that I guess –'

'But that dissipation was disturbing, too. Because now I was crushed by lethargy. The day ahead, the little tasks, domestic chores, admin, life – it all seemed so utterly futile. I was just another sleepwalker. Not even that: I stayed in bed, counting off the minutes, the hours. I was grappling with something I'd felt before: I can't stay here. But the alternative … well, I just had to stick it out, to come back to the platform.'

'You think this was fated for you?'

'Sometimes I do feel like there's a pattern to my life. A course, downwards. Probably everything's just luck. But they say you make your own luck.'

'Who's they?'

'Oh, sports pundits mainly.' Pardue rolls her eyes. 'I'm not sure where they stand on bad luck.'

'I think, maybe this isn't the bad part, what's happening to us here,' says Saria. 'I mean, these days, safe enough on the platform – they might be the best of it. And travelling home, that's just build-up. But getting home...'

'Do you have family?'

'My mum.'

'You need to get back for her.'

'To the island? I don't know … she might not even be there now. We were in the processing centre together for a while. I got moved to Camp Beta, but her case got held up. Then I got my KI work visa, and last I heard she was still stuck in processing. We haven't spoken for a few years now.'

'Why?'

'Ha! Just … issues. Don't you know my surname?'

'No, actually. That's odd, given the naming conventions around here.'

'I refused to conform. My name is Khittar. Saria Khittar.'

'Okay.'

'KHITTAR! THE! QUITTER!' She flexes her fingers in the air before her, flashes to punctuate each word.

'I don't … oh, what, the swimmer?'

'Ta-daa!' Saria deadpans. 'You are in the presence of a star.'

'The Games. Singapore?'

'Uhuh.

'I saw it live, I think. Saw you dive in, straight down and just –'

'Never come up.'

'It was really something.' Pardue recalls the scene: the dive-start, a single swimmer plunging down as the others resurfaced and eased into their strokes; a flickering figure, cross-legged on the bottom, blowing bubbles to the surface; competitors speeding back and forth above and the crowd buzzing in confusion. 'You were in my mind, you know. For some time afterwards. I wanted to know why you did it. And then, I don't really –'

'It was just before the tsunami, Oregon.'

Pardue nods. 'Yes, that's how I remember. It was the symmetry, I suppose. You there in the pool, protesting or whatever, and the whole world going crazy over it. Then later, breaking news, bodies floating in Albany. I had no idea. I mean, no idea that was you.'

'Should've kept my mouth shut. I've changed since. Grown up, and down – shed a bit of muscle. Anyway, we got our notice to vacate not long after that mess – citizenship rescinded, report for transportation to Offshore Processing Facility KI. I don't think it was cause and effect … could've been though.' Saria sighs deeply. 'We didn't have any place of origin, so it was limbo for her, Camp Beta for me. I qualified for a training scheme, diving and maintenance, got my pass to work out here. A final break between us. We're done.'

'In the camp: what was it like to –'

'Oh, let's not. Please.'

'Ah. I quite admired what you did there, at the Games.'

Saria ignores this. 'I've been on borrowed time here. A bunch more drones arrived on trial about two months after I did. I spent most of my days here sitting at a console watching them do the work. Sometimes I'd try to make them crash: to skew the data, and to have an excuse to get in the water. It wasn't easy – they are quite smart. Or they were, until their plugs got pulled. So anyway, I knew, it was only a matter of time before they took over, and then … back to the camp probably. Why didn't you want to go home to Melbourne?'

'I'm not a contractor, Saria. Going back to Melbourne meant a breach of sentence. It meant going to prison.'

'Oh.'

'You're shocked?'

'No, I'm just … surprised you would tell me that.'

Pardue shrugs. 'It's no secret. It's on my profile. Porter knows. I had a problem with a drug, a painkiller: moxodone.'

'How did you come to that?'

'Oh, I don't know … when I was younger, I spent some time overseas, Turkiye-Syria borderlands, at work in a refugee camp. I saw … things there. I came home, and the drugs helped, made me feel numb, disconnected. Sometimes I think they're still in there, traces still inside me.'

'But you're not –'

'I'm clean. That was my sentence: rehab, then out here to work.'

'For using drugs?'

'For stealing them. And there was a … situation with an old boyfriend of mine, a mix-up really. But the police were called, and away I went.'

'Wow. Well that's –'

'Do you miss her, your mother?'

'She wasn't much of a mother. She was a coach. Had me out of bed by 5am every day from the age of eight. "We only get one shot at greatness." She'd been a swimmer of … some talent. Well, you get the picture. I loved swimming when I was a girl, and she loved that I loved it. And I loved that she loved that I loved it. Ha. That's what it was like at first: this love, bouncing between us. She called me her water baby. Then I grew up, and I wanted other things. She wouldn't let me go, and it became apparent that it wasn't really love – it was something uglier.'

'You snapped. At the Games.'

'Kind of. Burnt out aged 16! I suppose … well, you've revealed your dirty compulsion, so here's mine: when you're under the water, everything external is muted, sound and sight, touch, all the senses. It's as though the only thing that truly exists is what's inside. The most succinct realisations, like epiphanies – they come to you in that vacuum. On that day, I saw … I saw the right and wrong of things with absolute clarity, total certainty. I saw the way of the world.'

'The way of the world?'

'Oh, I can't explain it. It's like a glimpse, a moment of pure truth: this is how everything should be. After that day at the

Games, I tried to shake it off, to cloud things over again. To forget it, because that seemed easier. The truth was … scary to me. I tried to find a new focus: religion, politics, reading, writing, ranting. Promiscuity, celibacy, anything that might pull me away from the water. But nothing worked. So I submitted to it. I came out here, and I went under again. And I realised what was so scary about it: I'm never more at ease than in the vacuum. Stay there too long, it'll kill you.' Saria's voice is growing duller with every word, and she is blinking heavier and longer. 'I need to find something else. A new way – a real way. When I said before that I'll make it home, I meant it. We're, I don't know, sixty Ks from the island? I reckon I could swim it.'

'Surely not.'

'Sure, why not? Haha.' Saria's eyelids have settled. She smiles softly to herself.

'The currents,' says Pardue. 'They're so fierce.'

'Mmm. The gyres, vortexes.'

'Yes, exactly … it wasn't always so menacing to me.'

'The sea?'

'I remember the first time I saw it.' Pardue can recall a hint, a tease: a shimmer between two forested hillsides as her parents' car had rounded a hairpin bend – there, then gone again, as though the landscape had shifted to reconceal its glittering secret. 'I was eight then. Seven or eight. One of my earlier memories. It still lifts me to think of it. But you know, I don't think you could swim all the way home.'

Saria stirs, shuffles up the bed and lies on her back, arms crossed over her belly. 'I could do it. That's what I tell myself. But I'd rather we went together.'

Pardue watches the young woman a while, waiting for movement or more talk. Finally, she stretches out alongside her, their bodies barely touching.

'Tell me a story,' murmurs Saria.

'A story?'

'You speak so well, Kathleen. Can I call you that? Tell me more. Tell me a story, Kathleen. Something nice, something ... somewhere away from here.'

'I've told you plenty. I don't –'

'Something else. Something fun, playful.'

'Playful? I don't know.'

'You struggle with the concept?'

'I don't know. The children in our block used to play – out the front of the building. When I was very young, I used to play there too. There was a courtyard with games marked in white on rubber tiles: a soccer pitch, hopscotch, that sort of thing. There was a climbing frame. They used to hang off it like monkeys, dresses flapping in the wind, lolling around up there, talking and laughing ... playing.'

'Playing at what?'

'Tag, maybe. Some sort of tag game – "quicksand" or something. Your feet aren't allowed to touch the floor. If you touch the floor, then you sink and die.'

'I don't know that one.' Saria is at little more than a whisper.

'I may not be remembering it right.'

'I like that in children, that imagination. You would have been up there, looking down at concrete, but you'd see quicksand. You'd really see it. Remember that excitement you could feel as a kid, that ... squirming excitement? So intense you could almost wet yourself.'

'It soon goes away, that feeling.'

'It goes with age. How many of you were there, how many friends playing games outside?'

'I don't know. It was different every time, I imagine. I don't really remember names, or even faces. I was younger than the others. Or that's how it always felt. I remember Foggy.'

'You had a friend called Foggy?'

'A dog. Foggy Dog – a stray. He had something wrong with his eyes. They were clouded over: foggy. But I don't think he was blind, not entirely. He would always be there in the courtyard, running circles around us, weaving in and out between our legs, chasing balls, sharing our sweets, barking up at us from the quicksand.'

'What kind of dog was he?'

'I don't know, just a mongrel, I think. He was brown and quite small, a terrier or something like that. Wiry hair. Lightning fast, so full of energy. He seemed well fed, like someone somewhere was looking after him. Or perhaps he was looking after himself, feral. Sometimes the girls would do his hair.'

'Aw.'

'They'd use elastic bands, make lots of little bunches on his head. He would run around with these things in his fur, and he would grin at me.'

'Grin?'

'Well, you know what I mean. I always took them out, the bunches – that didn't seem fair, him being a very boyish boy. Silly. I used to sneak biscuits out for him. Someone made him a collar from a handkerchief they pinched off a washing line. I'd forgotten all about Foggy.'

'What happened to him?'

'Ah, one day he turned up, and, well ...'

'Oh, no, don't say he –'

'He just sort of slithered out from the foyer nearest the playground. It was awful. He was down on his belly, creeping along, and he was covered in something: a thick, black goo. His fur was matted from snout to paw. We saw him crawling towards us and we rushed over. We gathered around, and he just collapsed among us. He shut his eyes and lay there, silent. We were all sobbing and wailing, wringing our hands and wondering who could have done this. But nobody moved, nobody went to help him. We just watched. I remember thinking, Someone has to do something, why isn't anyone doing anything? I was waiting for one of the older ones. But they just stood there. So I took off my cardigan and scooped him up in it. I could feel his breath on my neck, and the heat from his body. There was a hush, then a new sound. Disgust. That noise children make: "Ewwww." I didn't play out there again.'

'And Foggy?'

'I carried him all the way to the city. Found a vet.'

'Was he okay? Tell me he was.'

'Sure he was.'

Saria pouts. 'That was a pretty awful story.'

'I'm sorry.'

'I want a happy ending. Every story needs a happy ending.'

'Really?'

'Tell me more about the seaside, your first time.'

'I don't know.'

'Please. I won't bother you again.'

'What else can I remember? On our last morning there I said goodbye to everything: goodbye bed, goodbye ... oh.'

Now the ending doesn't matter. Saria is asleep.

****

Dreams of a life by the sea: it all started there, in a weatherboard shack out near the Otways, a week away from junior toils, from book reports and bullies. The house belonged to her mother's employer – their trip a bonus, cheaper than a pay rise. It sat close to the shoreline, beside a narrow inlet that rose and fell with the tides. On the slopes behind them, demarcated by rusty barbed wire, were fields dotted with cows, which she eyed nervously because of their heft and skittish clomping, and enviously because of their place among pasture – sun and salt air. In the mornings she woke in light, golden rays pouring through tall panes and settling across her legs. She would throw off her blankets and skip through to the living room, bare feet on cool boards. On the window seat were a pair of binoculars, and through them she watched plovers and oystercatchers dipping their bills in the flats and rock-pools. She counted them off, their number decreasing a little each day, the pattern apparent, but the reason beyond her. Occasionally a tanker would cross on the horizon, and she would try to track it down, to lock it in the lenses and follow its progress until it sailed from view. Eventually her mother or father, or both, would pad into the room behind her and she'd join them at the table for orange juice and milky tea, toast with jam, chocolate-covered cereal – things she'd had many times before but which tasted all the sweeter for their unhurried sharing in that crisp, light place. Later she would scramble over tufted dunes and down to the beach, to make castles adorned with seaweed streamers, or paw into wet sand and fill her buckets with cockles. In the evenings her parents would kneel before the fireplace to stack paper and wooden blocks. The rich, smoky smell clung to their clothes, and she'd sit between them, breathing it in, while the few unspoilt shellfish she'd collected boiled in a pot above the flames.

'We're living off the land,' her mother said. 'Just like the people who used to live here. Before invaders, before gold mines, coal mines, before ships and planes, factories and offices, before Melbourne. Before us. Not so long ago.'

The last day: goodbye bed, goodbye plovers, goodbye cockles, rocks and sand and sea, I will return, I'll see you again.

As their car pulled away from the ocean road, a few fat drops of rain thudded against the roof, thrown down by a single cloud. Her mother said how lucky they'd been with the weather, and she and her father nodded. Still, the sun was shining. She continued her goodbyes: goodbye fields, goodbye cows, goodbye gum trees and brambles and berries. Then her parents joined in, between laughs and knowing looks, until she chided them for being too silly. Goodbye broken gate, goodbye old fence, goodbye dead possum, goodbye cowpats, goodbye hills. Goodbye hills, that was the end of it. She told them off. 'Stop it, you two!' She was giggling, she didn't mean it, but they did stop.

They were inland then, up into the hills, the farms giving way to forest, giving way to service stations, then commuter townships, beige cladding and high fences. The road widened accordingly – track, B-road, two lanes, four lanes, six – and the sky darkened, clouds coming in mob-handed. Onto the Melbourne highway. In among Sunday traffic, and the rain came again, fatter and heavier, bouncing off steel and concrete, obscuring all sight and sound beyond the swish-thud of wipers on full-whack. It was still falling when they crossed the Yarra, still falling as they slowed to a single-file shuffle through the inner-city's glass slabs, still falling when they pulled up beside their tower block.

They loaded up with bags and boxes and sprinted for the lobby, kicking and shoving everything into the lift and rising, soggy, silent and shivering. Twelfth floor, apartment 1210. Tinned tomato soup for supper.

That night, she sat on her bed, blanket across her shoulders, willing the heater to work and trying to concentrate on her homework. But she couldn't. Instead, she watched transfixed as the rain dribbled across her window and the dampness on the wall below it blossomed from spot, into splodge, into patch. They built those towers to look good, but not to last.

Some days later, in an escalation of her attempts to ease Pardue's seemingly unshakeable post-holiday blues, her mother had asked if she wanted to return to the inlet next year.

'Can we go forever, Mum? Hide there. Live off the land, like the old people.'

Her mother's patience broke with a near-audible twang. 'It was just a holiday. You can't hide forever, Kathleen. And you can't really live off the land. Not any more.'

They never went back. Next spring, the great surge swept in and out, king tides heaving poison algae from the depths and leaving a noxious sheen on everything. The inlet was swamped, the shack was gone, and the fields were ruined. Goodbye plovers, goodbye cockles, sand and rocks. Goodbye to all that.

****

She wakes one more time in the night, terror chasing her into the liminal phase, tendrils pulling at her even as the nameless beast behind them retreats. She comes gasping and gulping across the threshold into reality. The light is still on. Saria has rolled onto her side and nestled her forehead against Pardue's shoulder. Her eyes are shut tight and she is sucking her thumb.

October 4: Blackout +14 days

Saria is gone, slipped away unnoticed in the pre-dawn. Pardue heads up to Control, but no one is there. In the canteen she finds Porter sitting alone, hunched over a table, chin resting on forearms and eyes locked on the rim of his mug.

'Good morning.' His gaze is unmoved, but his lips wrinkle into something approaching a smile.

When it reaches her, the aroma stops Pardue dead.

'I made an executive decision,' says Porter. 'I am still an executive of sorts around here … I guess.' He yawns. 'It's not the last of it – not quite. I just thought we could all use the help today. A little pick-me-up.'

'Thank you.'

'How was your night?'

'Disturbed.' She fills a mug from the urn behind Porter, sips tentatively at the scalding coffee and sighs. 'Damn. Do the others know?'

'I did the rounds. I couldn't find Saria though, and you didn't answer again. Where were you?'

'I was up in Control just now. Did you tell Seule?'

Porter frowns. 'Yeah, I told everyone.'

'Of course.' She takes a seat as the door behind her rattles open. Gill enters, pauses, filling the door frame.

'Oh.' He blinks, breathes it in. 'That smells so ...' He lurches for the urn, patting Porter's back as he passes.

Porter grins awkwardly, blushes. 'Well, it's a big day.' The smile slips. 'I thought, liquid breakfast – we'll push our meals back to midday. Something to look forward to.'

Gill takes a deep swig, lips and tongue apparently impervious to the heat. 'Oh, hell.' He chuckles, shakes his head. 'Shit. We might just make it after all.'

'We need to move,' says Pardue. 'Faster than we first thought?'

'Today's the day to get everything sorted. You should set yourself to packing, Pardue. There's nothing you can do on the boat. Pack your medical stuff, our food. Scour the facility, anything that might be of use on the journey. And after the journey.'

'Okay.'

Daws slopes in, head bowed low, as though sleepwalking. They watch as he fills his cup, takes a first sup, smacks his lips and emits a soft mewl. Only when the three of them fall into laughter does he look up. He eyes them warily, then snickers. 'Small mercies, I guess.'

Porter raises his mug. 'Cheers.'

They sip in unison. Another ripple of sighs passes between them.

'You're going to catch us a big fish today?' Gill asks Daws.

'I can try.'

'If they're out there, you'll get them.'

Daws stares blankly at Gill, scanning his eyes for sarcasm, his lips for a sneer, but he finds none. 'We should get you coffee every morning.'

'Huh.' Gill downs another mouthful. 'That's what my wife used to say. Every day. "Grumpy bear, have a coffee, then talk to me." '

'I didn't know you were married,' says Pardue.

'Yeah.'

'What's her name?'

'Gem. She was a teacher.'

'Was?'

'Yeah, she was a –'

Porter jumps in. 'Remember … uh, the teacher who came out here last year. What was that guy's name?'

'Professor,' says Daws. He is pecking at his drink, savouring every drop. 'You mean the professor.'

'Yeah, yeah, the professor. He was a geologist, I guess. He came here with his students, preppy kids out from Sydney. A field trip, you know. I asked him what it was all about. "Each generation must prepare the next," he tells me.' Porter's weary babble is addressed to Pardue, but he eyes Gill as he goes. 'We gave them the tour, me and Gill. We're explaining the extraction, processing, transport, how the platform works. Same spiel I gave you – bit more on the technical side, I guess. It didn't matter. The professor was cutting in, lecturing them on petrostates, the King Island deal; history, political stuff. We're out on the deck and I'm explaining the resupply roster, and Gill's talking them through engineering fixes … and then comes a ten-minute essay on the resource wars. That was one of his favourites. That and total auto – the end of us plebs.'

' "Oil and gas: the blood and breath of a civilised world," '

Gill's recitation is dull, distant. 'He was a zealot. A fossil fetishist.'

Porter nods. 'He's talking and talking and talking, and by the end of the tour, that's all there is left: him talking. We just moved them from one room to the next and let him go. Then we ended in the canteen here: questions and answers. Questions for the professor. One brave kid – brave or stupid – she asked us a question. "Mr Porter and Mr Gill …" God, now I can't remember what it was. But the professor, he was fuming. He's shooting filthy looks at this poor girl, and she's fixed forwards on us, kind of pleading with us to answer, and we're looking to the professor. Well, I choked. But Gill, he stood, and he said, "We bow to our masters, the rats." I remember that.'

Pardue looks to Gill, expecting him to challenge this odd anecdote, this apparent diversion. But he is lost in his cup; she can't be sure he is even listening. Daws, too, seems to have switched off.

'A strange story,' she says.

Porter furrows his brow, as though at a loss to explain it. 'I guess.'

She moves on. 'What's happening today, Gill?'

He sips, snaps into focus. 'Uh … we launch the boat. Me and you can do that, Porter.' The other man shrugs. 'We'll bring it up with the crane, prop it on the helipad. Then we strip out some weight, cut a hole for the mast. There needs to be some sort of rope pulley system for the sail. I'm not sure about that. It's Seule's thing.'

'And the mast?'

'We took a couple of struts off one of the legs. Real strong, light stuff. There's a nice roll of canvas for the sail. Seule says it'll do the job. We'll take what's left over for patch-ups … just in case.'

Daws shakes his head, says nothing.

Gill, either ignoring this or failing to see, continues. 'It'll come together. I know it.' He shifts eagerly in his seat and seems suddenly warm to the task ahead. Pardue knows why, she can feel it herself – a caffeine glow around her heart, a hot rush. 'I figure we're good to go in two days. Ready for launch.' Gill tips the final drops of coffee down his throat, plants his mug on the trestle and casts his eyes towards the urn.

Porter says, 'I'm going to check comms. Pardue, maybe you could find Saria. Take her some coffee.'

'Sure, sure.'

'She's up on deck,' says Gill, still eyeballing the urn. 'Said she was going to mark her cuts on the lifeboat.'

****

The cloud cover remains, an endless, billowing sheet. She follows the western walkway, the opposite edge to the lift and the fishing lines. At the northern end she sees Saria, hands on hips, staring up at the lifeboat's orange rump. Pardue is about to call out when Saria's head drops, shoulders slump. Her hands are drawn to her face, clasped over her mouth.

Pardue hesitates, then continues, calling out, 'Coffee's up.'

Saria seems to tense, as though caught in some illicit or embarrassing act. Slowly she turns. 'Coffee?'

'It's Porter's treat.'

'Right, great. I don't really like coffee, but –'

'Really?'

'Never developed a taste for it. I've never wanted to … take drugs. Sorry.'

'Consider it a prescription.'

'Okay. Would you like to share it?'

'No, no. I've had my fix.'

Saria takes a healthy slurp, grimaces.

'It's bitter, but it's worth it,' Pardue reassures her. 'Cheers you up.'

'Do I look so sad?'

Pardue shrugs. 'No more than anyone else. Less than some.'

'I'm sorry for stealing your bed last night.'

'That's okay. You left very early.'

'I wanted to see the boat, see what I'm working with.'

'And?'

'I need to get started.'

'Gill and Porter are on their way, I think.' Pardue casts her eyes to the pathway behind her, as though to illustrate that point. No one is there, but something else catches her attention. Something on the gunmetal panelling inside the walkway. A scarlet splash, and next to it a long smear of the same hue.

'Oh, yes,' mutters Saria, following Pardue's eyes. 'And there's that.'

'You've already seen this?'

'Yes.'

'What is it?'

'What do you think?'

'I don't know.' Pardue steps in for a closer look. 'You think it's blood, yes?'

'Don't you?' Saria moves up alongside.

'It could be anything.'

'I suppose.'

'It could be from weeks, months ago even.'

'You're the doctor – you've seen the accident logs.'

'I think you should be very careful,' says Pardue, failing to mask her irritation, the first stab of a caffeine comedown. 'I mean, are you going to start throwing around accusations?'

'Not yet. Tell me though: if you were going to kill yourself, would you … ah, this might have to wait.' Saria nods along the pathway. Gill and Porter are ambling towards them. Gill claps his hands together, rubs them eagerly. His eyes shimmer with intensity.

'These two are all over the bloody place,' murmurs Pardue.

'Ready for launch?' Saria asks.

'Yep, yep.' Gill grins.

'Ready as we'll ever be.' Porter is chewing on a thumbnail that is down to the quick, dried blood at the corners. He pulls a lever, jerks open the boat's rear hatch. The interior lights up and he clambers inside.

Gill follows and turns to seal the door, first addressing the women with another manic smile. 'Beware. The front rows may experience some splashing.'

Saria tuts. 'What's got into him?'

'Drink your coffee.'

'Will it make me act like that?'

'Hardly.'

After a moment, there is a deep clank as the brake is released, the rumble of spinning casters as the carriage tilts forward and the orange bullet slides along it, off into a free-fall. Pardue and

Saria step to the railings to follow its nose-heavy descent. The boat seems to drop for an age before piercing the surface and disappearing amid an explosion of white water. One second, then another, smaller detonation as the boat crashes back through and wobbles itself upright. They hear the engine snarl, and watch as the boat swings around and chugs away towards the lift.

'We have fuel, ignition, internal combustion, all that and more,' Pardue muses as she watches the boat go. 'Tomorrow it'll be a sailboat.'

'Well, they fitted it with a lawnmower engine,' says Saria.

'They couldn't imagine a situation like this. Whatever this situation is.'

'We can't imagine it either!' Saria beams at Pardue.

'No. How's your coffee?'

'Mmm. So, the mystery marks. What do you think?' Saria nods back towards the spatters. 'Broz. You don't think anyone here would do that? You don't think people are capable?'

Pardue is still staring over the railing. The boat's foamy wake is gradually receding. 'I know what people are capable of.'

****

No connection! Record offline?

'There is blood out near the lifeboat. A red daub – it isn't so much. But Broz is dead and blood is blood, so it's something, not nothing. I don't know exactly what to make of it, but ... I know what people are capable of. I've seen the work of masters: the maiming. Extraordinary pain inflicted by ordinary people.'

The recording continues, but Pardue falls silent, unsure of her purpose, of what she is trying to achieve here. Is this data log or diary? Catharsis of some kind? Does it matter?

'I'll just talk. I'll talk and see where it goes. It's just, I have a sense for man-made horror, its ubiquity and its ... boundless imagination. Even before I confronted it in person, it held a place in my mind. And I can trace that to a childhood as sheltered as anyone could wish in this world. Sheltered, safe, but still ...'

But still. There was the great surge, there was poor Foggy. Hints, then, when she was about ten, a lesson delivered via film clip – a link clicked while her mother chatted to a friend in their kitchen. She saw a narrow room, pale walls, tiled floor, a wooden door. On the right of the screen, his back to the camera, a man in a grey-blue uniform and wide-brimmed cap sat at a desk. He shuffled through some papers, then said something – a question, she thought – in words she couldn't make out, or a language she couldn't understand. On the left was another man, a barefoot figure in faded pink overalls. He sat on the floor, back wedged against the corner walls, knees pulled tight to his chest, arms wrapped around them and head bowed.

He's in trouble, she thought, and she began to cry.

The man at the desk spoke again – sharp words, identical in sound and tone. The man in pink was unmoved, and this seemed to upset the other; his shoulders drooped slightly, and he put down the papers. He opened a drawer next to his right thigh and pulled out something long and hefty, a black stick. He rose from his desk and, as his chair scraped back, the man in pink seemed to flinch and cower, shuffle further into his corner. There was a gasp behind her, firm hands scooping her up and snatching away the tab. She cried out, asked her mother, 'What is it, what did I see?'

'Oh, that's nothing, a bad clip, some grown-up thing, nothing to worry about.'

'But where is the man, the man with the black stick?'

And her mother, shushing and cooing and rocking Pardue in her arms, whispered through her hair, 'He's far away. Far, far away.'

So she knew: far, far away, terrible things were happening.

A year or so later came the famines. More images on screens, children with dead eyes and bloated stomachs, weeping mothers, skeletal men reaching out, pleading, and nothing she could do about it.

When she was fourteen, a coalition of prospectors and warlords set forth over an ever-expanding desert, blasting everything and everyone to rubble until even they were seemingly forced to pause and consider what they had wrought. Then the fightback began, a conflict of old ideals attached to new flags and symbols.

Pardue saw a woman – almost; probably she was only a teenager. She had dark hair, weather-worn skin, and she wore khaki. She sat on a sandy slope or banking, legs stretched out before her. Her eyes were lowered, as though bashful in the presence of the camera, and her broad smile suggested someone being lightly coerced into something she considered silly, or maybe even unbecoming. In the crook of her arms was a grenade launcher. Every day for a month, Pardue looked at this photo and read again the story of the militias holding the line against thieves and tyrants. They lived together and fought together, and they feared nothing. They spoke of a better world, an equitable world they would create when the peace was won. They radiated strength and righteousness, and a beauty she could understand. She wanted to join them. She sought updates – daily, hourly – from the dusty patches over which they fought, punching the air with each advance, sinking into despair when the setbacks came, sitting out sieges, plotting offensives, imagining herself there with them.

'But they have to kill, Kathleen. They have to kill people.' Her mother's words, a simple assertion, devoid of judgement or threat. Something to think on, as she knew her daughter would.

'I don't want to kill,' Pardue told her later.

'But you could heal.'

'Heal the world.'

'Aim high, that's the spirit. You can try.'

She was 18 when the dirty bomb went off in Shenzhen, and everyone said the world would never be the same again. But a couple of weeks later, it was. They had seen all the broadcasts, read the stories and the analyses, and made their donations. Everything that could be done was apparently done, and everything that could be said had apparently been said. Shenzhen became nothing more than a byword for economic malaise: the pre-Shenzhen boom, the Shenzhen recession, post-Shenzhen bounce.

Then came the immigration lock, and the visa rollback: deportations from New South Wales and Victoria. So bad things were happening at home, too, and undergrad Pardue took to the streets – more flags, more symbols, and healing to be done when the batons swung hard and the gas swirled.

Aim high. No one can deny she tried.

When at last she was trained and qualified, she posted herself to the front line, across seas and continents to a sprawling city of canvas and plastic on the edges of a red wasteland. On the horizon, across some invisible border, was another city – a real city, or the ruins of one. All they saw of it were mighty plumes, smoke signals that said, We're still here, we're still fighting.

They arrived in convoy, a squad of young doctors and nurses, unspoilt graduates squeezed into trucks filled with donor boxes and supply crates. They bounced out and began unloading, unpacking, working quickly, chatting excitedly, exchanging glassy eyed grins and hugs. That first night, she stumbled into her tent, wobbly with exhaustion. She smiled herself to sleep.

Every day another convoy arrived – from the opposite direction to hers. On foot or flatbed, the dispossessed came as the real, old city emptied and the false, new one swelled. In the hospital tents they vaccinated, re-hydrated, cut, stitched, dressed and delivered. She saw goodness there: her first patient, a young man, a boy really, fuzz on his chin, dirt and oily sweat across his brow, a bony body wrapped in baggy camouflage that had turned scarlet from knee to ankle. At first he grimaced and clenched, his hands grasping, his back arching as they teased slivers of shrapnel from his shin. Then came a loosening of limbs and muscles as the painkillers kicked in and peace washed over him for the first time since who knows when. As he slipped into sleep, he reached out and touched Pardue's neck. She said, 'You're saved.' She felt like a superhero.

She could treat the ill, feed the hungry and clothe the homeless, and tell herself they were through the worst of it. She could sit on the hillside at night and watch tracer fire arcing through the sky, and know it was the young lions and lionesses of progress who were lighting up the darkness, and she could think, I'm making a difference. Here is humanity, fighting back.

But then she looked to some of the older ones, the veteran volunteers, and she wondered, Will I last? Some did, some didn't. Like the paediatrician who stumbled from the tent after a 10-hour stretch, blinking in the afternoon sun. He cast his eyes across the camp before him, just once, left to right, as though taking it in for the first time. Then he checked his watch, turned on his heel and trudged towards the road. He sat there in silence and waited for the next truck out. When he was gone, some of them chattered and speculated. Others simply nodded and shrugged. And she thought, I don't want to go like that; that change, like a switch is flicked somehow.

For Pardue, it was the girl. She came with the final wave of a mass evacuation that caught them all by surprise. They began arriving in the early hours – a few trucks and cars at first, then pulled wagons and lastly, when the sun was roused and raging, the long, slow column of walkers. That girl, they tried and tried to remove her, to usher her outside, bribe her with chocolate and fizzy drinks, but she held tight to her mother's hand even as the surgeons worked, waving away their appeals with pursed lips and head shakes. Pardue sat with her, tried to distract her, to ensure she didn't interfere. When it was done, the girl set down her mother's hand, straightened it neatly against the dead woman's side and held it a final moment.

(Hand on hand, and in this Pardue saw something so weightily evocative, more triggering than even sound or scent could be: she saw a goodbye to her own mother, taken by cancer a few years previous. Hand on hand, and her crying, 'It's not okay, it's not okay,' as her mother was drained of life. It was her challenge to a proud, content woman's final words: 'It's okay, Kathleen. It's okay because you're okay.' Her mother had accepted her fate; Pardue had railed angrily against it to the last, and the tenderness and reassurance that should have heralded the moment instead came after it, in promises to dead flesh: I will be okay, I will aim high.)

When the girl let go, she met Pardue's eyes. She seemed different then, older or just altered, as though some layer had been shed.

In perfect English, she said, 'You did your best here.'

The girl left and, after a few seconds, Pardue followed, shrugging out of her bloody coat as she went. When she exited the tent, she thought she'd lost the child. Then she saw a figure picking its way quickly up the hill that marked the camp's southern edge – the hill they climbed each night to watch the fireworks. The girl was sitting at the top when Pardue caught up, gazing out over the dwindling column of refugees, across the desert behind them, towards her city. The child's sun-dress was printed with pink flowers, and her plastic shoes were flapping at the sole. As Pardue sat, folding her legs awkwardly beneath her, she felt a needle-sharp pain halfway up her back, enough to force a sharp inhalation. The first twinge.

The girl said, 'Can I have some chocolate now?'

Pardue patted down her pockets. Empty.

'Oh, it doesn't matter.'

Pardue asked, 'Who taught you this language?'

The girl jerked a thumb back down the slope. 'Her, of course.'

'I'm sorry.'

'Now she has peace. That's what she said on the journey here. She told me where she was going. She knew.' The girl sniffed hard and wiped away a tear, the first she had shed. 'It was her time. Now I'm alone.'

'The people here can help you.'

'No.'

'They can find you somewhere, a place to live.'

'I have a place. Over there.' The girl nodded towards the city.

'No, no. How old are you?'

'Twelve, soon.'

'Let them help you here. You don't have to go.'

'Yes, I do.' She sighed: no mum, no chocolate and now this. 'It's no safer here than over there. If over there goes, so will this place. And the next one, and the next.'

'We can help you find somewhere safe. A family, a new home … your mother must have wanted that for you.'

'Where? In your country, your home?'

'My home?'

'They would never let me in, I know. It won't be safe there, anyway. Not forever. You must know it. All this' – a sweep of the hand before her – 'will come to you.'

'My home's a long way from here. It's not like this.'

'Really? Maybe you're from some other planet? Some place where bombs can't reach.' The girl smiled, as though enjoying this little escape. 'Okay. I'll go there with you, lady. Where is your spaceship – is it near?'

'My name is Kathleen.'

'Ariman.' She wasn't smiling any more. She was gazing over the desert again. 'I know you, here to save the whole world.' The girl rubbed a palm in the ochre dirt, rolled the grains between thumb and forefinger. 'This is ours to save, not yours. Your fight is not here. It will come to you. So just let it come.'

'I'm here to help.'

'Ha.'

That night Pardue lay awake, tormented by the first pinpricks of disillusion, and thoughts of the child, everything shifting, ideals that were grand – global in their scope and ambition – giving way to something simpler, more immediate. She made a vow then. She would save the girl. A life, not just stitched up and bandaged, saved for another day, but changed, pulled clear of the blades. Yes, she would smuggle her out of the country, find her a family, whatever it took.

It's easy to make vows in the night-time; even easier to break them in the day.

Failure was the end of her. A truck out, flight home, gin-soaked tears all the way. As she queued at the passport check, her watch chirruped and burped and beeped under the strain of first-world data flows, and the screen walls relayed the day's news on a ten-minute loop: a royal wedding somewhere; business; sport; lottery numbers. The headlines fell on her like lumps of sludge, and she thought, I achieved nothing.

She took work as a GP down on the Peninsula, moved to the coast, reverted to it, searching – in vain – for her pristine hideaway. She found an uninsurable bungalow with crumbling walls and a dirt yard that terminated in cliffs, jagged edges and fissures that widened daily. The land was stark, and the ocean below seemed more swollen and stagnant than glittering and idyllic. The two stood as opposing forces, bent on mutual destruction.

It didn't take long – the unravelling, the disconnect. It began in banal fashion on one of those wintry days when the daylight hours seem a sliver, pinched on either side by a dawn that never fully breaks and a dusk that comes in early and eager. She was in the health centre, shutting up for the weekend, ticking off another five-day cycle in a life so tepid and colourless it made everything that preceded it – that precipitated it – seem all the more vivid.

She was exhausted, a tiredness born of inaction, too tired to think straight, just tired enough to let her mind drift to days past, before everything fell flat. She realised it was a year since she'd left the desert – to the month, not the day. Not quite a milestone, but it had heft in that moment, or gained it in the instance of minor injury and petty frustration that followed.

It was raining when she left the centre. She pulled her coat up over her head and trotted to the car, on tip-toes through wide puddles, fumbling in her bag for the key-card, and cursing because she couldn't seem to find it, then, with a great howl of anguish, turning and sprinting back towards the office – sprinting until she slipped, tripped and fell, ripping her jeans and skinning a knee.

Inside again, she examined the damage, the blood and grit, and she began to cry. The key-card was on her desk.

When she raided the pharmacy, she was looking for a dressing and diazepam or something similar. She saw the moxodone, and she thought again of the camp, of that young soldier, farewell caresses as he slithered away from his city of misery towards some opiate sanctuary. She could recall his fingers at her neck, beckoning.

She thought, What if I went there with you? Must be better than here.

It came on like a warm hug, growing from the inside out, filling her, filling the room, the world, nudging everything aside so that nothing mattered. Nothing: not orphaned girls, freedom fighters, shattered shins, bombs, bullets, nor the humdrum that followed – not a thing. Then she saw her, Ariman, an apparition in olive green uniform, pouched webbing and a red scarf. This was beyond the mind's eye; she was there in the room, and it seemed fine, seemed perfectly acceptable.

Ariman said, 'It's coming, Kathleen.'

She didn't mind.

After that, she embraced the numbness, and allowed herself

to become detached from a world she couldn't save and no longer cared to. She flaked before flickering plasma and waited for a tremor great enough to rouse her. She could live like this, she decided. And for some years, she did. She became, in this time, a creature of habits – the many flowing from the one. On winter evenings, she would drive into Melbourne, to park in a suburban cul-de-sac of gravel driveways and uniform warmth. At 6pm prompt, a family of four gathered around their kitchen table, and she watched them through a double-glazed screen framed by pristine UPVC. A cheeky-looking boy of maybe three or four years, a cherubic girl of four or five, a mother, radiant and smiling like the ad exec's dream woman, and Mark – her Mark – greying at the same rate as Pardue, wider in the face, swollen with contentment. The family would scoop food from communal bowls and pour themselves colourful drinks from an iced jug.

Each visit was supposed to be the last.

I just want to see it, she'd tell herself. I just want to see what it looks like: they're numb too, in a way. The same as me. The same, but different.

****

The weak voice dips and wavers, croaks and crackles through swirls of static: 'Don't come to ----. The disc---- ah, hell. There's nothing ---- here, it's ---- seven ----. We slept ourselves to death. It's ap----. Oh, my god.' Silence. One, two, three seconds, then static again, and the same words, the same pattern: 'Don't come to ----. The disc---- ah, hell. There's nothing ---- here, it's ---- seven ----. We slept ourselves to death. It's ap----. Oh, my god.'

'How did you hear this?' asks Porter.

'I just picked up the headphones and it was there,' replies Pardue. 'At first there was nothing, then I heard those words.

72

Only that, looping around.'

Porter plants his palms on the desk, bows over the console, as though to steady himself. 'Why were you –'

'I don't know. I finished boxing up medical supplies. I came up here to see if there was anything in the store cupboards – spare waterproofs, that sort of thing. I saw the comms set … you know, I just don't think we should stop listening. This thing with the boat, it might not –'

'I was on the set earlier. There was nothing.'

'And now there's something.'

'Did you change any settings? Because this is on analogue. Junk tech. I mean, how … it's just this? Only this?'

'I didn't touch anything. I listened to it a few times, I came and told you.'

'Where's Seule?' growls a now fully decaffeinated Gill.

'Still in his room, I suppose,' says Saria.

'That little bastard.'

The ghostly voice returns, words dripping from the speakers.

'This is new.' Porter's voice is high, tremulous. He prods a jittery finger towards the console. 'I mean, it must be new. I was on here myself. There was nothing like this. Nothing at all. He says seven –'

'If he's not working on the boat, Seule should be on comms,' seethes Gill. 'Little shit. Can we record this?'

'Uh … yeah, we already are. It's always recording.'

'See if you can reach out, respond. I'm off to talk to Little Lord Seule.'

'Um, no,' stammers Porter. 'No, actually, I reckon we should all nut this out. All of us together, I mean. Let's call Seule and Daws up here.'

Gill stares daggers at Porter, sniffs hard, then offers a barely perceptible nod. 'Suit yourself.'

The voice returns. '… Oh, my god.'

****

They wait in silence until Daws and Seule arrive, the boy entering last in a heavy trudge. His hair is mussed on one side, pressed flat by pillows.

Gill sets upon him as soon as he is seated. 'Did you hear it?'

'Did I hear what?'

'Hear what?' echoes Daws.

'So you haven't heard that message?' Gill's focus is on Seule alone.

'What message?'

'Message?' Daws' eyes flit wearily from speaker to speaker.

Gill asks again, 'You don't know?'

'Know what?' cries Seule, fear filling his features.

'You missed it.'

'What the hell?!' Daws slams a palm against the wall.

Gill jumps, the briefest of tremors through broad shoulders. He recovers, lets his mouth fall open, this time in faux shock. He deadpans, 'All right, old man.'

Porter sighs. 'Okay, okay. Look, Dawsy, Seule, there's a message on comms. Like a loop. A recorded *radio* message.'

He flicks a switch, lets the voice tell its story: 'Don't come to -- --. The disc---- ah, hell. There's nothing ---- here, it's ---- seven ---

-. We slept ourselves to death. It's ap----. Oh, my god.'

Daws nods. 'All right.'

'I never heard that,' says Seule. 'Never.'

'Well, sure,' says Gill. 'I mean, how could you? Had yourself a morning off, didn't you?'

Seule splutters. 'That's not fair! I thought we were done with comms. I thought it was all on the boat now. I was waiting for you – waiting to set up the sail!'

'Right.' Gill's lip curls into a sneer.

'I just don't know –'

'What do we make of it?' asks Pardue.

'It doesn't really change anything, does it?' says Saria. 'Something bad is happening. We knew that.'

'Something evil,' Porter says to no one in particular. 'Opened the doors to –'

Gill tuts. 'Sort your shit out, Porter. We don't need your hocus-pocus. Where might it come from, the message?'

'Oh … anywhere. A ship, another platform, the island, mainland even. No way of telling.'

'Now we each must decide,' says Daws.

'Decide what?' asks Pardue.

'To go or to stay.'

'To stay is to die,' grunts Gill.

'And to go?'

'We *have* to go,' Seule sounds frantic.

Daws shakes his head. 'No. You really have no clue. Boy, your money, status, it won't save you now.'

'What? It's not about –'

'This is war. Power down, and bang.' Daws flicks a finger at Gill. 'You know it. No ships, no planes, no defence forces – you hope. And you,' he turns again on Seule. 'You know it too, but … oh.' A knowing smile. 'Has Daddy got a bunker?' Daws reads the answer in Seule's face, they all do. 'Well, well. Of course! The executive suite. Cosy. Till the water runs dry. Till the food's gone. Then what? Upstairs to scrap it out with the proles?'

'It's not –'

'We can fight dirty too, kid.'

'It's not … fuck you, old bastard! Stupid old –'

'Don't even bother,' sneers Daws. 'I'm tired, not soft. I've killed bigger boys than –'

Gill cuts in. 'Ah, Seule. Where is it?'

'I don't even want to go there, believe me!'

'Where?'

'It's under the airfield.'

'The airport?'

'No, the airfield. The private strip, south of Pearshape. It's for corporates coming between the mainland and the port.'

'Pearshape? What is that, a town or something?'

'Just a place. Inland from the New Port.'

'Past the checkpoints,' Daws tells Gill. 'A contractor's visa wouldn't have got you out that far from the port.'

Gill ignores this, says to Seule, 'Can we get there? Can we navigate to the coast somewhere near?'

'Navigate?' Seule shakes his head. 'There's no map – no hard-copy map, no proper instruments. I can hit King Island, the west coast, by compass. I can get us close to the New Port, or Currie even. Maybe. I can't say. Look, who'd attack KI? I mean –'

'Who wouldn't?!' cries Daws. 'The Green Bloc, the other petrostates … anyone!' A pause, then, 'Anyway, corporates won't let you through. Into their bunker? No way.'

'If they want Seule, they get us too,' replies Gill.

'Oh!' Saria claps a hand to her mouth, as though to suppress a laugh. 'Wow, I'm sorry, is he a hostage now?'

Gill glowers at Saria. Seule says nothing.

'We have to get out of here,' says Pardue. 'Whatever's happening back there … we'll see. But we have to get out of here.'

Gill arches an eyebrow. 'The doctor has spoken.'

'What? I –'

'Everyone has to decide,' repeats Daws. 'Me, I'm done. I'm not of that bloody rock any more. KI, Australia. Whatever's happening to it, good or bad – or worse. It's all the same to me. I wash my hands.'

'Don't say that,' whispers Porter. 'Don't throw it in, Dawsy.'

'I'm not throwing it in, you fool. I'm making a choice. It's just about all a man has left.' Daws taps his chest. 'My blood, my bones, my decision.'

****

'We have to get out of here.' She is in the clinic, recording again. 'We'll take the lifeboat as soon as we can … so this is my final report. September 20, that was day one of my second rotation. Day one of the comms blackout. I was here in the clinic, taking stock, preparing a supply order for the next drop. I

77

remember my tab screen froze, glitched out. I checked my watch: there was no network connection. It wasn't a big deal, or it didn't seem like one. It happened a few times on my first trip too: five- or ten-second dropouts. Sporadic. I busied myself with something else for a couple of minutes, then returned to my screen. Nothing. I called up to Control, to Porter. Control was down, too. No communications. Porter sounded pretty fried; nothing so new in that either. He wasn't yet ... panicky, though. But it never came back, the connection. I went up to Control about an hour later. Porter was punching buttons with Seule at the comms desk. Gill and Sargent were in one of the side offices pulling out old docs, maps, charts – I didn't know what that was about. They both looked angry. Porter told me we could use the chopper's comms unit when it arrived with the ops team – the rest of our crew. We'd get a techie sent out. Until then, we were deaf and dumb.

'I am ... I'm relaying this all as best I can: who said what, who did what, who was where when it all happened. I don't know what is relevant and what isn't. I'm not pointing fingers, simply presenting an honest picture. That day – early on, at least – there was no real *fear* to it all. Or none that I perceived. For my part, it was only frustration – that feeling when something fails that usually runs smoothly, something you take for granted. Like when there's a power outage back home, you think, Okay, no lights, no flat-screen. I'll use my tab; no, the cell's dead. Coffee maker, oven; no, no. And so it goes.

'I went back to the clinic. I didn't even know about the ops team until dinner time. In the canteen, it was just the same group that had flown out earlier, minus Sargent. Saria told me the ops team were a no-show, and I think I laughed. It was absurd – maybe even a little exciting, intriguing. We speculated. Porter was worried the chopper might have crashed, but that wouldn't explain why our communications were down. Gill told us *all* comms had probably gone down and the flight was grounded. A solar flare, he said. That could fry electronic systems, apparently. They'd fix it. No operations team means no operations, and they couldn't afford the platform to be down too long. It seemed a good explanation. Plausible and reassuring enough. It never occurred to me I was being fed a line. Then we found Sargent, and his note: "It's all gone now." That was it, four words scrawled in felt-tip on his dorm door.'

****

Sargent. He holds the key, or rather held the key, she is sure of it.

She had marked him from the start, their first encounter. There was something in him. Certainly, his cold indifference to the crew, an attitude seemingly calculated to signal position and place of origin: up high, somewhere important. But it went beyond a conceited demeanour. Even his appearance somehow offended her. It screamed platinum healthcare, private stylist. He stood tall and thin, an arrow-straight back and vulpine face, neatly trimmed black hair. He wore polished leather shoes, pressed trousers and a burgundy roll-neck: his idea, perhaps, of dressing down.

Still, she can only wonder at the impression she might have made on him – if any at all – the morning they met, coming as it did after an encounter that had left her wrung out and questioning her grasp on sanity.

The night before Pardue's second rotation, Ariman had visited. Previously, the girl had appeared only through the fug of meds or alcohol, her presence easily dismissed as the product of an addled mind. But Pardue was clean, and so had assumed she was free. No. When she woke for the fifth or sixth time during a night of fractured sleep, there was Ariman beside the bed, solid and real, shrouded in amber from the street lamp outside. Pardue found

79

authenticity in the details: strands of hair escaping tight braids, crumpled linens, plump toes wiggling in leather sandals. She felt her throat tighten and flutter in terror – not of the girl as such, but of her presence, the madness of her presence. Her voice, when she found it, came in a croak.

'Are you alive?'

'Sure.'

'How can you be?'

'I don't know. I keep fighting.'

'But you should be much older now, a woman.'

The girl exhaled, long and loud, then dropped and sat on the carpet. This simple, childlike gesture – fed up, bored of silly questions – was somehow reassuring to Pardue. She shuffled up the bed, propped herself on an elbow. She even reached out, as though to touch the girl, before thinking better of it.

'Well, nothing can be done about it,' said Ariman. 'We're powerless, after all.'

'I could have helped you.'

'You answered to something greater than one person. Me too.'

'I achieved so little.'

'Only a few in this world can really change anything, and they never do. The less good they do, the stronger they become. Stronger all the time.'

'We can't win?'

'We can try – for a while. But our path is set, and our destination. That's all. It's not our fault.'

And Pardue knew then: This isn't happening. There's no phantom in my room proffering rationalisations that sound so like my own, placating me as the drugs used to. No, I have conjured this ghost. I'm dreaming, or she's a hallucination and I'm going mad. Is that better or worse?

Pardue lay her head on the pillow, and the figment child seemed to read her thoughts, because she smiled sadly and said, 'It will be fine. There are two things no one can deny you, Kathleen. One is peace. You'll find it.'

What was the other thing? She can't remember, or Ariman didn't say.

Pardue didn't wake again until dawn, startled into a confused consciousness by her screeching alarm. She dressed without showering and headed to the heliport.

Saria was already there, alone in the departure lounge. She lay on her back across the cushioned bench, and at first Pardue thought she was asleep. Pardue considered her a moment: scuffed hiking boots, jeans thinning at the knee, a frayed woollen sweater, all carried with a kind of effortless style.

Saria opened one eye, swivelled it in Pardue's direction. 'Hi.'

Pardue introduced herself.

'Oh, I know,' Saria said as Pardue settled on the seat opposite. 'You're the doctor, aren't you?'

'Medic. I don't think I saw you out there before.'

'No.' Eyes closed again. 'I spend a lot of my time downstairs. Way downstairs.'

'Yes. Saria, isn't it?'

'Still famous. How wonderful.'

'Porter mentioned you.'

'He did? Ah … a friend for the awkward girl. He means well, I suppose. Of course, now we mustn't be friends, else we'll prove him right.'

Don't worry, Pardue thought. We won't be close.

Next to arrive was Daws, heaving through the swing doors with a dropped shoulder, running a hand through wispy white hair. He had the sallow skin and hooded eyes of an addict – alcohol or similar, she had thought. Now she knows the truth: it's only sleep he craves.

'No ops this morning?' Daws said.

Saria didn't bother opening her eyes this time. She muttered, 'They're coming later. First chopper out is managers and us sundries.'

Pardue was glad. The ops lot – on their own, they each seemed fine enough, diffident almost. But they mostly moved in a pack, and then they were something else: beasts jostling for rank, snorting and braying. And at their head, the alpha, Gill.

He was the next one in that day, silent save for a cursory 'morning' as he took a seat slightly removed from the group. He stared out the window, across the pad, towards wire fence and office pods beyond, all gradually gaining definition against the retreating darkness.

Seule, she hardly remembers now. He was there, of course, but she can't recall his arrival. Perhaps he came in with Porter and Sargent. It was the latter who held her attention.

Porter announced him with due deference. 'Mr Sargent's down from Currie, coming out to have a look around, make sure all's as it should be.'

Hellos were muttered, waves half-heartedly offered. Even Saria looked up, nodded, then returned to her meditation. Sargent forced a smile. It looked like a gesture he'd heard described once but neither witnessed nor practised.

They sat quietly until the thud of rotors drew all eyes to the pad, a fat black bug wobbling down onto the tarmac. Staff from the A-crew, their rotational counterparts, began spilling out the chopper's sliding side door, dragging bags behind them and jogging half-bent away from the aircraft's slowing blades. Pardue began to gather up her luggage.

'No rush,' Porter said softly. 'It has to refuel before we can board.'

She said, 'We got straight on last time.'

'Yeah.' He looked to Sargent, but the company man had taken out a tab and was staring at it intently, oblivious to them and their talk – or hoping to appear that way, at least. 'There were spare helicopters then. We're just using the one now. It's a shuttle run: it goes out with some supplies, picks up half of the A-team, back here, refuels, takes us out, then comes back with the rest of the A-crew, and so on, till we're all where we need to be. Um … if you see what I mean.'

'Why?'

'It's complicated.'

'Cutbacks,' said Daws. 'More bad news on the way. Last year after the spills, they sold some helicopters, sacked a bunch more crew … I guess I'm still cheaper than a robot. Now we've had a botched raid on Antarctica, billions more down the drain. We're lucky not to be rowing out there.'

Porter winced at the mention of the previous week's military misadventures, and glanced nervously at Sargent. When he was sure the other was not looking, he caught Daws' eye and made the lip-zip gesture. Daws rolled his eyes. Saria, reading the awkward silence, offered a single, sharp laugh. Her eyes remained closed.

Seule said, 'It's efficiency – nothing to do with Antarctica.'

Porter changed the subject, asked if anyone had seen Broz. Heads were shaken.

'Hell,' he grumbled. 'That kid.'

'Screw him anyway,' snorted Gill. 'If he doesn't come out, he doesn't get paid. Simple as that. It's not like he does anything so useful.'

Broz made it in the end – just. They were loading their gear into the chopper's hold when Pardue noticed a blond blur dashing past the lit windows of the departure lounge. Porter saw him too and uttered an oath of relief. The young man emerged onto the tarmac, a gormless grin just visible through shaggy hair. He was soon past Pardue and offering half-hearted excuses, but she did not turn, because there was someone else in the lounge then, a figure at the window who raised a hand and placed a palm flat on the glass. Pardue mirrored the gesture, waved once, then looked in panic to the others. They were paying no attention to her, nor to Ariman at the window. When she looked back, the girl was gone.

The blackout had begun just a few hours later. The next morning, Sargent's message. Porter found it. And beyond the door, the man himself, gone by his own hand.

'Is it true?' she had asked Gill.

'I guess. The platform went into shutdown two days ago. Production's been drying to a trickle. But it shouldn't be. The reserves ... shit, I don't know. I just run the machines. That's why Sargent was here. He was investigating – all on the quiet, of course.'

'So, the operations team, were they ever coming?'

Porter insisted they were: 'Business as usual, or the appearance of. A-shift had been working to ID the problem. We were supposed to pick that up.'

And Gill, hushed, quieter than she'd ever heard him, added, 'But there's no problem to identify. The pumps, lines, the whole facility – it's working just fine.'

She knows Sargent's motivations will remain a mystery – just as he, it seems, intended. But she can speculate. He came, he saw, and what he saw was enough to take him to the edge and over in little more than 24 hours.

He had glimpsed his future, she thinks. But what did he see? A future in which KI Energy's results fell short of what was required to keep his job, his wealth, home, family? Perhaps, but the world is replete with failed execs living well enough off their severance packages. There is a point at which failure comes easily, and without consequence.

Did he, instead, see a future in which his cooked books and overstatements would lead to something else – something beyond negative numbers, something that could land even a man of his status in prison or worse? Maybe, or maybe he was just on the brink, for whatever reason, and nothing that did or didn't happen out here could have changed that.

Now, she supposes, another option presents itself. Another future foreseen by Sargent: a moment of illumination in those early hours of blackout. A future for them all, one he saw then and which she and her crew-mates are only just beginning to comprehend.

It's all gone now.

At first, they simply couldn't – or wouldn't – see how much trouble they might be in. Their supply drone failed to show on schedule, but it was another two days before they started to ration their food. It was a further day before Porter acknowledged the absence of traffic in the shipping lane a few kilometres to the south. On the sixth day, at breakfast in the canteen, Pardue asked about the lifeboat.

'It wouldn't work,' Porter told her. 'It has a tiny engine, just enough power to get clear of the platform in case of fire or collapse, or some such crisis. Then – theory goes – you sit there, switch on the beacon and wait to be rescued. So … no.'

She had retreated to the clinic, sought solace in its limited supply of moxodone, almost. It was more that she sought solace in the option. She knew what it would mean. A regression, a slide down the longest snake, all the way to the first square. And the devil in her said, So what? It doesn't matter now, does it?

That's what held her back as she sat staring at the open cabinet: giving in would be more than merely a setback. It would be an admission, an acceptance that something dreadful was happening, something that rendered all other considerations moot.

There was a practical case for abstinence, too. Only one sleeve of pills remained, and she knew from grim experience what was waiting for her when they were gone. So she maintained a tightly clenched resistance. On day eight, as she sat there chewing her lip and chasing the arguments and counter-arguments back and forth through her mind, there was a knock at the door. It was Seule, and he was suffering migraines. She sent him away with that last packet. It wasn't the right medication for him. But he needed something, and Pardue needed those pills gone.

****

Gill had said something earlier as they sat debating the radio message, that morbid loop, and she had ventured her opinion. The doctor has spoken!

The implication being, she assumes, that she has flitted passively – or worse – around the margins of this crisis, offering little, committing to nothing. It was a snide aside from him, a typically thoughtless shot. But there is truth to it, she can see that now. Her veins may be clean, but that numbness, that sense of detachment she courted after her retreat from the desert, has lingered. This realisation is born of acceptance – an acknowledgement now that no one will come, and that the boat is a real and singular solution.

Daws says he'll stay behind, and she can't understand that any more than she can the choices made by Sargent and Broz. But Daws was right when he declared they each must decide, they each must act.

Now, alone in the clinic, she surveys her work of earlier – several open boxes, into which kits, pouches and packets have been haphazardly slung. She sighs, as though considering the efforts of some slapdash underling, and begins rearranging the equipment, packing the remainder neatly, sealing full boxes with tape.

October 5: Blackout +15 Days

Morning, waiting for her midday meal. Something to look forward to, Porter had called it, but the anticipation builds only in blocks of discomfort. Stomach writhes, muscles cramp and chemical levels surge or burn to nothing. There is upside of sorts in the new schedule, though. It has her keen for work, for distraction. She stacks more boxes in the corridor outside her clinic, then moves to the kitchen pantry, where Porter and Daws have divided dry food packs into an array of meal portions. Pushing aside thoughts of theft and engorgement – and the gut-gurgles of encouragement – she boxes up enough for five travellers. The meagre remains will serve as a daily countdown to Daws' demise, unless he can produce life from a sea that has so far given nothing but death.

In Control she finds a well-padded kit bag. She heads out to the main deck, hears banging and clanging from the helipad, sounds of the others at work. Peering over the railings, she sees the fishing lines are in, but there is no sign of Daws. She stuffs tissue strips up her nostrils and enters the storage shed, moving slowly, uncertainly along the rows of shelving, perusing odd cans and unfamiliar packets, weighing their applications, their potential uses, and stepping carefully around the corpses at her feet. She takes a small can of lighter fluid, a pack of matches. She finds a pair of bolt-cutters, a crowbar, a reel of nylon rope, another of wire. She is about to leave when she sees something nestled on the top shelf, a blocky shape, barely visible in its dark, dusty corner. She stands on tiptoes to reach it. She grips the tool, turns it over in her hand appreciatively.

Back outside, and up two sets of stairs to the helipad, above and behind Control. Gill stands before the lifeboat, head back, chin in hand. She follows his eye-line to the mast, now pointing proudly through the craft's roof. He senses her approach, turns.

'What you got there?' He nods to her left hand.

'I thought it was a nail gun. Is it?'

'Yep.'

'I didn't see any nails though. Perhaps you should take a look in the shed later. I dare say I missed something.'

'Yeah, I will.'

'How are you getting on? This looks promising.'

Gill grunts. 'So far. We need to fit a boom on the mast there: kind of like a crossbar, I guess. Then the sail goes on. Lash it on. Did you see Seule?'

'No.'

'Shit.' Gill hawks, spits onto the ground by his foot. 'Kids, sleeping while the world burns.' He frowns. 'Ah, you don't think … he wouldn't –'

'I'm sure he's fine.'

'We can't lose him, you know. Not him.'

'Maybe you should tell him that,' Pardue says.

'Maybe *you* should.'

'It's not the same. Surely you can see how he looks up to you.'

'Morning.' Saria emerges from inside the boat. 'Oh, a nail gun.' Her eyes narrow. 'You getting ready for a rampage?'

'I –'

Gill gives a grim chuckle. 'Doctor Death.'

'Please don't.'

'You never know.' He offers his hand. 'Give it here. I'll find the right ammo for you later.'

'I picked up some other things. I'll put it all in Control. And I'll go find Seule.'

****

She knocks, but receives no immediate response. She is about to try again when she hears the faint thud of footsteps. The door opens a crack to reveal a grey face, lit by reddened eyes. Seule coughs, a dry wheeze that makes him wince.

'You again,' he says.

'You don't look so good, Seule.'

'I had a bad night.' He sniffs hard. 'I suppose Gill's raging at me again.'

'We need you now. The mast's up.'

'Yes, okay.'

'Let me come in. I'll take a look at you.'

Seule winces again, splutters into the crook of his arm. He looks feeble in pale yellow vest and tight boxers. On the bed behind him, off-white sheets are tangled and strewn. A musty smell hangs over the room. Pardue clears her throat, braces against this adolescent funk, and tells Seule to lie down. She perches on the bed and checks his eyes, throat, chest.

'You're a bit feverish.'

'A bit,' Seule sniffs. 'It started last night. A cough at first, really bad – like my chest was going to explode. Then I woke in the early hours in a sweat. Dripping with sweat, and my throat

90

was so tight I couldn't breathe. I thought I was having a panic attack.' He screws his eyes shut, purses his lips.

'And how about those headaches?'

'Stopped, I guess.'

'You've got a cold, maybe. It'll hit worse, because of the hunger, the weakness. Everything.'

'Yeah, I don't know. Pardue, I had a … uh, dream last night. Or it was a vision. I'm not sure whether I was asleep or awake.'

'You're feverish, like I said. And, you know … trauma does things to people.'

'No, no. Listen, I lived it. I lived out near a whole day. It was like that was real and this here was the dream.' Seule sits up with a moan, yanks the sheet over his prone body, then drops again, curls away onto his side, face to the wall and back to Pardue. She moves to leave, but he continues. 'I was lying here shivering and sweating. Eyes closed. Darkness. And then I heard this crunching sound. Clear as anything, unmistakable. Car tyres on gravel – just a lovely sound. My eyes were shut, and I heard this noise, and when I opened them I was gone from here. I was somewhere else. It was daylight, and I was standing outside a country hotel, the sort of place you drive out to on Sundays, old farmhouse style. You know?'

'Not really.'

'Oh, right. Well … it was real. A crisp, cold day. I could feel it, I could actually feel the breeze. And on the ground all around were autumn leaves, dry and crackling under my shoes. Crackling leaves and crunching gravel. Lovely. I was standing at the rear of our car. My mother was beside one door, adjusting her coat, checking her reflection in the window. My father emerged from the front seat. And there was a girl there too. A little younger than me maybe. She was my sister. I mean, I don't have a sister. But just then I did. In that moment, I knew she was my sister.

'Okay, well, I'm not sure what –'

'Father strode away towards the hotel and Mother went after him. My sister watched them go, and sort of smirked at me and rolled her eyes. This place, I didn't really recognise it, just its type: high ceilings, whitewash and silver, cool and soothing. The girl on the front desk asked Father if he had a reservation. The old man turned it on, all warm smiles and head tilts. 'No, no, we don't book, but …' And the rest is implied, no need to say it: You can see who we are. Mother checked the contents of her handbag. Me and my sister shared a look, like, oh, how embarrassing. The girl panicked, called her superior over, and we were taken to the private dining room. They poured red wine and we were served roast chicken, potatoes, veg, baked … oh, hell.'

'Don't.'

'I could taste it though, Pardue! I really could. I could taste it, feel it going down my throat, the weight of it in my belly. Oh –'

'Don't.'

'Oh. Afterwards, my father turned to me and he said, "You'll be back from the sea soon then?" And I didn't know what he meant. I said, "I'm back now, aren't I?" He says, "No, no, no. Back for good, across the sea and back to stay." I told him I didn't understand. I said, "I'm here, Father – that's all behind me now." He shook his head. Mother chimed in: "Your father's done so much for you." And Father said, "You won't last long out there. Not you, not with those people. You won't make it without us. You need to be here. There is a place for you. We look after our own, of course. It's the right thing to do." See how clearly I can remember all this? That's not a dream is it?'

'It seems a little cryptic – dreamlike, you might say.'

'I said to him – in the hotel, I mean – "I don't get you, I don't understand." My sister squeezed my arm. So then … uh, it's weird. We went for a walk, all of us together. No one said anything. Father got up, put on his coat, and we followed him: out the car park and up a dirt path. On our left there was a row of apple trees. On our right was a ploughed field that sloped up to a wooden fence, and a grassy hillside, very steep. The path curved away, around the far edge of the field and up the hill. We crossed a stile and we were climbing. I felt my breath getting shallower as the track got steeper and narrower. But I didn't want to stop, didn't want Father to see me struggling. We had to walk single file then. The weeds on either side were brushing our arms and legs, and this path just got steeper and steeper. About halfway up, I heard a horrible noise, like cackling. I turned and my sister was there, a bit behind me. She's stopped, hands on hips, and she's giggling, grinning up at me. She says, "What are we doing here? This is insane!"

'I looked up at my father and mother, him in a business suit and shoes, her in dress and heels. They were climbing on, oblivious. And my sister was laughing again. "This is nuts!"

'On we went. The climb ended on a cliff edge high above a beach of rocks and pebbles. The wind was stronger there – strong enough to blow you over if you weren't careful. We stood near the edge. And further along the cliff was a house. A hut really, like they have in the detention centres. It stood on an outcrop, sheer drops on three sides. Father pointed and said, "It's going to fall in. I wanted you to see."

'And my sister said, "Why didn't you tell us earlier? Why didn't you do something? Do something now!"

'Father just said, "You don't live there. Stupid girl, you should be more grateful."

'And I was glad – glad he snapped at her, not me. He led us back down. It was getting dark when we reached the car park. The hotel was shut up, and ours was the only car there. We climbed in. I remember the smell – leather upholstery, sharp in the cold air. The heaters kicked in, and I could feel my hands and feet growing prickly in the warmth. I leant back and shut my eyes as we reversed out. There was that crunch again, tyres on gravel. I … couldn't breathe. Then I was here, wet.'

'A bad dream. A fever dream.'

'I suppose. But honestly, I lived it. Every second, every minute. It passed in real time. I lived that day.'

'I'm going to try find something for your throat.'

'Are there any pills left?'

'No more pills. Gill needs you up top.'

'Really?'

'Tomorrow you're going to sail us out of here. We're all counting on you.'

'Right.'

When she returns with a tube of lozenges, he is showered and dressed, and flashes of pink are returning to his cheeks.

****

She heads back up, through Control, where she finds Porter sitting at the comms desk. His hands are clasped tight over the heavy headphone shells, fat digits quivering, knuckles drained to white. He has removed his glasses and is staring blankly out the window, unaware of her presence over his left shoulder. His cheeks are moist with tears. She leaves him be.

'Aw, fuck's sake!' Gill's cry is the first thing she hears as she steps onto the deck, followed by a guttural roar, a string of strangled curses from above. She sees Gill lean over the helipad. 'Get up here, quick,' he yells. 'She's cut.'

Saria is on her knees, bent double before the lifeboat, left hand clasped over right, a pool of blood forming on the gridded deck between her thighs. She is grimacing, growling. Pardue crouches next to her, prises away the shaky left hand to reveal a cut on the other, a deep, oozing slice down the fleshy pad below her thumb. Pardue hears Gill retching behind her.

'You hold it again.' She replaces Saria's good hand. 'Okay? Let's get you down to the clinic.'

'Stupid, stupid, stupid.' Saria is unmoved. Her whole frame is shaking now.

'What happened?'

'Tool slipped. Idiot!' Saria grits her teeth, wobbles forwards slightly. 'Argh, shit.'

'Come on. You need a couple of staples. Gill! Help me move her.'

'I, ah …' He looms above them, face drained of colour. He wipes his sleeve across his lips, steps forwards, rocks back, opens his palms. 'Uh –'

'Just help me support her! Like this.' She takes Saria's right arm, just below the shoulder. Gill nods and follows suit on the other side.

'I can walk,' snaps Saria.

'Of course, but we'll be here if you need us.'

They stagger down the steps and through Control. Porter has left.

In the clinic, Gill helps Saria onto the bench as Pardue rips into boxes she so recently packed and sealed. As she begins the job of cleaning, closing and dressing Saria's wound, Pardue hears Gill collapse, moaning, onto her desk chair.

****

'This day isn't going the way I'd hoped,' Pardue says when her work is done. 'No doubt you'd agree.'

Saria lies on the bench, stares at the ceiling. Gill has left, a wordless exit when Pardue pulled out the stapler.

Pardue asks, 'Does it hurt badly?'

'No.'

'Keep it wrapped, well protected.'

'Okay.'

'There's no point beating yourself up over this, you know. Nobody can operate at 100 per cent under such circumstances.'

'But we kind of have to. We have to operate at 100 per cent or we won't get through this. I mean, we haven't even got in the boat yet.' She laughs bitterly. 'So stupid! I really thought I was –'

'It could have been much worse.'

'Oh, and Gill really is squeamish. That's just great.'

'Well –'

'Maybe it is good news.' Saria sits, swings her legs down from the bench. She examines the bloody smudges across her grey sweater. 'You're right, it could've been worse. Could've hit an artery. I'm glad you were there.'

'You should rest. You lost a bit of blood.'

'No, it's okay.' Saria forces a weak smile. 'I can put my feet up tomorrow, when the cruise starts.'

'At least wait here while I repack these boxes. You certainly need to eat. I need to eat. I'll walk you back up.'

'Okay.'

'What did you mean, about Gill? About good news?'

'Oh.' Saria seems to weigh her answer – or maybe the wisdom in answering at all. 'Probably nothing. It's just … with Broz and everything.'

Pardue tuts. 'This again. Can't you accept –'

'Forget it.'

Pardue is happy to comply. 'What were you working on up there, before your accident? I thought you were waiting for Seule.'

'I was removing the back seats. I thought we could squeeze a mattress in, take turns to rest. I'm not sure how long we'll be out there, but –'

'More than a day … do you think so?'

'Oh, it depends, I imagine. On the weather, the wind. Could be a few hours, could be … well, I suppose if we haven't hit the island in a couple of days we're in some real trouble.'

'I suppose so.'

'Ugh, Seule.' Saria prods lightly at the dressing on her palm. 'Is he up to this?'

'Try to be supportive.'

'I want to show you something before we eat, Kathleen.'

'Oh?'

'Come with me.'

Saria's quarters are a tip. Her bed is unmade and jeans, jumpers, odd socks and boots are strewn around. Like Seule's, it is a teenager's room. The smell, though, is incongruous.

'What is that?' Pardue asks. 'Talc?'

'Oh, I suppose.'

Pardue smiles, shakes her head.

'Is that odd?'

'No. It's pleasant. So civilised. I ran out of everything a while ago. No toothpaste even.'

Saria looks hurt. 'You only had to ask.'

'I suppose. It never occurred to me. It didn't seem right, perhaps. Play the cards you're dealt and all that.'

'That's crazy.' Saria nods towards the bathroom. 'There's toothpaste in there. There's soap even. Take it – borrow it, I mean. You'll feel like a new woman.'

'Thank you.'

'There's something else.' She crosses to a cupboard, pulls out two hangers.

'A wetsuit?'

'Not quite. These are under-suits. Two-piece. I wear them beneath my dry-suit.' Saria pinches the grey spongy material between finger and thumb, lets it snap back into shape. 'Thin, but very warm, even if you're wet.'

'Okay.'

'Put it on under your clothes when we leave. Don't tell anyone. I only have two.'

'You think we'll be getting wet?'

'I was thinking about when we get home. Get to the island, I mean.'

Pardue examines the suit. 'Why are you giving this to me?'

'You're the right fit.' Saria hurries on. 'Look, what happened just now, I think I got a bit scared. But I want you to know, I don't usually lose it like that. It was just that the blood kept coming, and –'

'You don't have to convince anyone of anything.'

'But I do want you to know: when we get back, I'm strong enough.'

'I don't doubt it.'

Saria asks, 'What will you do back there?'

'I don't know. It depends.'

'I mean, where will you go, or try to go?'

'I would have to report to … if there's anyone … oh, I don't know. I think I need to work again. Really work.'

'Work? I was thinking more about living, surviving.'

'It's not just a job. It's a duty, a vocation. I've neglected it, and –'

'But if it's as bad there as everyone thinks, the time for duty might have passed.'

'The opposite, I'd think. Look, Saria, I just want to get back there. That's all I'm focusing on right now.'

'Yes, yes. But, I mean, Gill has a wife, Seule has a family. Seule has a bunker! Porter … I don't know. But you and me, nothing. Right?'

'We really have no idea what's happening. It could all be –'

Saria sighs. She drops her under-suit onto the bed and flops down on it. She stares into the corner of the room. 'Didn't you ever aspire to more? Family, friends? An anchor.'

Pardue's eyes drop to her own suit. She fingers a zip, pushing it back and forth across several notches. 'Someone once told me, "This will come to you." She meant the chaos and carnage of other places, other countries. I've been to those places, some of them. Seen it with my own eyes. And we've all grown up under that shadow, that vague notion – holocaust, apocalypse, whatever. Annihilation. But still, there's a part of me that thinks, Not us, not here, we stand apart from that. Oh, I know it's something bad, I can imagine crises. But something more, I don't know. Perhaps I'm deluded.'

Saria grins bitterly. 'I'm not sure what you're saying.'

'I don't really know.' She sits beside Saria. 'How's the hand now?'

'Stings a bit. It's fine. Thanks for fixing me.'

'Do you live with anyone, Saria?'

'Not really. I had a room in a block. There were other people there.'

'I once lived by the sea. Right on the edge. That's how I could afford it – because it was so close to going over. Open fireplace, low lights. Ancient. A place for blankets and quilts. The kind of place that makes you crave a cold winter. Things might have worked out for me there, if I'd stayed clean. You know, if everything turns out okay, if this is all just some giant screw-up, I'm going to do my time and I'm going to move back there. Try again.'

'I think that may go beyond hope. Fantasy.'

'Sometimes there are gulls in the garden. Little ones. I even saw a seal once – or thought I did. Impossible now, I imagine. But ...'

'Maybe I'll come visit.'

Pardue says, 'We should go and eat.'

'You go, Kathleen. I think I'll rest a while after all.'

****

Family, friends. An anchor. Question deflected, questioner deflated. But if Saria couldn't force a response, she has at least compelled Pardue, eating alone in the clinic, to consider one. The question holds weight. The answer: it was there if she wanted. It was there with Mark. But almost from the start, she had resisted, rejected what he represented.

For a while her push had been offset by his pull, and she had achieved an equilibrium of sorts, the midpoint between fight and submission, until the former overcame the latter. She often wonders whether the polarity could have been reversed, the balance found again and sustained. Hard to imagine, though. With Mark, life so often seemed comfortable, safe. All was right with the world, no need to worry – and that had worried her. The pull and the push.

It began with a scare.

She'd been walking home from the uni hospital one night, along footpaths that glistened with frost – a rare cold snap. Her breath formed white plumes in the frigid air, and she amused herself, in childish fashion, by pretending to be a smoker, building out her character from there: she was someone edgy, dangerous; she was off to some moonlit meeting of great consequence and risk; she was stalking urban streets. More fun than the reality: traipsing an arterial road on Melbourne's eastern fringes, urban outposts on one side, agri-plants and farmland the other.

In sight of her dorm block, she had heard a commotion in the field beside her: a thud, a bass moan, something awful, alien, then laughter, high chuckles, followed by hurried, grass-muffled footsteps and muddy squelches. She stopped, rocking on her heels, wondering whether to move, which way to move, and scrambling in her pockets for keys or anything else that

101

might do damage to a cheek or eye. Then, in the field, in the small sweep of streetlight amber, two figures emerged, wide-eyed and grinning. They stopped when they saw her, exchanged guilty glances, then veered away, back into the darkness.

'Idiots!' she hollered as she regained composure.

A private message: 'Kathleen, sorry about the other night. We didn't mean to scare you. We were drunk. I feel awful now. Mark, room 244.'

She didn't know him, and so his familiar tone had grated, as did the memory of that scare. She marched to room 244 and rapped on the door. She was angry, but hadn't considered how to convey it, and so she didn't as such. She simply told him not to bother her again, stomped away.

'I just want to chip away at the edges,' he told her later, and she was offended, of course. But part of her must have wanted him to succeed, or at least to keep trying. And likewise, she took it upon herself to sculpt him a little. Why else would she have returned to his room an hour later on that first day?

'Actually, I'm not finished with you.'

Lesson No.1: there is a fear known only to women alone in the dark. No.2: every cow has the right to sleep in peace without someone trying to tip it over.

'Do you have a thing for cows, Kathleen?'

'I respect cows.' She was angry still, but they ended up laughing.

He took her to parties where pinched prescription pills of the milder sort were washed down with cans of icy beer and tumblers of cheap wine, where vivid, vibrant undergrads circled and swayed from room to room, drifting on smoke and vapour, speaking easily to friend and stranger alike, as though it was nothing. She clung close to his side, and he was good enough to let her, to know she lacked the self-assurance to be alone in those places. Mark liked the hours around midnight, when the music was loud and fast, and the people were high and tightly wound. Pardue grew to crave the pre-dawn, when the numbers dwindled and the dancers fell still on their feet, then sat, then slumped under blankets; when the talking gave way to gentle smiles and shallow nods, and the music grew soft and dreamy, calling for introspection.

Drugs and booze, her first real tastes.

There have been times since that she has sought the easy out – blaming Mark for what followed, portraying him as a rogue influence, an opener of gateways to the bad, bad places she would later explore alone. But to do so is to cast herself as naïve and yielding. No, it was her choice to experiment, to dabble in a lifestyle. And anyway, the link is unclear. Mark and his friends, they dosed up to feel something new, something fun or wonderful; that's flawed in its way, but it doesn't have to precipitate the awful other – doing the same to feel nothing at all. In truth, if Mark was a gateway, it was to nothing more than a mellow middle age.

During their time together, the nights were his. In daylight, she showed him her world. She took him to sit-ins, dragged him along on marches, because this was the time of the border protection act, the basic income repeal and the union ban. Time for action, hitting the streets in solidarity and fury. She tried to open his eyes to the true state of things: allies and enemies. He must have found something to admire in her idealism, just as she was half-charmed by his cheery indolence. Sometimes he would read over her shoulder and ask for bullet-point primers on whichever subject was gripping her, and he'd say, 'It's unbelievable; it's awful, I never knew,' and she would be at once thrilled and oddly dismayed, as though she had taken something from him. As though it were her corrupting him.

She took him to the coast too, to unspoilt spots, to blow holes, caves, arches and stacks, then up to precipices, where the roar of the wind and the clawing of the sea below demanded silent contemplation. He would grin at her earnest appreciation for it all, and she would tell him, 'These places, they're worth struggling for. Our world and the good people in it – all worth the fight. I used to want to live in a place like this. One day, maybe.'

Mark's nods affirmed nothing but uncertainty. He was, she always knew, wondering where he fit in this picture. And she never told him. The push.

He figured it out in the end.

'We could buy a place. Think about starting a family.' His words, graduation day. Then silence and a sad half-smile, an acceptance that their moment had passed.

He couldn't win her over. She had, by then, made her choice: committed to the desert, to her war, to freedom fighters and whatever else awaited.

****

'There's something out there.' Porter is at the south-east corner of the helipad, staring out across the water, landward. His voice is flat, dispassionate. 'Something's coming.'

Pardue draws up beside him, just in time to hear the pronouncement. It doesn't quite register, though, because she has more pressing concerns. He has missed his meal, and this is inexplicable.

'I've got your rations here, Porter.'

She reaches for her pocket, but he grunts, waves her away.

'What's wrong with you?' she asks.

'There's something coming.'

'I can't see anything. What are you talking about?'

Porter points. 'On the horizon there. It's just a spot. I wonder what it is.'

'Are you sure you're not just … seeing things?'

'No. There's something out there. It's moving. Bigger now, I reckon.'

'It's hard in this light.'

Porter glances skywards, then curses under his breath. 'I've lost it now. Have I?'

'It's probably just flotsam. Or is it jetsam?'

'Probably.'

'Are you okay, Porter?'

'Yeah, yeah.'

She makes to leave, to join Gill, Saria and Seule, who are gathered on the roof of the lifeboat, grappling with the tarp that will form their sail.

'There it is again.'

She looks back towards the horizon. 'Oh! Yes, I'm with you now. I saw it straight away this time. Is it in the water? Is it floating?

'Yeah, I reckon.'

'Okay. Uh. We shouldn't get our hopes up though. I mean, it could be anything.'

'I'm not hopeful.'

A cry comes from behind them. 'Are you seeing that?!'

It is Saria. Pardue turns to see her up on tiptoes, right hand cupped over and around her right eye, framing her vision. Gill and Seule remain crouched behind her. They stare up at Saria, mouths agape. Then they too are slowly standing, peering out over the ocean, squinting, straining, as the half-mounted sail flaps limply beside them. Pardue sees Gill's lips moving. Saria shakes her head. He steps up alongside her, closer to the boat's edge. He nods. Behind them, Seule is tottering and craning, seeking a better view.

Pardue turns and again locks on to the shadowy shape, larger now – closer. It is floating: she can see it rise and fall in time with the swell. Up, tip and dip, the pattern repeating, holding their attention, mesmeric almost, and promising something: a great revelation. Finally, a shift. A twist, a turn, the slightest change of course that reveals – for a moment – a soft silhouette, a definite shape. Context.

'Oh, my …' The words stick in Pardue's throat.

Behind them comes the heavy clang of boots on steel, Gill dropping to the deck and rushing to their vantage point. More clangs, more boots following fast behind.

'That is a fucking boat,' Gill pants as he pulls up alongside them. 'Do you … oh.'

The shape has shifted again, its edges melting away to nothing.

'We saw it,' Pardue reassures him.

'Is it heading this way?' asks Saria. She and Seule have completed a five-strong front row, all hands clasped on the railing, 50 whitened knuckles.

'It's coming for us,' says Porter.

'It's getting closer, for certain,' says Pardue. 'We're looking at the front of it. I can tell that now.'

'The prow,' says Seule quietly. 'We're looking at the prow, and there's a wheelhouse up top, I think – like it's a little dinghy, a pleasure boat or something. It's got no business out here.'

'But it is here,' says Pardue. 'This could be our way home. I mean –'

'Home's what they're running from,' Porter whispers.

'What's up?' Daws has arrived behind them. 'I heard you shouting.'

No one turns, but Gill replies, 'A boat's coming.'

'Oh. Well, that's interesting.'

****

Gradually, the vision forms: snub prow, dirty white fibreglass, the narrow, open-top wheelhouse and, inside, a dark form, shoulders, a head – just a smudge really, shrouded perhaps by some hood or hat.

Pardue and the others shuffle in unison along the railing, adjusting and readjusting their position to match the boat's expected point of arrival, dashing down to the main deck when it becomes apparent it will reach them under the crane. When they hear the splutter-chug of a diesel engine, they begin to signal, to shout 'Hey!' and 'Ahoy!' and to wave. The skipper remains bowed over his controls.

It comes on quicker now, the detail: the figure's greasy green cape and sou'easter, the odd boxes and plastic drums piled up behind him, wide spatters of sooty muck along the vessel's flanks. Only when the boat is almost directly beneath them does the skipper raise his head. Their cries fall silent. A face: bleached

107

skin hanging loose from sunken muscle; empty eyes; darkened maw. The man raises a hand, extends a bony finger and draws it across his throat.

Then he is gone, the engine muffled as the vessel passes under the deck. Porter exhales, long and loud, from somewhere deep within, and he begins to sob. Daws simply closes his eyes. Gill, Seule and Saria turn and run to the other side of the platform, Pardue following, arriving in time to see the boat emerge below her, its course unaltered, its pilot unmoved.

'Tell us!' screams Gill, voice cracking with the effort. 'At least tell us!'

They watch in silence as the boat leaves, course unaltered.

Finally, they return to the eastern deck.

****

Daws is staring to the heavens, a puzzled look on his face. They follow his gaze to see Porter sitting astride the crane's narrow arm, several metres out from the deck, hands clasped to the metalwork, legs dangling over the water.

'… and now I'm done,' he is telling Daws. 'We're cursed. Or we are the curse, a curse on this land.'

'It's your choice,' Daws tells him.

Porter nods, mouths something, but there is no sound.

'Now what?' groans Gill.

Porter glances back over his shoulder, then continues, louder, shouting almost, addressing them all. 'We've failed, everyone. Humanity! I've feared for us, for myself. Now I'm tired out. Done in. What's the point in going back? Nothing much there before, and whatever's left … lord, we wouldn't even deserve that: a life of fear and misery. No, we don't even deserve that much.' He tilts his head to one side, as though weighing his own argument. 'You tell yourself you do good, that you're a good person. But all of us … we slept ourselves to death! I understand now. That voice, it's like it comes from within.' Porter wriggles a little further along the arm. 'This isn't how it used to be here. Everyone just scrambling, grubbing, from start to finish. No thoughts for the world of tomorrow … or even of today. No cares for what we're doing, how we're killing ourselves. It's like we're blind. Or perhaps we can see, we just don't want to. Bunker mentality. Hey, Seule? What do they think – *your* people? "Oh, our kids needn't worry." Wrong! The flood has come, and their ark isn't ready! They should have built more platforms instead. Haha! Nothing touches us out here.'

'You're giving up are you?' Gill slaps his hand against the crane cab, punctuating his question with a metallic clank. 'Giving up like Daws? Is that it?'

'Ha! Nothing you say now …' Porter shakes his head, leaves the sentence hanging. 'Maybe there's a way out. Salvation, somehow. God, I hope so.'

Daws trudges away. He flops down on the helipad stairs, jams his hands between his knees and stares at his feet.

Gill continues. 'This isn't for you, Porter. You know what? You're right. Those people, the bunker crowd – you're dead right about them. Screw them. Don't you get it? This is the time. You're mad, and you should be. Look what they did to us – all of us. This is the moment to wake up, open our eyes. Fight, man.'

'No, no, no. It just starts again. Same old … people. That's the problem. It's in you too, Gill. Dictator in waiting. It doesn't take much.'

'Fuck off.'

'You know it. It scares you, I'll grant you that. But it's there. It's in you, in all of us, I reckon. We're always on the brink.'

Gill slams the cab again, then sets himself to mount the crane's latticework. 'I'll drag you down myself!'

Porter throws back his head and roars to the sky. 'Do not come up here!'

Pardue moves up alongside Gill, bound to act, to placate the patient, Porter. But she has no sense how to proceed, no words seem to suffice.

Saria beats her to it. A high yell – she sounds, for the first time, shaken. 'Stop!'

'Listen to her, Gill,' says Porter. 'Or we'll both go over the side.'

'Porter!' Saria is half-pleading, half-raging. 'This isn't right! This isn't the answer. It isn't the right thing to do!'

'I can see now, that's all. The scales have fallen. Is that what they say? I heard the voice: seven seals. And I've seen the messenger, the throat-cutter. We all know what that means, sailing away into the nothingness. We know. We knew all along. Knew the end was coming. But we figured it would fall long after our time. Some other guy's problem. Why? Someone had to cop it … and now it's here, it's for us. I've listened and looked, and I've felt it, in my bones, in the ache in my belly. Smell and taste, they're all that remain: salt, I suppose.'

Porter's shuffles a little further forward, then his right shoulder dips, pulling the rest of his body behind it. He sends a yelp into the abyss, then tumbles after it.

****

Four sit in the canteen, silent in their thoughts.

Seule rests his forehead on folded arms. He is the one to break the quiet. 'Now what?' he mumbles into woollen sleeves.

Pardue glances at Gill, expecting him to respond in typically bullish fashion, but he is staring glassy eyed at the floor beside him.

Saria answers. 'It'll be dark soon. We should get some floodlights on the helipad. We're almost finished with the sail.'

Seule lifts his head. 'We're still going tomorrow?'

'What else? Stay here? He's right on one thing.' Saria nods at Gill, but he remains unmoved. 'We can't just sit here.'

'I mean –'

'This place will do for us all. If there's hope, it's at home … the island.'

'That thing in the boat didn't think so.'

'Thing?'

'Didn't you see?'

'I saw a very sick, old man.'

'Sick? I saw Death. Damned … skull face.'

'Death? Please, don't.'

'It was a man; I know that.' He thumps a hand on the table. 'I know it was a man! But he came from the place we're going to, and he didn't look so good. I saw –'

'Saw Broz there,' mutters Gill.

A flash of horror courses through Pardue. 'You saw what?'

'I saw Broz. Porter saw something that made him go up the crane. Seule saw Death. I saw the boy.'

'Oh, I knew it,' groans Saria.

Pardue rubs wearily at her eyes. 'Why did you see Broz?'

'Uh ...' Gill blinks hard, as though shaken by his own revelation. He purses his lips, sealing them against further indiscretion.

Seule whines, 'What are you all talking about?'

Saria tuts loudly. 'Let's hear it.'

Gill swallows hard. 'He had food. He had taken our food. I caught him.' He adds nothing, as though the rest is self-evident.

'Go on,' Saria demands.

'Uh ... he had chocolate too. Chocolate! I didn't even know we had chocolate here. Maybe it was his, from home. That makes sense. But, fuck – the situation. Our situation. Ah ...' Gill clasps a hand over nose and mouth. He meets all their eyes in turn, imploring. 'He cheated us.'

Pardue asks, 'What did you do, Gill?'

'Executed him,' Saria sneers.

'No!' Gill's head shake is vehement enough to set his cheeks wobbling. 'No, no. He went for *me*. I was holding him off me. Pushing him away. And he hit his head. That's all. Uh ... he went limp. Bled out.'

'You tossed him over the side?' asks Pardue.

Gill gulps again. 'And I hosed it away, all that blood.'

Seule shakes his head. 'Oh, no ... why are you even telling us this? We don't need to hear this now! We need –'

'Leader Gill!' cries Saria. 'Fearless leader Gill. The great dictator. Yep, Porter was right about you.'

'Stop.' Pardue shoots Saria a pointed look.

Gill sniffs, clears his throat, wipes a sleeve across his eyes. 'I didn't mean it, you know. But –'

Seule interjects. 'If he kept stealing food, we'd have been done days ago.'

'So thieves must die?' scoffs Saria.

'He's right though,' reasons Pardue. 'It's not just stealing, is it? It's more –'

Gill whispers, 'It wasn't punishment.'

'Why throw him over then?' snaps Saria. 'Why dispose of the evidence?'

'I don't have to answer to –'

'I think you do. If we're all getting on that boat tomorrow, I think you do. I don't want anyone else thrown overboard.'

'Oh!' Gill's bearing shifts. His eyes narrow, and his teeth are suddenly bared. 'Fuck you. Oh, you perfect little –'

'Ah, he's back.' Saria meets his glare.

'Please.' Pardue sighs. 'Stop this … baiting.'

Saria is incredulous. 'He took a life! How can you be –'

'It's not getting us anywhere, Saria. We are getting on that boat tomorrow. Everything else will have to wait.'

Saria glowers at Pardue. 'This is nowhere near over.'

But for the moment, it is. Saria submits. Seule lowers his head to the table top once more, and Gill returns to his dead-eyed meditation.

'I caught this.' Daws has entered quietly behind them. Cradled in his arms is a large, silvery fish.

****

She prepares the dregs of the coffee while Daws swiftly fillets and begins frying the fish.

'This will be a little weak,' she tells him.

'It's worth it just for the smell,' he says, breathing in deeply.

'Yes, I suppose.'

'Oh, that smell. It takes me back to so many places, so many times. Safe places, good times – some of them. If I shut my eyes now, I could be away from here, just for a while. But that's the last of it, hey – last of the coffee.'

'I'm sorry.'

'I know what you're thinking, Pardue.'

'You do?'

'I know what you think about me.'

'You seem content now.'

'That bothers you though. Scares you maybe. You should know, I'm not giving in. That's not what this is. I'm at peace is all. I'm just at peace. We all have to find a way, our own way of dealing. You're right to get in the boat, I'm right not to. Porter did what was best for him. He believed – hoped, I guess – there was some good place waiting for him. It gave him some comfort.'

'Did it? Because I'm not so sure … not so sure he jumped. I mean, I think he might have fallen.'

A shrug. 'I don't know how long I'll last out here. Could be days, months – years even. If I'm going to spend my last days fishing,' he nods towards the sizzling pan, 'well, now at least I know. It's not futile. That's something.'

'You'll be alone.'

'I accepted that long ago, long before all this. Ah … accepted might be the wrong word.' Daws takes a spatula, flips the fillets, revealing a perfect golden crust on each. He hums appreciatively, begins tracing concentric circles in the hot oil, staring down into the spiral shapes that form, then fade, form again. 'Adapted. I've had my time, had my chances. Some I took, some I missed. Can't complain. And, you know, there's nothing so awful as loneliness among crowds, is there? Out here, I can be the last man on Earth.'

'You said you had killed.'

'Yeah … yeah. So that's another thing. Whatever's happening out there, I know: it's just more of the same. This world's been at war forever. Certainly as long as I've known. Maybe this is the final battle. But I've had my say in it all. It feels like a lifetime ago, but I can't forget it. I've done things, seen even more, same as you.'

'Same as –'

'I know where you've been.' Daws puts down the utensil and meets her eyes. 'It's okay, no one told. I just know, because I've been there too – long before you, of course. The trauma, it's there in you. On you. It's like a mist, a cataract or whatever. No one walks away unscathed from that place.'

'You were in the borderlands?'

'Went there to save democracy. That's what they told me anyway.'

'They told lies.'

'First person I ever put down, first one I know about anyway, we …' Daws tails off, frowns, then continues. 'We were raiding apartments, looking for some bigwig, I think. I didn't even get inside the building, because they opened up on us from the rooftops, pinning us down in doorways, hugging the walls. We backed out of the street and tried to swing around behind them. I turned a corner and there he was, rifle on his hip like some bloody movie star. He let go a wild burst – nothing doing. I didn't have time to think on that. One round from me and he was down, and I knelt over him as the others ran past me to the next one and the next one and the next one. The boy was shaking. I pulled a hypo from my webbing and jabbed it in him. I shouldn't have done it, shouldn't even have stopped with him. But sometimes you make your own rules, for wrong or right. All the hardness and hate went from him. He smiled at me, and it didn't matter then that I was the one who made him hurt, because I was the one who stopped it too. He started to say something, one word over and over, and I don't know what it meant, but to me it sounded like "love". I held his shoulder and stroked his hair and I nodded as he repeated that word over and over: love, love, love. Then he was gone and I had to move again, because I was alive and he was dead. End of. Later that day we shot three more of them because our CO wouldn't take prisoners. Bloody hell.' Daws' sniffs hard, takes a long breath. 'Whatever anyone did out there, it was either too much or not enough.'

'It's right to try, though. It's right to try.'

'So there's a drop of hope left in you, hey. That's good. It means there's still fight in you, too. That's why you get on the boat.' He turns back to the pan. 'Me, I'm all fought out, and that's okay as well.'

'Daws, I think you should know. Broz –'

'Nah, I heard – I listened to it all outside the door. I doubt you're getting the whole truth on it. But who am I to judge? Who are any of us now? Sometimes you make your own rules. There's no anger in me any more, Pardue. When I saw that thing out there in the boat, I thought, That's it for me, that's really it. I release myself from the … ah, the duty of care. It was a relief. Now I'm … I don't know.'

'Disconnected.'

'Yeah.'

'But I'm not sure that's truly possible.'

Daws grins. 'Not while you still have hope. If you're running low, look to the girl, the boy even. Draw from them … if you want.'

****

The group eat and drink in silence, eyes widening and muscles relaxing as the sweet, supple flakes momentarily cleanse minds and memories. No one demurs when Pardue splits Porter's unused lunch between them as a side.

When they are almost done, Daws raises his mug. 'Here's to you, then. Good luck, I guess. If all's well, maybe you'll come back for me.' He smiles feebly as the others tilt in their cups.

'You should come,' says Seule, raising a final forkful to his lips.

'Huh. I absolve you, boy. Remember that. Now … time for bed. I'm so tired I might even sleep. You'll be needing a crane driver. I'll see you all at dawn.'

'There isn't time to train you,' Gill whispers. He is staring at the floor again, as though expecting something to emerge through the linoleum.

'I know how to work a bloody crane.'

****

Alone in Control, she watches as the clouds that have shaded their days of late begin to shift and fracture on a landward breeze, revealing flashes of sunset sky beyond, violets descending into blood red. Saria and Seule are up top, securing the sail and applying other last touches. Gill is below. He slipped away after the meal, no further questions.

A killer among them, and a journey ahead. On both matters, Pardue seeks brief sanctuary in deflection and denial – primitive tools, but useful enough. She reaches for the headphones, waits for the message to loop around again. She will fill in the blanks, solve the puzzle. But the message is gone, fallen from the airwaves. She flicks through the channels, searching for something, finding perfect silence, a semi sensory deprivation that ushers her towards a near meditative state. She gazes into the shifting sky, focus slipping, lost in the kaleidoscope of colours and shape chaos. Lost in a void – a vacuum, Saria might call it: her place for epiphanies and absolute clarity. The latter holds little appeal, though. Clarity now means fear.

Pardue is chasing the opposite, but doubts she will find it. She recalls once trying some kind of edible. While those around her found camaraderie and laughter, she found paranoia and self-loathing. Mark was there, and he had put aside his own high – brushed it off at will, it seemed – to hold her and talk her down, and as the edge came off, she had, so briefly, felt something like bliss, which she attributed to him more than any psychoactive.

'Maybe that stuff just isn't for you,' Mark told her later.

He meant the drugs, but she'd wondered if perhaps it was ordinary, pointless joy in the company of others that was beyond her.

Now, in sun dapples among the rupturing greys, she sees pink flowers in a featureless field. This fires the synapses – she feels it: the heat across her neck, sweat prickling at her skin, the throb of overworked shoulders. The music, the way the bass hits her chest. The scent of strong and exotic tobacco that seems to make a dry throat feel ever more parched.

She thinks, This isn't a good place.

But she's there now, living it again. The day after her first encounter with Ariman, promises to be kept. She starts in an aid agency HQ, an orphan dorm. But the girl, she is told, has gone – slipped away, disappeared among the tent city's shifting laneways. So, in the noon sun, Pardue sets off to find her. The camp is quieter during these baking hours. She sees some children, though: pearly grins on grubby faces as a handful of stick figures career around a corner before her, screech to an uncertain halt, then sprint past, giggling, bobbing and weaving between jerrycans and guy ropes in some game of chase or hide and seek. Ariman isn't among them.

I should have brought water, she thinks.

It's an annoyance at first, a discomfort. But soon she is near delirium. Her vision begins to fracture, a silvery shimmer on the edges, slowly closing, narrowing towards the centre. And suddenly she is sitting, unsure whether she has done this willingly or not. She shakes her head in cartoonish fashion, screws her eyes shut. She can hear the blood pulsing past her temples – a steady beat, like music. Then she realises, it *is* music. She feels it too, thudding up through the ground and rattling around her pelvis. She forces herself upright, feels the wobbles begin to fade, some strength return. In the absence of other cues, she stumbles off towards the music, and as she gets closer the sounds shift and grow, gain definition: an electronic squall, rising and rising, and a feminine voice, high-pitched vocals, indecipherable. She finds a circle of awnings, doorways to the centre, spaces in the perimeter blocked by old oil drums topped with sandbags, creating from fabric and empty metal the illusion of something secure and militaristic. She follows the perimeter, the music growing ever louder, until she reaches a gap in the wall, a metal pole slung across two barrels barring entrance to the compound within. Before this flimsy checkpoint, a group of militants sit in camp chairs around a sound system and stack of rifles. They are swapping bottles, smoking cigarettes and somehow making conversation above the din. One of them, a man, sees Pardue round the corner. She halts, and they stare at each other in puzzlement – her because the camp is supposed to be civilian-only, and she has believed it to be so; him because people like Pardue apparently are not expected to venture this far into the settlement. One by one, the fighters turn towards her – cold expressions, free of malice but devoid, too, of the goodwill usually inspired by the red patches on her sleeves. Another man rises and approaches.

'English? Francais?'

She can barely hear him above the tune. 'I speak English.'

'Hmm.' He looks her up and down, makes some sort of assessment, then raises his bottle, tilts it towards her. She nods gratefully, takes a swig of the coolish beer. 'Why do you come here?'

She tells him.

'Huh. Lots of girls in this place. She could be anywhere.'

'I know.'

He offers a cigarette. She declines, waits for him to light up.

'Maybe she wanted to join your group,' Pardue tells him. 'I think she did. She wanted to go back to the city, to fight.'

'Okay.'

'She's only eleven.'

The man shrugs. 'Then she will not fight. We are not like that. There is a life for her, with her people. Her time will come, when she is older. If she wants.' He flicks his hand in the general direction of the front line. 'This war will wait for her.'

'She's lost everything. Don't you think she deserves a break?'

'Yes. We all do.' He must see the next question forming on her lips; he goes on, 'Here is the tragedy of it. You remove one, and what then? You cannot save all. You are a medic, yes?'

'A doctor.'

'So, this is why you are here. Now you should go – back to your hospital. Do your thing. It is a good thing. But we must do our thing, too. It is all part of the same. You understand?'

'I didn't know you were here – your people. I mean, soldiers. We see some, of course, but this is a … base. Should you be here?'

'Sure. What happens if they come – if the enemy comes? Nurses and doctors will not protect this place.'

She looks over the other fighters. They are again absorbed in their bottles, their jokes and laughter, their foot-tapping and head-nodding.

'Neither will you,' she says, words she instantly regrets, fearful they may anger him, wound his pride. 'I mean, you don't seem to have many people.'

'We would die for sure. But they would … busy themselves with us. This is how it goes. We keep them busy. No matter – they will not come. Not yet. Really, we are here to rest. A break, like you say. Some days from now, we will go back to the city. Others will take our place here.' The man takes a long, last pull on his smoke, and she notices for the first time the patchy down on his top lip. He drops the cigarette, watches it fall, come to rest by his toe. He seems, for a moment, rapt by the smouldering butt. 'You know, if the children here now do not grow to fight, that place over there – that city – it disappears. Very bad people trying to get in there. You realise this?'

'They're fascists.'

'Hmm. They will win, and that is the last of it. No city, no more children. We here today, fighting – we are the unlucky ones, that is all.'

'I don't want her to kill.'

'You do not want her to kill fascists?'

'Fascists can die. But she's –'

'What do you think is happening here?' He meets her eyes again, but if there is a new edge to his words, his face shows none. 'Huh? It is good you are here. But if you come, you should know. If you come from your place to visit us in hell … and this is a hell of your making, no? If you come to us in hell for a while, you should know. I also do not want to kill. It is damaging. But these people here,' he gestures behind him. 'They are my family now – all that remains. I kill for them, and they for me. We kill for love. Do you see? In this way, it is …' He cannot find the words.

'Her name is Ariman. If you see –'

'We kill for love. Do you understand me?'

'I don't know.'

'I will tell her you came. She will find you … if she wants.'

As she leaves, she glances back to the checkpoint, to the huddle of young fighters and beyond. A group of figures are crossing the compound, a moving copse of brown, green and grey, and in the middle, pink flowers. She lets her go.

The heat, choking dust, and the ache inside. It was too much then, and it is too much now. She forces herself to find something, to ease that pain, to switch off the synapses. Block it out, straight bat. That was the formula: opiates and cricket – opiates and over rates. It worked then, and she bids it to work now. She takes to the clifftops, where everything is a distraction.

Saturday evening, lying on the couch, eyes locked on screen, fingers clasped around controller, click, click, click, wading through endless streams of slurry, desperately searching for a portal to some better world, an escape for an hour or so. Click. She sees a lush field, static figures in pristine white. And across it all, a sound: the gentle drone of a crowd at ease. Then comes a singular burst of movement, a one-man charge, a dance of odd angles, elbows and knees, pumping action. Now a reaction – a reciprocation of sorts from the masked man opposite. A distant roar from the observers in white, a lustier exultation from the crowd. Smiles and back-slaps, high fives, fist-bumps, and a voice. A flat tone, a one-word verdict from a jaded judge: 'Gone.' She watches for three days straight, until she almost comprehends. It ends in a draw. A shrug. No matter: next match, because at almost any time of the day or night, week or year, somebody in some bright, faraway corner is playing this ancient sport. And if they aren't playing it, they are arguing about it. She gorges, and she learns, she decodes the commentary, the jargon, and teaches herself to read the scorecard, the alpha-numeric highlights package. In her wilder moments of make-believe, she imagines herself buying a bat, learning to bowl, joining a club.

There is a flaw in this game, of course – a scourge that strikes at random and from which no one can escape. The washout, the bad light: nature itself. Ominous skies, blackened and low, nimbus fleets arriving on fierce winds, threatening great danger and curtailing everything. They come to thwart, to kill.

****

A tap on the shoulder yanks her clear with an eye-widening snap, a strangled cry. She blinks dumbly up at Saria, who is speaking. She slides off the headphones.

'… and you're just sitting here staring at it.'

'Huh?'

'The storm! The huge storm coming up.' Her voice is pointed, accusatory, as though Pardue's ignorance is somehow exacerbating matters.

'I wasn't really here.' Pardue peers through the window again. The sun is almost down now, but she can see enough – a skyline torn in two: still clearing above, a phoney improvement; to the north-west, a surging cloud mass, an obsidian slab marbled by lightning. 'Is the boat okay?'

'Seule's up there securing it. But when that thing hits … I don't think we're getting out of here tomorrow.'

'But if –'

'I'm going to bed,' snaps Saria. 'Maybe everything will be different in the morning.'

****

She watches, waits for the moment of impact. The rain arrives first, flat slaps delivered with great force, escalating until the noise is all-enveloping, a crescendo of rainfall and the staccato creak of doors and windows shifting in their frames. All that can be seen is squall, then darkness – the storm squatting over the platform, smothering what remains of the day and leaving Pardue to face her reflection, which strobes in and out with the lightning.

Seule is yet to come down.

She checks the time: almost an hour since Saria passed through. She rises mechanically, pulls on coat and hat, gloves, scarf from throat to cheekbones, goggles, whatever she can find on the racks. Only when she grasps the door handle and sees her alien avatar in the plexi does the task to which she is committed fully register. Too late to reconsider, though. And so, as one gust gives way, and before another finds its mark, she puts her shoulder to the door and heaves – too hard; it gives easily and she stumbles out into the jaws of it, the screaming and the howling. Now the wind finds her, ripping the door from her fingers and driving it back into the frame. The gust knocks her back with it, down onto a knee as the rain strikes like scattershot. She waits for another lull, but it shows no sign of arriving, so she wraps an arm around the nearby railing and begins shuffling up the flight of steps, to the lip of the helipad deck, where opposing spots cast a wide, irregular arc of light. In the centre, the lifeboat stands wrapped and lashed to its scaffold, undisturbed by the tempest, save a slight warp through its mast. The deck melts into blackness on all sides, and there is no sign of Seule.

She is still a while, weighing her next move, an advance into open space, shy of shelter or anchor points. When she goes, it is at a crouch, a crab-creep to the safety of the nearest spotlight. She swings the beam, left to right, each short jolt revealing a new vista of swirling droplets and bare steel. Another ferocious gust catches her square, striking with force enough to empty her lungs, to tear one hand from the spotlight and push her back on her knees. She gasps, a silent cry of terror. When she has recovered her grip, and when her mind's fear-babble returns to coherent thought, she thinks, Oh, he's gone. He's gone over the side like the others.

But on the light's next sweep she finds him, some way from the lifeboat, closer to the deck's edge than centre. He lies still, belly down, feet towards her. His coat is open, caught on the wind. It flaps wildly over and around his head. She screams his name, but she can't cut through the storm. The light seems to rouse him, though. His head lifts, and his frame curves, tilts towards her. He raises an arm to pin the coat by his side, a hand to shield his eyes. Now he is moving, slowly turning, righting himself within the beam. He begins a slow crawl towards safety.

****

'Was I right on the edge?' Seule sits on the floor, huddled and shivering beside the heating vents. He stares at his boots, the steamy puddles forming around them. 'I thought I was on the very edge of the platform.'

Pardue stands over him. 'What happened?'

'The wind took me. Spun me around. It threw me right across the helipad.'

'Were you hurt, knocked out?'

'I don't remember.'

'But you were still. You were just lying there.'

'I couldn't see the lights anywhere, so I thought, I must be right on the edge of the deck. I had no bearings – no idea of forwards, backwards. I couldn't move.'

'I don't think you were on the edge.'

'But it felt like –'

'So, you didn't dare to move.'

'Don't tell them that.'

'Why would –'

'Don't tell anyone!' He turns on her, a snarl at his lips – and a wobble there, too. Pardue glares back, and it is Seule who breaks away.

She mutters, 'Ridiculous.'

'Huh?'

'You're ridiculous! You're …' Pardue holds her tongue. She takes a seat and sets herself to watching rain trails form on the

126

window pane. She sucks in a deep breath, continues, 'What's with the headphones?'

'I don't –'

'You told me before, they were making you feel bad, yes? Headaches.'

'So?'

'I was wearing them earlier. The silence. It was odd. Unnatural, I suppose.'

Seule considers this a moment, then asks her, 'Are you okay?'

'Yes. It felt like I had … folded in on myself.'

'Uhuh. Are you feeling okay now?'

'Never mind. Are you all right, from that fall? Not hurt?'

'No.'

'Only your pride.'

'Everyone thinks I'm so soft,' grumbles Seule.

'They don't think –'

'You all think I'm spoilt, soft. I know it. And you hate me because of what I am. Where I come from. Money and –'

'No!' Pardue raps a fist on the desk, drawing a flinch from Seule. 'No. Not now. None of that matters any more, Seule. It's gone. If people have a problem, it's because of your actions. It's *who* you are.'

'That's not –'

'I mean, who *are* you?'

Seule considers this a moment, then answers, 'I don't know.'

Pardue has no response to this cold assessment, and Seule himself seems forced into further introspection.

After a while, she says softly, 'You're not your father … and you're not Gill, either. It wasn't so bad, Seule – up there, you weren't on the edge. But I understand, it would have been disorienting. So you froze. Fine, who cares? You were up there doing what had to be done. And you're still here, alive.'

'I needed to be rescued.'

'Forget all that. Just forget it. How's the boat? It'll be secure in all this wind?'

'I suppose.'

'You suppose. Great.'

'So long as the storm doesn't get worse.'

'Sure. Have you ever sailed through a storm like this?'

'Yeah. Yeah, I've sailed in storms before, but … the lifeboat isn't really a sailboat. Not really.'

'What's it like, sailing in wind like this?'

'Oh. It's … fun?' Seule stands, moves up beside Pardue, catches the eye of her reflection, then looks to his boots again. 'It can be fun.'

'It can?'

'The speed. *Harnessing* the speed. And the hustle. Everyone working in unison. It's exhilarating.'

'I didn't figure you for an adrenaline junky.'

'No. It's not that, not really. It's more … the process. No talk, no bullshit. You have a task, you carry it out. You're part of something. Something good. But there's always, you know, tethers, life rafts, emergency beacons. All the kit. And I've never been too far from land, so –'

'Maybe when we're out there, heading home, you'll show me the ropes. Show me how to sail.'

'I'm not much of a skipper.'

'You can show us all – just the basics.'

'Sure. But,' Seule gestures at the window, 'we're not going.'

'We'll have to, eventually.'

'In that boat, in this weather. It's certain death.'

Pardue sighs. 'You should go to bed.'

'I don't suppose I can –'

'You'll sleep. In the morning, we'll see. I think this will blow over. Storms like this move very quick. I've seen storms like this blow over in a night.'

'Really?'

She doesn't answer immediately. She is mulling her response, gauging her feelings towards him, a needle flicking furiously between pity and frustration, into anger even. Eventually, Pardue says, 'See how easy that is?'

'I don't –'

'To reassure someone. Just a simple, empty reassurance.'

October 6: Blackout +16 Days

She sleeps on and off, until the off-switch sticks in place. She returns to Control before dawn, and when the new day comes it brings a brightening around the edges, enough, at first, to inspire hope. But it's soon obvious that the light – the little that penetrates – means nothing. The elemental bombardment continues.

Daws pokes his head around the door, offers Pardue an apologetic smile. She replies with a shake of the head, and he withdraws.

Saria arrives next. 'Not happening.'

'It may clear up.'

'Too late. We need to leave first thing – now. To get all the daylight.'

'I suppose.'

Saria fastens her coat, pulls it tight around her neck.

'Where are you going?' Pardue asks.

'Where do you think?'

'Why though?'

Saria opens the door a crack, allowing a burst of wind and rain to infiltrate. Pardue ducks away from the spray. When she looks again, Saria is out and leaning into the gale. The door slams shut behind her.

She returns soon enough, raw cheeks, runny nose and eyes. Another icy blast follows her in. 'We'll rot here.' She stamps away.

Pardue gazes at the internal door, waiting for Saria to return with some PS, either an escalation or move to reconciliation. Then, envisioning a more likely flashpoint, she follows, out from Control, down two decks towards the dorms. She was correct – she can hear it from the stairwell, above the natural tumult outside: a furious pounding and shouting in the corridor. She emerges to see Saria outside Gill's room.

'... open! Come out here!'

Saria doesn't acknowledge Pardue's approach. She maintains her attack on the door, her rattling at the handle, kicks at the jamb and challenges to the man within.

Pardue fixes Saria with a weary, withering glare. 'What's this?'

Saria unleashes another, more intense flurry of punches and kicks, then lets her forehead fall against the unyielding door.

'I want to know,' she pants. 'I want to know, Gill!'

One last punch, then she retreats and drops, spent, onto her rear, back up against the wall opposite. Pardue sits beside her, descending with a creak.

'Is he even in there?' asks Pardue.

'Ha.' Saria examines her bandaged hand, blood spots blooming over the aggravated wound. She presses at the dressing, winces slightly. 'This hurts.'

'We'll redress it.'

'Do you think I'm losing it, Kathleen?'

'No.'

'I might be close.' She sniffs. 'I just want to know what happened. I want an explanation, a reason.'

'Okay.'

'All this death. I just want answers. You don't care?'

'I don't know,' concedes Pardue. 'Will an explanation change anything now? A confession? Everything that has happened – Sargent, Porter, everything. Broz and Gill is just another piece of it.'

'Porter. It was awful … and I've barely given him another thought.'

'There'll be time for that, maybe. Time for reflection, remembrance. Whatever it takes to … recover.'

'But this,' Saria jabs a finger at the door opposite, 'is something different. No one has that right, to just take another person's life like that.'

'Maybe there'll be time for justice, too.'

'You defended him yesterday.'

'No. I was defending us. All of us. We're going in that boat together.'

'Are we? I think this storm goes on forever.'

'It'll pass,' Pardue tells her.

'It's worse this morning than it was last night.'

'Things get worse, then better. That's the cycle. It will pass.'

'You know all this?'

'I feel it.'

'Oh. I feel like … it's all slipping away.'

'I want to know something,' says Pardue. She doesn't wait for

Saria to respond. 'I want to know what you saw in the pool, at the Games. I want to know … not abstracts, not "truth". What did you actually see there?'

'Why?'

'Upstairs last night, I had a … I'm not sure how to describe it. I've had … episodes in my time. But this was something different. Memories, but relived: vivid and immediate. The heat, the smells, I was back there. And I thought –'

'Back where?'

'The desert, and … it doesn't matter.'

'I didn't see the past,' says Saria. 'I saw the future. Or a future. They said, "Take your mark." I took my mark. Then I thought, Why am I doing this? They say move and I move. They say jump and off I go. But I don't want to. I don't want to jump, and here I am, I'm about to jump. And in the time between taking my mark and hearing the buzzer, I saw … another life. I saw the faces of strangers: men, women, children, warm faces, beckoning me forward, downward. It felt like they were calling from my future. I thought, Go to them. And I did, and they were there with me in the water. All of us together, united. It felt right. There was a … sanctity to it. But that future, it hasn't come to anything, and now it probably won't.'

'It's something to fight for.'

'Maybe it's just madness. The first step towards madness: becoming lost in the past or in some fake future. Anywhere but here.'

'Like Seule's dream.'

'What dream? Oh, never mind. Listen to that wind, Kathleen. It's like bombs falling. I wonder, will I starve first, or lose my mind first?'

'We shouldn't think like that.'

Saria is up, leaving.

Pardue calls after her, but she doesn't respond. Pardue continues anyway. 'You said you'd swim. You won't try that will you?'

'It's impossible.'

Saria is gone, five doors down, into her room. Pardue's bed is only a little further along the corridor, but she can't draw the energy to stand. Her eyelids fall.

****

A sensate spike, a jolt; then a hand on her shoulder, a summons to the conscious world. Now an aural awakening, a tuning in – the barrage beyond the walls, and a voice: 'Hey, hey, hey.' Vision sharpening, Gill's frantic face looming large over hers. 'Hey! Come on, Pardue.'

'What is it?'

Gill is crouched before her. He lets his legs crumple beneath him, slumps back with a jarring thud against the opposite wall. His dorm door stands open. Pardue sees splintered wood, cupboards and shelving units ripped free and torn apart, sheets and blankets lying in ragged strips, walls cratered by foot or fist or shoulder.

'What happened?'

'Huh?' Gill's chin rests against his chest.

'You smashed up your quarters?'

He straightens, glances over his left shoulder and into the room. 'That was days ago, that was …' He shrugs. 'I came out and saw you there. You looked dead.'

'I don't know why I slept here. It doesn't make any –'

'I slapped you just then. Sorry.'

'Oh.' Pardue feels for her cheek, a slight sting there.

'You wouldn't wake.'

'It's okay.'

'I don't want to scare you.'

'I'm not scared.'

'Good.'

'You need to explain yourself, Gill.'

'I thought you were –'

'Explain what happened with Broz.'

'I did.'

'No. We can't go on like this. People are losing their minds now. It needs to be out, needs to be straight.'

'I told you what happened.'

'Tell me it all, and I can tell Saria, the others.'

'I told you. He was stealing food. Wasn't even the first time. I'd caught him the night before sniffing around the canteen, the kitchen. I gave him a kick up the backside then, sent him packing. Next night, I kept an eye out for him. I caught him again, down here, coming back to his room with pockets bulging. He clocked me, turned and ran, back up the stairs. So I'm chasing him. But he's faster – too fast for me. I lost him. I searched every damn room. It was so dumb. Why hide?' Gill closes his eyes, shakes his head. 'He was outside. I found him holed up in the lifeboat. Wrappers everywhere, crackers, spreads, our stuff – he'd thrown it all down his throat. I was so fucking furious. It wasn't just the food, it was the running: the cowardice. Greed and cowardice. The little shit, I reached in and ...' Gill's brow creases at the retelling, as though something there seems newly incongruous.

'You said he hit out at you.'

'Yeah. Yeah, that's right. And he bumped his head, in the struggle.'

'Struggle?'

'Defending myself. He hit his head – on the door of the boat, I think.'

'And you threw him over.'

'Panicked.'

'You're sure he was dead.'

Gill gulps, puffs out his cheeks as something ascendant is forced back down. He nods. 'Mm hmm.'

Pardue waits for more, but Gill, it seems, is done. She considers his statement a moment, then says, 'You must be more desperate than anyone. To get home – beyond self-preservation, I mean.' Gill's face is blank. She prompts him: 'Your wife.'

'Oh … no, she's gone.'

'Gone?'

'She died. Uh … about seven months ago.'

'I had no idea.'

'No. I didn't really tell anyone about that.' Gill shifts his weight and, for a second, it seems he is about to up and leave. Instead, he stretches his legs out before him, settles. 'I did talk to Porter about it – at the time. He didn't know what to do or say. I don't know what I wanted him to do or say. What could be done? He tried … oh, carve that on the man's tombstone. He tried. Kind words … empty. And I got mad at him for it. Hit him … oh. After that, I just kept it to myself.'

'What happened to her?'

'She got sick, that's all. We met too late. Way too late. I wasn't much of a man till she found me. We met at a march during the general strike. I was close to getting arrested again. That would've been me: jail, deported even. She talked me down.'

'I was on those marches.'

'Yeah? That makes three of us – ask Daws. It was a good fight, a good cause, even if we got our arses kicked. And I met her, so … yeah, fine times. Gem saw something good in me, and she brought it out. She was the only one who could do that. She made me better. Because she was better: better looks – oh, sure – but better mind, heart and soul. More … ah, just more than me. She had friends, family. She was loved, and I had nothing and no one. But still she wanted me! So … well, we had a good few years. The best years.'

'That time together, it counts for something.'

'A small victory. Sometimes I feel like, when Gem was taken, all the goodness was ripped out of me.'

'I'll talk to Saria.'

'Huh?' Gill starts, as though roused from restfulness. He rises, fixes his eyes on the dorm five doors down. 'Ah, no. You should get some sleep, Pardue. Real sleep. You look like shit. I'll come wake you in a few hours. We'll … reassess, I guess. See what the weather's doing.'

'But –'

'I'll talk to the others. I'll do it.'

'I don't know if that's such a good idea, Gill. I don't –'

'It's on me. I'll make it right.'

'But you have to –'

'I promise.'

'You have to get your story straight.'

****

A normal slumber, content almost – the dreams muted. She glides easily through a landscape of disjointed imagery, of fleeting, faceless interactions that prompt only the shallowest ripples of emotion: frustrations and anxieties, the barest of disturbances. And, between these, long stretches of relative calm, like the ocean – the ocean they must hope for. She is not so deep, not deep enough to fully shed the weight of reality. And so, when she wakes, that weight is there and it is familiar, which is preferable to the alternative – those micro-moments of ignorant bliss that often greet the waking. It is not Gill who wakes her, nor any other interruption. It is, rather, an absence, a change that has triggered some internal alarm. Her room is dark, but only as dark as it was before. The difference, she realises, is in the sound. In the wind, in the rain. They are the absence.

October 7: Blackout +17 Days

Pardue and her travelling companions gather on the helipad, four sets of fiery eyes and wan scowls, shivers and twitches, coughs and splutters. The clouds that remain – rear guard to the great storm – leer over them, capturing the mood below: fragile peace, and the threat of further disturbance.

Daws arrives with a limp salute. He stands aside, disengaged, as they load bags and boxes into the lifeboat. When the last package is stowed, Gill clambers in and takes his seat. He doesn't look back, and Daws is equally unmoved by their parting. The old man offers a brief handshake to Seule, who opens his mouth to speak but summons nothing; Daws is already moving on. Saria pulls him in for a hug, drawing a wobbly smile that looks, for a moment, as though it may herald tears.

Daws watches the young woman board the boat, and says, to no one in particular, 'Hard to find words for this.'

'There are no words for this,' answers Pardue. She is glowering at the ocean's gentle eddy and swell, unconvinced by the show of innocence.

Daws shrugs. 'Au revoir?'

'I hope so.'

An empty chuckle. 'These little lies we tell ourselves. I never really understood why people do that. I get it now. It's comforting, that's all.'

Pardue turns away from the sea and says, 'Goodbye.'

Daws reaches for his pocket and pulls out a scuffed-looking mini-tab, thrusts it into her palm. 'That's me, Pardue. It's all in there. You can look after it. Battery's running low, mind. Won't seem to hold a charge these days.' He leans in, whispers, 'Keep an eye on the girl.'

****

There is a clunk, a judder, then a jerk as they are hoisted clear of the platform. She grips the arms of her seat, digs in her nails as they hang there and as the dangers inherent in simply launching the vessel become apparent.

'Is he really trained to do this?' she asks Gill through gritted teeth.

'I guess.'

The boat rocks gently on its long axis and then, with a horrid lurch, they swing out across the deck. Once in position, Daws lowers them slowly to the water. There is a welcome thud below their feet, and a shocking list-wobble that self-corrects to relative stillness.

She peels her fingers from the armrests as Gill opens the top hatch and turns them loose. Seule is up next, to check the wind, raise the sail. He begins pulling and tying off ropes that pass through notches cut close to the roof.

Nothing much happens. They bob there a while, three passengers watching in silence as Seule makes his calculations and adjustments: tighten, loosen, tie off again. Apparently satisfied, he flops down behind the wheel.

'We're moving,' says Saria.

Seule grunts.

Pardue can't see it – and then she can, through the circular window to her left: the platform's north-east leg just visible at the front edge; fully visible; passing by; gone, away behind them. Only ocean now; she flinches away from it.

'Look.' Saria is at the rear window.

High above, visible only now they have distance from the platform, Daws stands before his fishing reels, coat wrapped tight around him, hood up.

Pardue feels a beat of nausea, something like vertigo. She wants to be up there with the old man, shivering in cool air, contemplating a dash back inside, a steaming shower, breakfast, hot tea or coffee – and here she is lost, because these last luxuries are no more available to Daws than to her. He is waving, hand carving wide arcs through the air, jaunty almost, reassuring, like a father bidding farewell to his children on their first day of school. He thrusts his hand into a pocket and turns away.

Pardue's panic kicks harder, becomes almost unbearable, and with it a realisation, an absolute certainty: We'll die in this boat, we'll float infinitely, sealed and alone.

Daws is gone, and now everything is gone, everything is grey, like a shroud has been pulled across her vision, and she thinks, Oh! I'm going to pass out again – just like in the camp. Just like in the helicopter that time, too! The perfect bookends to my arrival and departure. Just perfect.

'Oh, perfect!' Saria's voice, then another sound, a guttural hack, a splatter.

Pardue blows hard, expels her demons, and staggers around to see Gill on his knees in the centre aisle, a thin string of bile hanging from his chin.

****

The lifeboat pulls away, slowly, but certainly forward, eastward until the platform has almost disappeared, lost over the world's curve. She watches it going, noting its diminishing heft, its sharp lines and angles growing furry and indistinct, colours fading to monochrome, until it is no more than a thumb-smudge on the rear window.

Gill lies at her feet, on the mattress he has claimed for a sick bed, retching, spitting, rehydrating, repeating, each cycle sounding like a lurch further into hell. His keening moves up a key, and she breaks away to tend to him. When it is done, the platform is gone. She resists the urge to kick out at the pathetic lump before her. No going back now.

She takes a seat and pulls out Daws' mini-tab, turns it in her hands, feels its old-model weight, deep scratches across the screen. She flicks on the power and waits for aged circuits to warm up. The front cover contains a single doc tile: Book of the Dead. She clicks through to the opening page.

Peter Daws age 46 my dad. The first body I ever saw. The one I knew best. But I learnt more when he was gone than in his life. I remember flashing lights outside my bedroom. I looked and I could see him in the gutter. There was a smashed bottle there and a pool of blood. It changed colour in the blue and white lights. Better in the blue…

'Oh, goodness. Look!' Saria is leaning across her, flapping at the porthole.

Pardue sees nothing there but rolling water. She moves to brush the young woman away. A few metres from them, a curved blade breaks the surface, followed by a broad crescent of smooth, black skin, slicing through the ocean, up, down, gone again. Now another, slightly further away, and a third, a little to the rear.

Pardue emits a guttural noise, somewhere between gasp and gag.

Seule calls back, 'Orca. We're okay in here. I think.'

Saria's face is lit with joy. 'The sea is alive, it's really alive!'

Featureless, yet somehow open and expressive, vast yet sleek and elegant, the orca begin to swirl and swoop, circling around and under the boat, creating wakes that rock and roll the humans, nudging them forward, cajoling, as though the vessel's gentle progress is frustrating them. Pardue is rapt, mesmerised by manoeuvres that seem calculated, communicative. And in her, something stirs, an opening, a blooming from the centre, enveloping her and carrying her away, back to hills and inlets, herds and flocks, tides that come and go with certainty. Perfect natural order.

Oh, but we must be somewhere else now, she thinks. We must have crossed over. This isn't our world, because this quiet communion between apex beasts couldn't happen in a world as cold and cruel as the one we've made.

****

After a stay of some hours, their message delivered, or their curiosity spent, the visitors slip away.

Saria darts from window to window, seeking signs of re-emergence, before settling opposite Pardue.

'The light's fading,' Saria says.

'Perhaps it's their time to feed. Time for hunting.'

'They were hunting us. Sizing us up.'

'I didn't think so.'

143

'I don't care if they were.' Saria dabs at her eyes. 'They were a family.'

'Maybe they'll come back.'

'Sitting in here watching them, it reminded me of a story I once heard. No, not a story. It was a poem I read.'

'Tell me.'

'It was at school, I think. I don't know. Where did you go to school, Kathleen?'

'Nowhere special.'

'You must have been a good student.'

'Not really. I raised my game towards the end. My mum got sick, so I straightened out.'

'You used to get in trouble?'

'Not so much. I just … coasted, I suppose.' Pardue leaves the conversation there, and Saria returns to gazing out the window, a picture so forlorn it obliges Pardue to continue. 'I got in trouble once. Only once. When I was about fifteen, before Mum became ill. They called us in to meet the principal. I was sick with worry. It felt like the worst thing that could happen. My father had left by then – it was just the two of us. I think Mum was as nervous as me. We sat before the principal's desk, waiting while he read through something on his tab. He said to Mum, "She's never quite fitted in – doesn't seem to gel with anyone. Now this thing." He pointed to the tab, and we couldn't see the report, but that didn't matter. "This fight." And I told him, "Don't call it a fight, it wasn't a fight. If you don't hit back, it's not a fight." He said, "But you do have a problem with people, with the other children. What is it?" And I thought, and I told him, "They're monsters." He laughed at me. Mum stood and took my hand, and she told him, "It's a worldview." And to me, she said, "Let's go. It's fine. This will be fine." But I'm not sure it was. Tell me about your poem.'

They play out a fast back and forth, a frantic rally that begins with the verse, half-remembered, before veering into chatter, pointless yet pointed – the mechanism more important than the product because they must fill the silence, make reassuring sound while sight grows duller. In the end, though, the former fades with the latter. They hang torches from the ceiling, but the swinging beams create nightmarish flash-frames and dancing shadows, and Pardue is relieved when the batteries are drained. Finally, they submit to the night, which is total and feels somehow terminal.

****

Sleep brings no relief. Ariman visits, an older Ariman, a woman with taut, pointed features. She sits in the foot well beside Pardue, her back to the wall, knees pulled up tight.

'You grew up,' Pardue whispers, fearing the others might hear.

'I told you it would come,' Ariman replies.

'You came to gloat?'

'No. I wish I was wrong. But how could I be?'

Pardue says, 'We've crossed over.'

'No.'

'But I felt it before, when the orca came to us. I was so happy: good for you. You've survived. Everything this world has thrown at you, every abuse and indignity you've suffered in silence, and here you are, alive and strong. And now you come to guide us, to guard us even. I thought, We must have crossed over. We must be on some other plane – another dimension or timeline. And I didn't care, Ariman. I didn't care. I thought, It's not about us any more. It's their time and their place. Superior beasts. And us – we're done.'

'We are the unlucky ones.'

'Have we crossed, have we passed from one place to another?'

'No.'

'Then I do want to care. In this world, I want to do good, and I want control. I should never have stopped believing in that. You have to leave me alone now, Ariman. Leave me alone, leave me alone ...'

She repeats this plea, over and over, through sobs and curses. She can't stop, and she realises the boat is rocking in time with her utterances, as though the words are waves, calm at first, growing in strength, pitching and heaving, slapping and smashing, and finally threatening to overwhelm everything. Leave me alone, leave me alone, backwards, forwards, up slope, down slope. You learn to adjust, she thinks. To shift your weight with the to and the fro, lean in to it, lean out of it, riding the gravity. Yes, you adjust ... until the swing is too deep, and the lean too severe. Over we go ... her knees are up, buckling, tumbling back and towards her head, and all the weight seems to fall on her neck, bending and cracking, tired structures giving way. There is a roar from outside, from all around, a bellow: 'Where are you going!?' And now cries, more immediate, but not hers, someone else: 'This is it, this is it!'

But it is nothing.

Everything is still again, and all she feels is the cold and the wet, sweat. Ariman clasps a hand over Pardue's shoulder, and with the other begins to stroke her hair and cheeks.

'It's okay, Kathleen,' she whispers. 'Don't be afraid.'

Awake, and she knows it isn't Ariman who comforts her, but Saria. The young woman holds her a while until she slips again into dreams – dreams of waking, coming around to something else: sunlight streaming through blinds onto crisp, white sheets; the sound of Mark padding across the room, scratching his belly, yawning; music playing in an adjoining room; the smell of coffee brewing; bacon. Then awake for real, to darkness and damp air, to the smell of vomit and urine, to their undulating world.

This pattern repeats. Sleep again, dream-wake again, wake, a cycle of dashed hopes, until finally she sees a man: a slim silhouette, sharp relief against a corona of golden rays. She sees the outline of brow, nose, jaw, and in them a sort of rigid determination. Robert Seule, the captain at his bridge, hero of the hour – a man now, his own man. And she realises, this is a real dawn with real light and real possibility.

October 8: Blackout +18 Days

'I have to eat now,' Pardue whispers. 'I can't wait. I just can't.'

Saria is curled up on the double seat opposite, hugging herself tight. She nods in response, a solemn, sickly gesture that seems to settle more than merely a morning's schedule: Yes, Kathleen, that reward is ours now, it says; and we won't speak of the night, of whatever occurred there in sleep or otherwise. Leave it to the shadows.

Seule is unmoved.

'Have you been at the wheel all night?' Pardue asks him.

'I guess so.' He doesn't look back.

Pardue drops from her seat, crawls back to the boxes and unpacks rations: clumps of cold rice, a cracker each. She throws hers down where she kneels, slugging back water to ease its passage. She rises to a crouch and shuffles forward to serve Saria and Seule, who starts at her presence, as though waking, as though their previous exchange took place an age ago.

When they have eaten, Saria opens the ceiling hatch. Now, fresh air, UV and carbs combine to produce something like a burst of euphoria, giddiness – uppers straining against the downers of ill health and fatigue.

Seule secures the wheel and begins to show them the ropes: how to find what little breeze there is, how to capture it, to tighten the sail or loosen accordingly, how to tie off knots, read the compass and maintain their vague course. He offers instruction, they try to absorb it, and then he repeats each lesson with a chuckle or wry smile when they ask questions that have already been answered. It's clear that he won't be able to sleep, but Pardue and Saria persist with the pretence, and Seule plays along. When they take the controls, he spreads out on the seat behind them and closes his eyes.

Minutes in, the sail falls slack. The breeze is lost and can't be recovered. The women exchange knowing looks, part regret, part amusement. Pardue prods Seule's elbow. He doesn't open his eyes, but grins and asks, 'What took you so long?'

As Seule resets, they talk. There is no crisis planning now, no measuring of dread nor weighing of moral uncertainties. It is not forced, thrown up as a shield against some fast-encroaching foe. They just talk, chat. Inconsequential recollections of life before the blackout, or fantasies of beds and baths. They compile lists of the things they will do on their return, and for once they avoid speculating on what they are returning to, or the dangers that may yet halt their journey. These frothy interactions continue until Gill wakes with a dry hack and a rattling sigh. Pardue goes to him, and the other two fall into silence.

'You having fun up there while I die down back?' Gill's throat creaks, a warning against further exertion.

'You're not dying, Gill. Seasickness never killed anyone.' She has no idea if this is true. She doubts it.

She helps him drink, take in a little mushed-up rice. He notes the way she eyes the remainder of his portion, huffs to himself and drops, turns away from her.

'Share it,' he says. Or at least that's what she hears.

'Later … maybe.'

A cry now from the front of the boat, Saria's voice. 'There!'

Saria and Seule are at the wheel, craning their necks to peer skyward through the sloped windscreen.

'A bird!' says Saria.

At first the possible significance of this is lost on Pardue, but in a beat or two it hits, and she moves to join them. She sees thick clouds, pewter sky, nothing more. Then it passes overhead, gliding serenely from their rear-left to front-right. Some huge gull or goose-type thing, a plump, perfectly white body, fat feet, all hanging improbably from narrow, grey wings of great length.

Seule mutters, 'Forget that. It doesn't mean anything.'

'How do you know?' asks Pardue.

'That sort of bird … it doesn't stay close to the land.'

Part 2: The Island

October 9: Blackout +19 Days

'Oh, we were lucky.'

Pardue's body forms a stiff Z, head near the centre aisle, torso across the double seat, legs bent awkwardly in the foot well. She winces as she straightens, flexes her spine. Saria is still asleep in a pose mirroring her own. Gill is sprawled on the mattress. She watches him a moment, acknowledges the heaving of his chest.

'The sun's out,' she says to no one in particular.

'That's what I mean,' slurs Seule. He is up at the wheel. 'We got lucky. Come and see.'

She squeezes past the mast, to a position over Seule's left shoulder. The clouds have cleared, and the once-filthy water has turned a glistening blue. White foam bursts below the prow, showering the windscreen with heavy droplets that land with a satisfying thud.

'We're really moving,' she says.

'The wind came on an hour or so ago. We'd been drifting for so long. Now it's right at our back. The sail's really working.'

'You said it would.'

'Hmm. An empty reassurance.'

'Oh.'

'That's not what I mean, though. Look there.' Seule flaps a finger weakly towards the horizon. 'Can't you see?'

'What?'

'Cliffs.' Seule coughs, wipes at his mouth. 'Cliffs and rocks. If it was night, we would have sailed straight into them. We were lucky.'

'Oh!' She clasps his arm and laughs, an adrenaline-charged bark. 'We did it, you did it!' Oh my –'

'I think I need to sleep.' He slides from the chair, gestures Pardue to the wheel. 'Just keep us on this course.' He taps the compass.

'I'm sorry, I slept longer than –'

'Wake me when we're … I don't know, a K away. We'll put the engine on, find a beach.' Seule's eyelids droop and his body sways, as though he might sleep where he stands. He giggles. 'A day at the beach.'

'What's happening?' croaks Saria. She is throwing off blankets, fumbling in the aisle for discarded boots. 'What's up?'

'We're there.'

'We were so lucky,' says Seule.

****

When the engine kicks in, the boat rears, lurches. She looks to Gill. He is awake but seemingly undisturbed by the turbulence. He is staring at a dark, damp patch on the mattress beside him. He traces a hand along grey, cracked lips, tries to swallow, grimaces. She leaves Seule at the controls and heads back.

'Here.' She passes him a bottle of water, raises her voice above the mechanical roar. 'Have as much as you need. We're almost there.'

'We are?'

'Look.' She helps him shuffle up against the wall, allowing

him to see out the window opposite. Seule is wheeling the vessel around to their right, running parallel to the land, scouring the coastline for a safe place to disembark. 'See? Cliffs.'

'Oh, yeah. I'd forgotten.'

'You forgot?'

'When I woke just then,' Gill takes a long pull on the bottle, 'I forgot. I didn't know where I was.'

'Kathleen!' Saria is calling her forward. 'Help me – we need to lower the sail. It's slowing us.'

'I'll come back,' she tells Gill.

Seule eases off the throttle as Pardue unties the ropes. Saria unscrews the top hatch, ushering in sunlight and a saline mist. She gasps as the droplets find her, inhales deeply as cool air begins to fill the musty cabin. Now she carefully ascends the ladder, until all that remains visible are legs and rump.

Pardue watches a moment, tugs at Saria's sweater. 'Make room.'

Saria shuffles aside, leaving her left foot on the ladder, planting her right on an armrest. Pardue scrambles up, squeezes through the opening beside her, mirroring her stance. They lean into one another, bracing. Pardue is gripped by the chill, but she is grinning, laughing – they both are. They reel in the sail, shovelling it down through the hatch, stamping it beneath them, giggles and whoops passing between them with every blast of spray, every gust of icy wind.

When the sail is stowed, Pardue ducks down and tells Seule, 'Go for it!'

He smiles wearily. 'Are you staying up for the ride?'

'I don't know –'

'Hold on tight though.'

She returns to her position and wraps her arms around the ladder, nodding at Saria to do the same.

Saria throws back her head and roars to the sky as Seule reapplies the throttle. She is laughing deliriously.

The cliffs to their left are grey-black, tall and sheer. At their base, deep water heaves and swirls. Seule keeps his distance, holds his parallel line. A couple-hundred metres away is a headland, an angular outcrop of grass-topped rock. Saria points to it, mouths something indecipherable. Pardue follows her finger.

'Birds!' screams Saria.

Pardue sees them: gulls, hundreds, thousands probably, drawing wide circles above the headland, swooping down, looping around.

'It's so beautiful!' cries Saria.

There is movement on the clifftop, too: frantic flaps as adult birds skid to a halt among the tufts of scrub; grey blobs, fat, juvenile bodies bobbing, necks craning up towards sustenance.

When they are closer, they see gulls breaking away from the circling flock, tilting their wings and arrowing towards the ocean below, plucking at the surface with barely a splash or ripple.

The scene holds their attention until they round the headland, only to discover another stretch of unbroken cliffs and, in the distance, a similar promontory. Their smiles slip, the fun is over. Pardue drops into the cabin, Saria follows. Seule is hunched over the wheel, peering through the windscreen, right hand planted in his hair, fingers kneading at his skull.

'Can you see anywhere to land?' Pardue asks.

'No.'

'How long do we have?'

'On the engine? I don't know – five minutes?'

'Maybe after the next headland.'

'Maybe.'

'And if not?'

'I don't know. The sail goes back up, I guess. Damn, damn, damn.'

Saria lays a hand on Seule's shoulder.

They plough on in silence. As they round the second headland, Pardue and Saria lean forward as one.

'Come on,' whispers Pardue.

Seule sighs. They are at the mouth of a shallow cove. At its apex, a kilometre or so away, the cliff line drops and retreats behind a strip of sand. He swings around in a wide arc, turning front-on to the beach, and lifts the throttle.

Pardue returns to Gill. He sits as she left him, propped up and staring blankly out the window.

'We're coming in now,' she tells him.

'Yeah, I gathered.' As he speaks, his chest heaves and his throat seems to contract. Gill moans, turns away and dry-retches into the corner. He spits, wipes his chin. 'There's nothing left in me.'

'We'll get some food in you, as soon as we're on land.'

'I won't stomach it.'

'You will. This passes quickly, sea sickness. I think it does, anyway.'

'Is that all it is, sea sickness?'

'Of course. You think it's something else?'

'I don't know.'

'Brace yourselves,' calls Saria.

The engine is cut, the boat settles into a slow glide. There is a jolt, a bang from below, a scraping and scratching as the vessel grinds to a halt. Seule guns the engine again, throwing them forward, rocking Pardue and causing her to slump against Gill. Then all is still, and the only sound is the gentle rush of waves all around.

'That's it then,' she says as she rights herself.

Gill's laughter devolves into a rasping cough. 'Now for some real fun.'

****

She wades through light surf, luggage stacked high on her shoulders. When she is clear, she collapses in a heap on the sand. She grasps at the grains, clutches two fistfuls and watches them drain through the gaps in her fingers. Checks her watch: no connection. She breathes in the beach, fills her lungs, then begins pulling out their rations. She offers Gill two crackers, a palm-full of rice, and watches as he forces them down, pulls greedily at his water bottle. She notes the first flush of colour returning to his cheeks.

Seule lies flat on his back, eyes closed.

Saria scans the cove. 'I'm not sure how we get off this beach.'

'Must be a path, steps or something,' grunts Gill. 'Look at this place – it's untouched, a frigging beauty spot. Probably a private beach. Let's try the far end.'

Pardue nods towards Seule. 'Wait a moment.'

'Shit … hey, kid, are you awake?'

She glowers at Gill. 'He didn't sleep last night. Or much before that.'

'I'm awake,' says Seule, eyes still shut. 'There won't be steps, a path. I think we might be near Seal Rocks. South of there, maybe? No one ever comes down this way.'

'You need to rest, too,' Pardue tells Gill. 'We should all eat. Let's double up, have a real meal.'

****

When they rise, it is to a chorus of grumbles and groans as legs are stretched and joints flexed.

Pardue transfers medical supplies from boxes to bags, hands out the remainder of their ration packs, and they set off for the cove's southern corner. Saria trails. She is turned around, stepping carefully backwards and staring into the sky behind them.

'What kind of birds are they, Seule?'

'Huh?'

Saria gestures towards the white whirlwind. 'Those birds.'

'Why are you asking me?'

'You don't know? Come on, you went to a good school, didn't you.'

'That doesn't fucking mean … oh, forget it. I think they're probably silver gulls.'

'Silver. Hmm.' Saria spins around, skips forward to join the others. 'Did you notice them before, when we were in the boat?'

'Yes. I've never seen them like that – never seen so many flocking together like that. They're thriving.'

'They have a good thing here,' muses Saria. 'A haven! It's wonderful. Don't you think, Kathleen?'

Pardue turns to take in the colony. 'It reminds me of … oh.'

'What's wrong?' asks Saria.

'Look at the boat.'

They all stop, and they all see it: water lapping higher at the vessel's flanks, waves shaking at its rear, up, down, side to side, prying it from the slope on which Seule had secured it. A fast-advancing tide. They switch their gaze to the cliffs, and the perfect plane about three metres up, a horizontal divider in the granite: blackened below; bleached clean and freckled with lichen above.

'We've got to move,' says Pardue.

'Should have moved straight away,' spits Gill. 'Come on.'

'Wait, let's just –'

'Let's just find a damn path.'

'I don't know –'

'Come on!'

'You.' Saria delivers the pronoun in a low, slow growl, lip curled in disgust. 'You are not in charge here, Gill.'

'Oh, for fuck's sake. Have you got a better –'

'I can see from here there's no path. No steps. It's either back in the boat or we're climbing.'

Pardue eyes the cliff face: 12, 14 metres. 'Saria, I'm not sure –'

'I'll go up and send a rope down for you.'

'I don't think we should get back in the boat,' Seule says in a voice thick with terror.

'Gill can't anyway,' scoffs Saria.

'I mean, we got lucky finding this place. We shouldn't push it.'

'And where do we climb?' demands Gill. He rounds on Saria. 'What are you, the damn spider woman now?'

'I'm more than you'd know. Over there.' She points him to the southern end of the bay, where the cliff line switches almost at right angles out towards the sea. 'In the corner. See? It's not sheer. It's a slope … mostly. There's a ledge halfway. It's all I need.'

They take in the features she has described. Gill huffs quietly, turns and trudges onward, kicking at the sand as he goes.

When they reach the end, Saria ditches her rucksack, pulls the rope from Pardue's kit bag and slings it over her shoulder. She begins scouring the face for handholds.

'Watch how I go,' she calls. 'You'll need to copy me.'

She reaches up, digs in her fingers and begins her ascent, shoulders rippling as they heave her body, boots kicking and scraping until they find purchase. Then repeat. In three jerky movements she has negotiated the initial, near-vertical sector and found a place to pause. She hugs the rock where it leans away into a more accommodating slope.

'Oh, wow! That's the hardest part,' she reassures them between deep breaths. 'It's easy from here, I think.'

'Ah, shit.'

Pardue turns to find Gill down on his knees. 'What is it?'

'Ugh, sick again.' He waves her away. 'I'll be fine.'

'Have you been sick?'

'No, it just came over me. Same as earlier. Thought I was going to black out. I'm fine … ah, look.' He nods to Saria, who has passed the ledge and is clambering rapidly. 'She really is the spider woman.'

'Can you manage this?'

'Yeah, yeah.' Gill pushes himself upright, wobbles slightly, doubles over for a moment, hands on thighs. He straightens again, forces a grin. 'All good.'

There is a whooping from above. Saria is gone. They wait for sight or sound, then the rope flies over the edge, uncoiling as it drops, slapping back against the rock, its tip settling just above the vertical.

'Oh, boy.' Seule is peering up, scratching roughly at his jaw.

Saria reappears, head and shoulders craning out over them. 'You should smell it up here! Grass and dirt, earth!'

'Screw it.' Gill strides to the face and searches for Saria's handholds.

'Gill, wait,' calls Pardue. 'Don't you think we should –'

'I'm going, before I have time to think.' He grabs at the rock and, with a great roar, makes his first lunge upwards.

'But your bag –'

Saria shouts, 'Come on then, tough guy!'

Gill says nothing in response until he is on the slope. He stops there, as Saria had before, clinging tight, left cheek pressed to the surface. He is panting heavily, and when he calls out, his voice wavers. 'This rope better be tied tight!'

'Move!'

Gill wraps the cord around a wrist and starts picking his way up the slope. At the ledge he pauses again and retches.

A wave crashes in hard behind Pardue and Seule. They watch as the frothy wash crawls up the beach, tainting dry sand. It stops just short of their boots, and retreats.

Pardue makes to call out, but Gill is moving again.

'We have to get these bags up,' she tells Seule. 'I'll take Saria's, Gill's. When I get to the rope, throw the kit bag to me too. I'll tie it on. You bring your rucksack.'

'Ah, okay.'

Gill disappears over the lip, hurls the rope back down. Pardue slings one rucksack over each shoulder, ties them off around her waist and begins her climb, moving slowly up the route signposted by the other two, clenching her jaw and groaning with each advance. At the slope, she lashes the rope to her left arm. As she shifts her weight, everything goes – pain like lightning, coursing through her and frying every circuit. Her knees buckle, forcing a mad scramble as hands rush to take the strain. She bites her lip, screws her eyes shut and waits for the back spasm to dissipate.

Seule shouts, 'Are you okay?'

Pardue ignores the question. 'Throw up the bag.'

She watches as Seule feels the bag's weight, begins to swing it back and forth in a long arc. After four swings, he lets go. The bag slaps into the rock about a metre below her and drops with a heavy thud. Seule shakes his head, murmurs something to himself. The second attempt is higher, but still short, and pulled too wide. A look of despair passes across Seule's face. The third effort falls lowest of all.

He buries his head in his hands. 'I can't –'

'It's okay,' Pardue says.

'I'll carry it.'

'No, it's too heavy. Too awkward. You need your arms free.'

Seule appears not to hear. He is wrestling with the handles, pulling them over his head, trying to force an arm up through the narrow loop and push the load down to his back. 'It's almost there, I can do it!'

'Try another throw,' says Pardue. 'You were getting closer.'

'Hell, I don't … oh. I can't throw it.'

'You can.'

'No.' His voice is wobbly, shrill. Another wave washes in, and now the water is bubbling around his ankles, drawing a yelp of alarm.

'Leave it,' Pardue tells him.

'No! Just get moving. We don't have long. I can do it.'

'Seule! Listen! Take off the bag.'

'But I –'

'Do it, drop it.'

He falls to his knees, bends forward and lets the bag slide from his neck into the deepening pool.

'Open it. Seule?'

Shaky fingers fumble at the zip.

'Come on, good. Some of my things are in there. Take them out, put them in your rucksack. Okay? Rations, my spare boots, clothes, whatever's there of mine, whatever you can fit in your rucksack. Make room, find a way.'

'What about the other stuff?'

'What is it? Just the tools? We don't need those now. They were for the boat. We don't need them here.'

'Uh, lighter fluid?'

'If it'll fit in your bag, take it.'

'And this thing?'

'Can you fit it in the rucksack?'

'I think so.'

'Okay, yes, we'll take that. There's a carton of nails in there, too.'

'I see them.'

'Good, that's plenty. I'm going up. Okay?'

'Okay.'

At the top, Saria is waiting. She plants a foot, leans out and takes Pardue's arm, pulling her up and over. Gill lies motionless on the ground.

Pardue whispers, 'Is he all right?'

'Huh? I suppose.' Saria does not bother to lower her voice.

Pardue takes in the view: a rolling field of scrub, jagged rocks, scree slopes, sandy depressions, and further inland, where the ground appears to even out, a screen of taller brush. No tracks, no signs of civilisation.

'I know,' says Saria. 'I was hoping to see houses or a road or something. Look though: I anchored the rope on an old fence post. So that's something.'

'Sure. Well, we walk inland, I suppose.'

'Is Seule coming?'

Pardue glances down the slope. There is no sign. She hollers to him, but there is no reply.

Saria scratches at her temple. 'That first bit is tough.'

'You don't think he can do it?'

'I don't think he should have been last to go.'

'Oh, hell. I wanted to get the bags up. I just left him behind. I shouldn't –'

'I'll go pull him up. Oh, hang on. Is that him?'

'Where?' Pardue's eyes are fixed on the point at which she topped the vertical climb. Saria points her to a space a metre or so left. She sees Seule's right hand scrabbling blindly for a hold along the slope's edge, skittering back and forth for a moment, then dipping out of sight.

Saria mutters, 'He'll never make it up that way.' She grabs the rope and begins backing down. 'Seule! Don't move, I'm coming!'

Pardue watches her descend quickly and confidently, retracing their upward route. Now she pauses and shuffles sideways, away towards Seule's doomed line. The surface there is smoother, the way unclear. Saria slows, tightens her grip on the rope. She makes two slithering, sliding plunges, barely controlled, and holds up close to the rope's end. She leans in tight to the surface and, with her right foot – her leading foot – she sweeps the rock below, searching for purchase. She glances up towards Pardue, grimaces, then calls out. Pardue opens her mouth to respond, but the cry is not for her. The disembodied hand rises again: a brief, panicked wave. Saria says something, but Pardue cannot hear the words, nor Seule's reply, if there is one.

Saria inches tentatively down, until she is almost at the rope's end. There, she seems to find a more secure footing. She says something, and again the hand appears. Saria stretches her right leg until boot meets palm. Seule grips her ankle, lifts his other hand and grabs her calf. There is another pause, another exchange of words. Then a head and torso heave into view and Seule finds the rope. Saria speaks, Seule nods. Saria speaks again. Finally, he swings up his right leg, pulls his left knee in behind it, and brings himself level with Saria, face to face over the rope.

They stay flat to the rock and begin dragging themselves up

and across, Saria first, inching towards the safe route, turning occasionally to grab at Seule's jumper and move him along. When at last they can rise to a stooped walk, Pardue exhales, a breath held throughout the slow rescue. Saria grins, raises a thumb. Seule's hair and clothes are plastered to him, sodden. His eyes are watery. He is shaking his head, muttering something, and smiling.

When they are up, Pardue takes Saria aside. 'What did you do?'

'He did it, not me. I just talked him up. I told him to remember the boat. Told him he got us here, we'd all be dead without him. I told him he was our hero.'

'You're bleeding again.' Pardue nods to Saria's injured hand, its soaked bandage.

'Oh yeah.'

On the cliff edge the breeze blows stronger and colder. They change into dry clothes, pull on hats and coats, and rest on the grass, gathering themselves for the hike ahead. They watch as the water chips away at the lifeboat's mooring.

Gill is sitting now, resurgent, slurping water so keenly that broad streams tumble down his chin. When he is done, he belches, nods at Pardue and asks, 'What's with your back?'

'What do you mean?'

'Your back – you're always clutching at it, bothering and bending.'

'Does that annoy you?'

'No! That's –'

'It's a bulged disc, I think. A slight bulge. It's fine, nothing.'

'Does it hurt all the time?'

'It comes and goes.'

'It's getting worse though? Is it going to pop? I mean, it could happen at any –'

Saria emits a sharp hiss, but her invective is cut short.

'There it goes,' says Seule, dragging their attention back to the shore. On his cue, a great swell knocks the boat loose, driving it forwards, then jerking it back and claiming it for the ocean. The boat wheels, dips, then rides another wave, and further submits to the currents. 'It was a good boat.'

'We never gave it a name,' says Pardue. 'Perhaps we should have.'

'It's a lifeboat,' says Gill. 'I mean, it's The Life Boat.'

'Oh. Yes, it's as good a name as any.'

Seule coughs, offers a feeble wave. 'Bye then.'

****

As they walk inland, the bush seems to fold around them, to pull them in among clutches of reedy grass, then shrubs and eucalypts.

'Where are we?' Gill stops, hands on hips. He checks his watch, throws his arms out wide. 'Where in the fucking world is this place!?'

'Should we turn back?' asks Seule. 'Go follow the cliff line? Or –'

Gill ignores him. 'Isn't this bloody place supposed to be golf resorts from coast to coast?' he cries, with an unhinged giggle. 'I mean … bloody hell.'

Seule again: 'Those are all up north, around Currie.'

'Oh.' Gill sighs. 'Ah, shit. I guess we should push on. We'll come out the other side soon enough. Hit a farm or something.'

'It's rewilding, it's –'

'I don't think we should turn back,' says Pardue. 'It'll get dark in … however many hours. We don't want to be stumbling about near cliffs.'

'We don't want to be stumbling about in the bush either,' says Saria.

'But we'll come out the other side. Surely.'

Saria shrugs. Gill walks on, muttering as he goes. Pardue falls in behind him, and only she hears: 'Bloody bush, no connection, no people. Fucking fucked.'

A couple of hours pass before they find the path – little more than a desire line. In either direction, it curves away and disappears among the scrub.

'This way must be north,' says Seule, pointing to the leftward route. 'I mean, if we've kept a straight line since entering the woods, then this way is north.'

'And …' Gill's eyes widen, expectant.

Seule offers a grim grin, shakes his head. 'And what?'

'Which way?'

'Left is north. Right is south.'

'So …'

'So that's it. What more do you want from me? I mean … goddamn it!' Seule stamps in exasperation. 'What does it take?! What do you want from me?!'

Gill blinks hard, taken aback.

Pardue says, 'It depends where we landed. Right, Seule?'

'I don't know! Ah … really, I don't know. I think we came in south of the New Port. But I don't want this pinned on me. I think we came in well south.'

'Toss a coin,' grunts Gill. 'Why the hell not?'

'Let's go north,' says Pardue.

****

'Who's Ariman?'

They are single file on the track, and Saria's voice, low lest the others should hear, comes from over Pardue's shoulder. Pardue doesn't turn, doesn't answer. She can't. She can only process the question, the name on another's lips, where it has no place.

Saria continues. 'You spoke of her on the boat. You spoke to her. On that first night. Oh, that was the worst night, somehow. Worse than the second. I suppose we just adapt to things and –'

'I don't want to talk about this.'

'But I was there with you. You were talking to me, but you were saying that name instead. And some of the things you said were … scary to me.'

'We left all that behind. We had a deal.'

'A deal?'

'An unspoken ...' Even as this argument forms, Pardue is aware how ludicrous it sounds. The morning after that night there had been a demand for food, and there had been a nod. That, surely, was the deal – that and nothing more.

'I remember. I know what you mean. But that was then. We're here now, and it's okay to talk –'

'I don't want to talk about that.'

Saria slows her step, allows herself to drop back on the track, further behind Pardue. 'I helped you that night,' she whispers. 'You needed help.'

****

They almost miss it, almost walk right past it. A wooden hut, worn boards blending in with the trees. It sits some way off the track, its dirty green door flanked by two scratched and smeared plastic windows draped in creepers and spider webs.

'It's a start, I suppose,' says Pardue.

Saria begins picking her way through the brush. 'Not quite civilisation.'

'A human touch though.'

'Wait,' calls Gill. 'Pardue, where's the gun?'

'Really?'

'Really,' Gill hisses. 'We don't know what's going on here. We don't know where we are, or who –'

'It's in Seule's rucksack.'

They all retreat, even Saria. Gill stations himself behind Seule, roots around in the bag until he finds the tool. He loads nails, checks the power cell, the safety. He glances at Saria, perhaps expecting some admonishment, challenging her to deliver one. Instead, she steps aside, allows him to approach the shack.

He grips the gun two-handed, creeps up and places his shoulder against the door, leans forward to peer into the nearest window. Satisfied, he backs up and checks the other one.

He returns, checks his watch. 'Shit, must stop doing that. Anyone got a timepiece that isn't networked?'

'No,' says Pardue. 'It must be mid-afternoon, at least.'

'Yeah. So –'

'Late afternoon.' Seule shields his eyes and scours the leaf canopy, clear sky beyond it. 'We've got a few hours' daylight left.'

Gill nods. 'Then I reckon we stay here the night.'

Again, he seems to invite a reaction from Saria, but she declines. She edges past him and goes to the door, shakes gently on the handle. It won't give. She places her right palm flat on the wood, as though to stroke or soothe, backs up a pace and delivers a sharp kick to the lower half, near the jamb. The crack of splintering wood echoes through the bush.

They follow her into the room, grubby floorboards, bare walls – more shed than house. Dust motes dance in the light streams cast by door and windows. In the centre of the room, a wood burner sits below a wobbly tin flue. Either side of this are couches, foam bulging through tears in dark tartan print. A tall cupboard completes the furnishings.

'An old hiker's cabin or something,' says Gill.

Pardue collapses onto a couch, wheezing with relief as the weight falls away and it occurs how close she must be to the limits of her endurance.

'Oh, my goodness.' Saria has opened the cupboard. 'Oh, my word!' Without turning, she raises her right hand to reveal the treasure within. 'Baked beans. There are … one, two, three cans here.'

'Oh!' Seule is laughing, incredulous. 'Are they okay to eat?'

'Wait.' Saria turns slowly to face them, blocking the shelves with her frame. Her smile is broad, playful. 'There is more.'

They cry out for answers.

'Ready?' She cocks an eyebrow, prompting a fresh barrage of expectant curses. She turns again, slowly, taking great care not to reveal the cupboard's contents. She pauses for effect before completing a full 360. 'Ta-da!'

In each hand is a can, taller than the bean tins, red wrappers adorned with a winking cartoon cow and chunky brown lettering: Chilli Beef.

There are few words – only more laughter, and groans and moans of delight. Seule drops to his knees and bows in front of Saria, supplicant before his new god.

'I've never eaten canned beef,' he half-sobs.

****

They gather kindling, larger branches. They fill bottles from a hand pump out back. By sunset the fire is burning well, filling the hut with a wearying warmth. Wet jeans, socks and boots are laid out to dry.

'Maybe we shouldn't eat it all,' Pardue says as Saria peels open the first tin.

'We still have rice and crackers for tomorrow. Ugh, I can't even – oh …' Saria's eyes widen as the smell of congealed meat and fat reaches her nose.

Pardue says, 'I've never eaten beef. But –'

'Let's just finish it,' says Gill. 'It'll give us strength for the morning. If we follow this path, we have to hit something. Everything should fall into place.'

'Maybe save some beans, for breakfast,' offers Seule, wincing slightly at the immediate implication of this.

Saria sighs. 'Good idea.' To Pardue, she says, 'You've never eaten beef?'

'Have you?'

'Once or twice. But you earned money, you were a doctor.'

'I just didn't feel … I didn't want to eat cows. Not since I was a little girl.'

'But why –'

171

'Never mind. I'll eat it.'

Saria bites a lip. 'Fine.' She turns away irritably, hair flicking behind her, and calls on Seule to help prepare the meal.

'It'll be faux anyway,' offers Gill. 'People who can afford beef – they tend not to want it canned, you know?'

The hot food is divided, consumed in silence as the light fades. Within minutes of eating, Seule and Saria are asleep at opposite ends of their couch, legs bent tight at the knee, feet slotting in around each other, filling every available space. Pardue and Gill sit opposite, transfixed by the fire's final glow.

'What do you think about tomorrow?' Gill whispers, words tugging Pardue back from the brink of slumber.

'I don't know. Maybe … I don't know. I still wonder, perhaps everything will be okay. Mostly okay, I mean. It's just a network failure, or some huge data breach. Everything's connected, it could happen. Something bad, but not –'

'Mm hmm. And we roll up, and we say, "Hey, you forgot about us!" And they slap their foreheads.' Gill acts out the reaction. ' "Sorry, guys! Our bad." '

She shushes him, nods towards the younger pair.

'Oh, they're dead to the world,' Gill reassures her. He claps his hands, clicks his fingers, but there is no reaction. 'See?'

'Let them stay that way then.'

'Well, it's a nice idea, Pardue. I think it's something more. A sequence, a cluster-fuck. And then … have you heard of the Cataraqui?'

'The what?'

'A ship. It wrecked just up the coast from the New Port, over 200 years ago – middle of the 19th century. Ship full of immigrants from England got caught in a storm on the way to Melbourne and broke up on the rocks here. Hundreds dead. That sort of thing, it's always fascinated me. Morbid fascination. Those folk on board, they were so close. Months at sea, plain sailing. Ready for a new life, a new start. Full of hope and expectation and … plans. Bang. Forget your plans; now it's every man for himself. Jump in the bloody sea and swim for dear life. Imagine that … shift. It must be there in us all, just under the surface: that animal instinct. It rises when it has to. Everything else is decoration. Look outside, Pardue. Have you ever seen a night so dark?'

'We're in the middle of a forest.'

'I know that, but still. The New Port throws up a *lot* of light. Usually.' Gill is gazing at the window. 'I really had no idea there was a forest out here.'

'Seule said it was rewilding.'

'Huh.'

'I've been having this feeling.' She wavers as Seule shifts on the seat opposite. She lowers her voice further, then continues. 'It started on the boat, a feeling we were in the wrong place, wrong time even. As though somewhere on the ocean, we had … crossed over. And then again and again. Like a series of invisible gateways taking us further and further from reality. Now, it's like we're alone here, we've come to a place and time that is somehow wiped clean.'

'And you're scared.'

'Yes. And no. It's felt like a great weight has been lifted from me.'

'Why?'

'I don't know. I haven't wanted to think about it. Maybe

everything would be easier. Not better, just easier. If it's not my world, then I have no duty to it. When I was younger, I felt this great obligation to serve, to organise, to make things better. Idealism. And everything else was secondary to that. It's still there … lingering. I know all this "crossing over" nonsense, it's a fantasy. This is the real world and the real time, and whatever has happened to this place, it's still mine. I must own it.'

'I guess. Weren't you ever in love, Pardue?'

'Uh … once, I think.'

'Love can change things. Change perspectives.'

'If you let it.'

'Who were they?'

'We met quite young, we were at college together. Too young, I suppose – the opposite to you and Gem. Is there a right time? It all feels like an age ago now, as though it happened to some other person.'

'What happened?'

'I don't know. Like I say, I had an idea then of what my life should be, and what I should be doing, and he didn't fit. It doesn't sound much like love when I describe it like this. I was loved by him – I believe that. I think about him a lot.'

'That does sound like love.'

'A painful kind.'

'Hell, that's the only kind there is.'

'Oh? When you were talking about Gem before, back on the platform – that didn't sound like pain.'

'Everything ends though. Every day of happiness is a step towards pain. I guess if you're lucky, then the end, when it comes, it comes quick: much happiness, little pain. She wasn't lucky. Neither of us were. She just started acting strange: switching on a stove top and forgetting about it; packing a suitcase when we had nowhere to go; getting lost walking the streets near our home. She would get into these states, then snap out, and she would try to laugh it off, tell me not to worry. But I could see the fear in her eyes. Her moods shifted. Sadness and anger would come over her. A meanness, like I'd never seen before. I made her go to the doctor. She went, but it was like, "If I must, if it'll shut you up. But then …"

'I'm sorry.'

'It can come on quite young … well, you'd know. I've never spoken to anyone about that part.'

'You don't have to.'

'No matter now. They say you should talk. That it's good to get it all out.'

'Sure.'

'Imagine being told that. Your brain fading, your … self. I can't fathom it. It went bit by bit, pieces falling away. Sometimes she'd see me and she'd cower. She was scared of me, had no clue who I was. And, well, look at me: big lump, scary. She would hit me, call me terrible things. And then she'd come back to me, just like that, and she'd hold me and ask why I was … you know, crying.' Gill's voice has grown thick, and he has turned away from the ember glow, away from Pardue. 'I looked after her at home, best I could. In the end though, those clear moments, they were like drips, drying up, stopped. Authorities wanted to put her in one of those aged care places. So I quit the wind farms and moved us both down to KI – bigger bucks for me, better care for her.' He drums out a sharp tattoo on his knees, clears his throat. 'And now here we are!'

'She's free of it now. It might be for the best.'

'Oh, I know. Sometimes I think, I'm relieved she's gone. She was too good, you see. I can do "every man for himself". Her, I'm not sure.'

'I didn't mean that. I meant, best that she's free of the pain. And you can remember her as she really was. That can give you strength. The strength to go on, perhaps.'

'Maybe.'

'I once knew a girl. She'd be about Saria's age now, I suppose. No, a little older. She promised me I'd find peace. And I know it didn't really mean anything, but it stuck with me, all the same.'

'Mm hmm. And you're looking for that.'

'I suppose. Isn't everyone?'

'I'm not so sure. I think, maybe I'm on the edge of something now. If there's a fight coming, count me in. Because Gem does drive me on: I'll fight to make a world fit for her, for folks like her. I don't care much about myself, so I'll fight. Let the good stay good, and the rest of us can wrestle it out in the dirt. No, I'm not thinking about peace so much – not for me, anyway. I'm done. I remember … our last night together, in our KI apartment before she went into care and I went on my first rotation. I was sleeping on the couch. It was about midnight, and I woke up, I could hear her moaning, crying in the bedroom. It happened all the time: she woke up and didn't know where she was, or who she was. That happens to us all, hey; for just a second or two. You know, that moment of waking, blankness before your brain fully fires up? But imagine that for five minutes, ten minutes, half an hour. I went in to her, and she was … her mouth was hanging open, eyes wide. Terrified. She was staring at the wall, holding the covers up tight against her. She didn't even notice me. I sat on the bed next to her. I had this routine by then, I guess. I'd say her name over and over, as soothing as I could.

First, it'd be like I wasn't even there. But then the name, or maybe just the sound, it would bring her around, and she would start to relax. Sometimes she would let me hold her – she did that night. I moved up closer, and pulled her towards me, put her head on my chest, put my arm around her shoulders. I stroked her hair, and started to think of all the times we'd lain there like that, with smiles on, just filled with ... dumb happiness, and thinking of the next day and the next night, and on and on forever. And then I realised: this is the last time I'll hold her. Here in the dark, and the smell of hair conditioner and clean sheets. Oh yeah, that hair conditioner she liked, expensive ... like flowers. And the sheets, I'd changed them that day; why did I do that? I started crying, and she said, "Oh, silly. You were always one to worry so." I didn't know if she was talking to me or to someone else – some long-lost friend or relative. Because that's how it was sometimes. She said, "I'm going away soon." I told her, yeah, she was. And she said, "You'll still be here though." Yeah, of course. She smiled at that, and she was quiet for a time. Then she stiffened in my arms, started to pull away from me. She shouted, "What's going on here!?" I told her, it was okay, it was okay. "Fuck you, J.J." First time I heard her really swear like that. And the last time I heard her say my name.'

'But that wasn't really her.'

'I'm done in. But ... you know, Porter and Daws, they gave it up. I can't do that, so ... I'll still be here, I guess. I'll fight.'

Pardue places a hand on his arm, pulls it away again, uncertain. 'You should sleep. We both should.'

'I'm a bad guy. It's plain as that. I don't care though. There are good uses for bad guys. This thing with Broz ...'

'Yes.'

'I'll answer for it, Pardue. If I have to, I'll answer for it. I told Saria the same. "Truce now, and you'll get what you want in the end." But that whole situation – that's what I mean by a place for the bad guys, the dirty work. Because I don't think many people will walk away from this thing clean.'

'Sleep.'

October 10: Blackout +20 Days

They are along the track, about two hours distant from the hut, no end in sight. Pardue is the first to speak in a long while. Her question is an offering, cued by the nagging sense that a reconciliation of sorts is required, and by a night spent reliving – in wakefulness and sleep – their journey from the platform.

She says, 'Do you remember the killer whales, Saria?'

'Of course.'

'Do you remember what we spoke about when they'd gone?'

'Why?'

'I was trying to recall it. I feel like there was … something to it. But I can't remember. We spoke a while. I don't know if it was something important, or –'

'This is pre pact of silence?'

Pardue sighs. 'I just wanted to remember. I just –'

'We spoke about nothing,' says Saria. 'Talking for the sake of talking. You were sad because the orca had gone. I was too. I think they had lifted us. It was a high, then a low, a … comedown. We spoke of life back home, school days. A poem. Probably the only poem I've ever read, or the only one that stuck. That's it.'

'Okay.'

'Not what you were looking for?'

'Forget it.'

Seule asks Saria, 'What was the poem?'

'Larkin. It was about a man. An older man who sees a young couple, lovers. I think he's stunned by their beauty, and their vibrancy. And he realises, they have something he never did. A new kind of freedom, I suppose. So it's wonderful to him, and somehow heartbreaking. He wonders if anyone ever envied him in the same way. Ah, but I don't know, I'm not even sure I read it right … sometimes, I think I should have been that girl, that young lover. I mean, we should all have that moment.' Saria shakes her head, rolls her eyes. 'Or whatever.'

Gill, a few paces ahead, chuckles. Saria flicks him a single-digit salute.

'I know what you mean,' says Seule.

'Must be an old poem, is it?' asks Gill, without turning.

Saria mutters in the affirmative.

'Things used to get better. Step by step, that's how it went. Take this world and make it your own; then your kids will do the same. It's slipping, always slipping now. My grandparents lived better lives than me. My parents had it worse than them, but better than me. What have we – Pardue and me, your own folks – what the hell have we left for you two? It isn't right.' Gill spits into the dust by his feet. 'Maybe we've bottomed out now. Maybe this is where it turns. Who knows?'

Neither Saria nor Seule respond. Instead, Saria asks Pardue, 'Is *that* what you were looking for?'

'No. I don't know. I just wanted to remember it all correctly. The whales, they were something special. To think of them now, still out there, it's hard to comprehend. It's like they were tied to that moment. Tied to us.'

'But they are still out there – safe in their pod. Still swimming free, still hunting, and we're long forgotten.'

'Like Daws,' says Gill. 'Still fishing.'

'I hope they leave some for him,' says Seule. 'I hope he's okay, I mean. It's not too late to send someone out for him, is it?'

'We'll see,' murmurs Gill. 'He's a tough old bugger, you know, Seule? He's a fighter is Daws – an actual fighter. Fought for the wrong bloody side, I'd say. But still –'

'The wrong side?'

'Could have picked his battles better. He paid the price in the end. He knows it. That's why he stayed on the platform, I figure. Doing his penance.'

'What would you know?' asks Saria.

'Oh, I know enough. Fifteen, twenty years ago, in the union rights days, me and him used to walk the same picket lines; opposite sides. Shit, he probably cracked my skull – plenty of those boys did. Probably took a swing at Pardue too. He'd tell you if you asked. It's no secret. He started out fighting resource wars in the desert, wound up back in Melbourne beating down his own people. So he's getting on a bit now – so what! He isn't some doddery old angel.'

'A paedophile too, is he?' Saria snarls.

'Of course not.' Gill shakes his head in irritation. 'I didn't start that. Those bloody ops boys. That shit shouldn't have happened. Not that it bothered Daws. Sticks and stones, and all.'

'How do you know?' pleads Seule.

'Nobody could hate Daws more than he does himself.'

'I wish I'd told him sorry.'

'Sorry? Hell, Seule, he wouldn't – couldn't – think badly of you for being a little shit. You're a kid. And your shittiness pales next to Daws in his own youth. I'm not saying he's all bad. But he's done some bad … oh.'

They have rounded a bend to find the end of the track, and the end of the bush. The ground drops away into a narrow valley, a shallow channel cut across their path, extending as far as they can see in either direction. No more trees, nor scrub; only rocks and dust.

'Like a moon crater,' says Saria.

'A quarry?' muses Pardue.

'Is that smoke?' says Seule, pointing beyond the opposite slope. 'Or cloud?'

They pick their way down the rubbley hillside, descending into shadows cast by the tree line behind them. Halfway across, they stop to pull on coats. Saria sips at her water bottle.

'I wish we could have stayed in the cabin,' she says. 'It felt like a holiday there.'

Gill laughs. 'Hell, what kind of holidays do you take?'

'I've never really had one.'

'You've never had a holiday?' blurts Seule. He blushes, seems to recoil at his own words. 'Oh, no, I didn't mean –'

'It's okay. Where did you go when you were a kid? You must have been to some slick spots.'

'Oh, well. I don't … it's not –'

'Come on, I'm interested. I asked you. It's not bragging.'

'Yes, I know. But I –'

'Come on!'

'You have to tell us now,' says Gill.

Seule eyes his feet, smiles bashfully. 'Well, we didn't go abroad too much. We have … an islet.'

Gill chuckles. 'You've got your own island off *this* island?'

'Um.' Seule scans the older man's eyes for scorn or derision, finds only benign amusement. 'North of Currie, near Whistler Point. I mean, it's only a little island.'

Saria laughs – a single, sharp ha! – and claps a hand over her mouth.

Seule grins, as though his modesty was intentionally absurd, the reaction desired.

'That must be wonderful,' says Pardue.

'Oh … I don't know. It used to be a nature reserve or something, but the sea's taken most of it. My father built a holiday house on what's left. He does love it. The only way to get there is by helicopter; I think he feels like a super-villain or something. It's rocks on all sides. Nowhere to land a boat.'

'What did you do there?' asks Saria.

'Nothing much. A bit of gardening. Walks. Father goes hunting – he took rabbits over; and the sea birds, totally illegal. "Those rules aren't for us." '

'Your dad sounds like a dick,' says Gill.

'Actually, he is. I don't like him.' Seule scans the valley. A shiver grips him. 'Let's get out of this place. It's giving me the creeps.'

They clamber up the opposite slope, red-faced and sweaty as the sun again catches their backs. They are on toes, scrabbling for footholds, hauling themselves forwards on those rocks big enough to support them. Saria pulls away, a few metres ahead, and is first to crest the grass-topped ridge. She stops there, seems to stagger slightly. She turns, doubles over, hands on knees, as though bracing against dizziness. Gill breaks into an awkward jog. The other two follow, and they see what Saria has seen.

Gill is the only one to speak. 'So now we know.'

****

King Island New Port, the newest of ports. A town of towers built on a foundation of fossil sludge. From afar, Pardue had witnessed its birth, its early years after Australia sold the territory to the petro-conglomerate. The '66 divestment, the world's biggest carbon offset: oil and gas flowing out from the bight to all parts that still use it; kickbacks streaming up across the strait to Canberra, and deportees sent the other way, disappeared into detention camps or put to work. The oil barons had been proud founding fathers. In part, anyway: Try not to look at our outputs; don't think too hard about the inputs either; but here's our sleek, super-smart company town, everything connected, data-driven and run by fabricated minds. This is the future, and we're part of it.

Singed circuits now, and all that data drifting skyward in poison plumes. She sees smouldering beams, scorched shards, melted panes and polymers. And dotted around the flattened, grey grid, fires that seem set to rage forever, flames dancing through gaps in the wreckage.

It's not the first time she has stood on a hillside and witnessed a community's final moments. In the desert, they used to drink beers and chat and sometimes even laugh while chaos raged on the horizon.

You can do that if you're far enough removed, she thinks. But not when you recognise yourself amid the ruins.

Places she has known, however briefly. The vague outline of the gasworks, the refineries and dock offices burnt black; the engineering institute, and the tower where the students lived, its upper half sheared off to leave a crown of polka-dot cladding and bent metal; the commercial quarter, the plaza and, hidden by blazing debris, the school precinct. On the other side of town she can make out the airport terminal, steel arches exposed to the sky, ribs stripped of flesh. And on the other side of that, unseen, in what passes for suburbia here, is her dorm block, and inside it her bed, her mattress, her sheets, her clothes and a few possessions, her scent on them all, a part of her lingering.

The destruction defies explanation. She recalls Daws' assertion: 'This is war.'

Maybe. Is this what it would look like, destruction along such a narrow sweep, razing the urban but sparing its surrounds? And where are the people, the survivors? Would there be any? She can see no crowds in the outskirt streets, no huddled clusters seeking safety in the parklands and playing fields there; no emergency services, security.

'Where the hell are we now?' she asks. And she means, Where is this place, this ridge, overlooking the city? She means, I don't remember this place. I don't recall coming here, or ever casting my eyes southwards and seeing this ragged peak. But, oh, things so often look different in a new line and light. Maybe the ridge was always here. Maybe the city was always burning: we could walk down there now, and everything would appear quite normal.

She realises she is sitting, and this development is somehow fascinating, worth exploring, a more palatable puzzle.

Here I am sitting on this boulder, she thinks, but did I really sit, or did I slump, collapse even?

She has no recollection. Certainly, no decision was made. Self-preservation through muscle memory perhaps, like when she was 17 or 18, on a long trip up to NSW, her first solo journey. She drove an old manual car and, once clear of the city, with a hundred or so kilometres of featureless highway behind her – near lane, straight line – she thought, I don't remember anything about the past hour. Not a thing.

Now, on her boulder, she realises something else: My eyes are closed, and I don't remember doing that either. Oh! Now I can't breathe, I simply can't inhale.

She determines that if she doesn't open her eyes, she'll never open her throat.

This is a loop! Find something, break it!

She does, she finds something – somewhere, rather. Leaning against a white railing around a perfectly manicured oval, sun at her back. Springy turf under open sandals, blades tickling her toes. In the middle, the facing batter is scratching at his mark, dragging a foot through the dirt. The bowler is striding away, head down, consulting the globe, scouring its surface for a route to riches. Now the bowler stops, as though struck by some startling realisation. He turns smartly on his heels and breaks into a trot, a smooth sprint. The fielders drop to their haunches, ready to pounce. The batter braces, paces forwards then back, rocking on his heels, playing out a dozen or more shots in his mind, betraying his nerves. The bowler is in, leaping, lunging, unfurling into an inelegant whirl of arms and legs, and somehow, from this mess, the ball is delivered, a ferocious flash, fast and short. The batter is forward, then snapping back, head whipped up and away. And he is down, bat clattering to the ground, body following, melting at the knees and hitting the deck before the crack of leather on helmet has even reached her. The close fielders are rushing in towards the prone figure, an act of sporting prowess as pure and perfect as any wicket-taking delivery or drive for four runs. And she is running too, kit bag in hand, gestured in by frantic waves from the men in white. And on the inside, she is smiling: I'm in the game now, I can help, I can help … I can open my eyes … I can breathe.

The crew are all sitting now, four in a row. She watches their eyes flitter across the shattered landscape, tracing their own routes, reaching similar destinations. Her flash of panic has passed unnoticed.

'This is really happening,' she says.

'It's an answer, at least.' Gill loosens his watch, flings it to the dirt.

There is a stillness to it all. Up here beyond the ring of flames and sepia smog, there is a serenity of sorts. She watches a dragonfly zip between the weeds at her feet, carapace shimmering in the sunlight, wings beating at an improbable rate as it plots a course that rejects interpretation or prediction: it goes wherever it goes, does whatever it does, and that's all. She could watch that forever. Serenity, beauty, until the insect darts up and away, past Gill, taking her eyes to his. What she sees there – more absence than presence – is enough to make her look again to the city.

KI Energy Tower is mostly intact, while the gardens beside it seem, from this distance, to have been bled of colour. Central Hospital is simply erased – either that or she is mistaken, has lost her bearings and can't place it. It should stand north of the office block, twice as tall. Instead she sees there a single tower, deep crimson, smooth yet somehow crooked of aspect, as though warped by design, built to an alien aesthetic or new geometry. It seems almost to pulse, to throb. It calls to her, draws her in and holds her. Livid clouds curl around the structure's trunk, wisps escalating to billows that creep upwards, suggesting some flashpoint at or around the ground. The clouds shift in shade and density – smoke to dust – and the structure's pulse becomes a more definitive sway and tremble. She almost expects it to rise, to rocket up and away. Instead it comes down, falls quickly in on itself, disintegrating into powders that mushroom high and wide. The noise, when it reaches them, is a crackle, a cackle.

'What was that?' she asks.

No one has an answer. Seule buries his face in open palms.

Saria, watching him, says, 'Let's get out of here.'

****

They follow the ridge east, away from the city, down a scree embankment and into parkland on the urban fringes – into the catastrophe now, no more observing from on high. The grass grows ankle-deep, through and around a carpet of cans, bottles, shredded tents, bags and scraps, clothing.

The New Port is there, awaiting investigation, but with every step they put it behind them. On the only road out, north-east towards all other points of population, they pass the darkened homes of middle-ranking types whose status has taken them out of the port but no further. Some of the houses are ruined and gaping, some untouched, locked doors that hold their counsel. There are a handful of cars on the outbound lane, immobilised and abandoned. And the litter trail grows thicker and wider, fanning out on all sides until it too fades and nature reasserts itself. Crows line the roadside crash barriers; they hop and caw at the passing humans, then settle back to their vigil. The crewmates pass all with no thoughts of intrusion, of picking for sustenance. Instead, they pick up the pace, eager to put the scrapyard behind them. They reach an unmanned security

188

checkpoint and push on, their visas breached.

In the evening, deep into the countryside, they find a lone minivan and manage to rive it open. They roll it to the nearest field, settle in for the night. They have not seen a single soul – dead or alive.

October 11: Blackout +21 Days

She lies on the back row of seats, hands cupped over eyes that will no longer stay shut. Her palms are lined with dust and muck, nails tipped with black crescents. Gill is stretched across the front row, one foot wedged on the dashboard, coat draped over head and shoulders. Behind him are Saria and Seule, side by side on the middle bench, bodies tilted inwards, her head nestled on his, his on her shoulder. Saria is sucking her thumb again.

Pardue rises, creeps past them to the door and steps out into dew-flecked grass. She gulps down the dawn air before searching for a sheltered spot to pee.

When she returns, Saria is up. She is stretching against the van's bonnet, palms spread on the metalwork, chin up, arms locked, back straight, one knee bent, other leg trailing behind her. She breaks, switches legs, then assumes the position once more.

'Hey,' says Saria, without breaking her pose.

'Did you sleep?' Pardue asks.

'I'm not sure. In and out, I guess. You?'

'The same.'

'You would have seen the stars.'

'Yes.'

'I've never seen anything like that sky … not on land, anyway.' Saria steps out of the stretch, shakes her limbs, rolls her neck. 'You should be doing this sort of thing, you know. For your back – stretch it out, loosen up. I can show you.'

Pardue grunts, a nothing response.

'Fine, whatever. You know, I was going to show Seule the stars. I was going to wake him. But I decided not to. I realised it was … awful.'

'Awful?'

'Yes. You know what I mean, don't you?'

'It made you feel alone.'

'Maybe that's why we lit up the planet in the first place. So we wouldn't see how alone we are.'

'Seule needs someone looking out for him.'

'We all do. He's better now, don't you think? He's … himself. I think he's pulled free.' Saria nods towards the motionless Gill. 'Stopped putting it on for that one.'

'Yes.'

'I suppose we all put up fronts – we all put it on,' Saria continues. 'No need for that now. Do you know, you never answered my question.'

'Question?'

'On the platform, in my room. I gave you the under-suit, gave you soap … oh, I didn't mean that to sound like you owed me anything. But I asked you, "What happens when we get back?" Because I wanted it to be … oh, I don't know.'

'What do you mean?'

'Nothing. There was no question, I suppose.'

Saria's shoulders tremble, and she tilts her head, allowing her hair to fall like a screen between them.

Pardue wobbles on her heels, comes forward and takes Saria by the arms. She pulls her closer, resting the young woman's head awkwardly against her shoulder. Saria submits for a second, then gives a sour laugh and steps away. Her cheeks are wet. She sniffs, rolls her eyes.

'You give the lousiest hugs, Kathleen.'

'I'm sorry –'

The van door opens with a clatter. Seule steps out, plastic container in hand.

'I'm down to my last meal,' he says, tapping at the lid.

Pardue clears her throat. 'We should be at the airfield in a few hours, I suppose.'

'Shall we risk it? Eat up?'

'I don't know. What sort of supplies do they have at your bunker?'

'It's not my … never mind. Years, I think.'

Pardue says, 'It's a fair hike still. No sense running on empty.'

Seule isn't really listening.

'Are you okay?' he asks Saria. 'You look like you've been, ah –'

Saria forces a smile. 'Fine, yes. Hey, let's eat! You're going to see your family. This is a big day. We should celebrate with cold rice and crackers.'

'Oh, sure.'

Saria ducks into the van, rummages in her bag.

'I suppose I never thought it would actually come to this – the bunker,' Seule tells Pardue. He rubs at his eyes, grinding middle and ring fingers deep into the sockets. 'I know it doesn't matter now. I mean, everything that's gone before. Family problems.'

'I don't know –'

'I know what we need to do. But I suppose I thought this whole thing might present ah … an opportunity for me.' Seule shakes his head. 'Do you remember I told you about that dream?'

Pardue nods.

'When I woke up, and I realised I was back on the platform, it was … a comfort. I was almost happy.'

'So?' The question drips with irritation.

'I –'

'I think you're right. Family: at least you'll have one.'

'Oh, I know! Compared with –'

'Actually,' she closes her eyes, takes a deep breath, 'I'm sorry, Seule.'

'No, I'm –'

'You saw the city yesterday.'

'So many people must have died there,' he says. 'From where we were watching, it looked empty. Did you think so too?'

'Yes.'

'But if we'd have walked down there, we'd have seen things, smelt things –'

'Yes. We might never have come back from that,' says Pardue.

'We're lucky. I'm lucky, I know it. I do.'

Saria returns and they sit beside the van to force down their cold portions. When they are done, Saria straightens her back, cranes her neck, peering into the van, searching for signs of movement from Gill. He remains motionless.

'What a mess,' she whispers to herself.

'Exhausted,' replies Seule.

'I don't really understand. I thought, everything he has done, it was all for his wife. That's his "greater good", you know? His mission. I could make sense of that. It didn't make it right – Broz and all – but it was something. Then he saw the city and he just … walked away. We all did, but wouldn't he want to know, for sure? Wouldn't he do something, say something?'

'What do you mean?' asks Seule, lips aquiver.

'His wife.' Saria lowers her voice further still. 'He's given up on her, just like that? How could you walk on when you have someone …' Her mouth hangs open, as though the next word is stuck there, and her eyes lose all focus. 'I just mean …'

But she can't finish, and the tears return. Seule places a hand on her knee, but Saria doesn't seem to notice. She wipes her cheeks and addresses Pardue, a story tumbling out.

'I saw the processing centre – the place they held us when we first arrived here. Flattened. The rooms used to have these awful curtains, bright green. And interiors to match – the doors, skirting. Ha! Fluorescent green! Such a cheery colour, and over the months that we were locked up together in that place, I learnt to hate it. Visceral. Even thinking of it makes my stomach heave. And thinking of Mum … the same. I felt it again yesterday. I couldn't understand, and then I realised: I can see the colour, there among the wreckage. It doesn't seem possible, I know. From so far away. But I saw the colour, I swear it. And Mum … it was there, stuck in that small room together, that we really lost each other. Feels to me like she was still in there; like she's gone.'

'Maybe,' says Pardue. 'But Saria, you know there was nothing you could do for her. And trust me, Gill knows the same.'

'But –'

'You mustn't carry that with you. You mustn't.'

'How could anyone not?'

****

On the march again, the city smoke palls at their backs. Gill leads, setting the pace, as he has since he shrugged off his seasickness. They have branched away from the main road now, through another abandoned checkpoint and onto a road of newish tarmac. The only sound is the crunch of boots and the flutter of tiny wings among the verdant foliage that flanks their path.

'Feels like we'll be there in an hour or so,' declares Gill.

'Less than an hour,' replies Seule.

'Oh?' Gill wheels around, but the younger man is unbowed, and Gill seems to catch himself, soften his response. 'Why so sure?'

'I know this place too well. This lane here, I must have taken it a hundred times or more, into the city, out of the city, every trip up to school in Sydney, shadowing Father in Canberra. I know everything about it, every curve and contour. Everything.' He closes his eyes, summoning the images. 'I know these shrubs, weeds. I know their density, shapes and colours in the Wet and the Dry; where they flower, where they don't. I was born after the divestment. The flora around here – it kind of grew with me. The rewilding. The company paid off the farmers, built the detention camps and gave the rest of this place over to nature. They sell it as conservation, but I know – it's because nature doesn't talk of what it sees. I watched these gums come up, and that tea tree ahead – the road bends there: Father's car slows to 23, 19 at night. It's a tight curve, and the road seems too narrow. The brakes come on quite hard, and I always think, We're going to crash. But we don't. After that, the brush will get much thicker and taller, two or three metres high. It closes right in on you, over you. It screens out the sun, and then it ends, just like that. There's a wooden pillar on the right, an odd thing, like a totem. It's an old power pole or something. Then there's a large house – odder still. It has a mock-Doric frontage, five white columns. Set back behind lawns, a pond and fountain. That plot belongs to a trafficker, or so they say. And after that it's open fields, clear along the flightpath.'

'It's peaceful here,' says Saria.

'Further north, there's real forest – quite thick. Plantation, I think. Right up until you hit Currie and the golf resorts.'

'Bloody golf,' mutters Gill. He kicks at the tarmac, takes a couple more steps, then pulls up and sucks hard through gritted teeth. 'Can we rest up a while?'

'We're so close though,' says Pardue. She hasn't noted his pained expression.

'Yeah, it's just, I've got blisters. I think I bust one.'

'Oh. Take off your boot.'

'No, no.' He waves her away. 'A quick breather, that's all I need.'

'Let me see it.'

She points him to the verge. Gill flops onto his behind, grumbling as he pulls off a boot, cursing sharply as the leather brushes his heel. He pushes a finger down the back of his sock, eases fabric away from skin.

She kneels before him and raises his leg, supporting the calf.

She whistles softly, asks, 'How long have you been struggling like this?'

'Since the hut maybe. Doesn't matter.'

'Why didn't you say something?' She takes the shared backpack from Seule and pulls out gauze pads, tape.

'They were fine until that little bastard burst. Ow.' Gill recoils at the touch of her finger. 'I didn't want to … argh, just leave it! It'll be all right.'

She tuts. 'It's one of the few things I can help with. I don't know why you'd put yourself through this.'

She dabs away puss, applies cooling cream and patches up the foot, then helps Gill replace his sock and boot. He seems to hold his breath as they do this. He rises slowly and nods as the weight falls on his heel.

'Huh. That is better.'

'Of course. If it hurts, if the others burst, you have to tell me.'

'But we're not far off, so …' Gill bites his bottom lip. 'I mean, thank you.'

'That's what I'm here for.'

He sniffs, wipes his nose with the back of two fingers. 'I do mean it.'

'Good,' says Saria.

Gill looks to the younger woman, drowsy eyes slowly sizing her up. He nods gravely. 'You're right as often as not, Saria. I'll give you that. Yeah, I'm sorry.'

'To me?'

'To everyone. That's never enough though, is it?'

Gill turns, continues limping along the lane.

****

The Greek House is a ruin, its windows blasted through, alabaster frontage streaked with soot and possibly worse; contused and cut to expose wounds of grey plaster and concrete. The driveway is marked by a dozen or more shallow pits and accompanying piles of dirt and gravel, suggesting an ill-fated treasure hunt. Something lies dead there, too. A dog probably, Pardue tells herself, but the charred body is too far gone to identify from the gates, one of which hangs askew from a single intact hinge.

They hurry on. Far beyond the property, they can see the airfield, or rather its control tower, a squat disc atop a concrete stalk.

'There's someone in there,' says Pardue.

'How can you tell that from here?' Gill peers across the intervening fields. The grass and earth has been churned up into a series of channels, a dozen or more tyre tracks that have dried to a dark crust.

'I think I see a figure there. Movement.'

'I see it too,' says Seule. 'More than one – two or three people, I think. Movement at the windows. See? There's one in the middle window now, and one in the next one along, to his right.'

'Hmm. I guess my eyesight isn't up to it.'

'I think they see us too,' says Pardue. 'I think the one in the middle there – he has binoculars.'

Saria moves up to her shoulder. 'Why do you say that?'

'I don't know. I think I saw his elbows come up – up and out by his sides, like this.' She mimics the action. 'Maybe he's looking back at us. He could be reading our lips.'

198

'Hi there, guy,' says Saria, with a nervy laugh.

'I bet it's my father,' whispers Seule.

****

The airfield's main gate is locked. The fence on either side is high chain-link topped with razor wire. On the distant landing strip, they see a chopper slumped forward on its skids, chin buried in the tarmac, rotors drooping. Beyond that, hangers and warehouses, the control tower – unpopulated now, it seems.

'I wonder what happens to a helicopter when the signal is cut, when the nav system shuts down,' says Pardue. 'Falls to the ground, I suppose.'

She is considering this when she hears a whip-snap sound in the field to their right, and a near simultaneous crack from afar, up near the buildings.

Seule steps off the road, peers into the grass where the first noise originated. Gill is umming and ahhing, weighing some half-formed insight. Another snap-crack, and a clod of dirt and turf leaps into the air near Seule's feet.

Now Gill has an arm around Pardue's shoulder and he is pushing her and Saria to the ground, shouting to Seule, 'Gun! Down, get down!'

Pardue is stunned into inaction, pressing herself into grass that is long but too short, she clenches everything and does nothing. There is another shot, perhaps, and Seule flops to the ground before her, too close to show as anything more than a block of denim, but with that crumpled look, that deflation she associates with corpses, and she thinks, That one got him, that one got him. This mini-mantra spurs her forward. She makes to move, and Seule moves too, a knee sliding up past her face, a boot pushing against the dirt, scrambling forwards, or

199

backwards – back the way they came, and now she can see Gill and Saria ahead of the boy, rucksacks wobbling over them like bright targets, and everyone moving faster than her. She orders her arms and legs to work, actually voices the command: 'Go, go, go.'

She sees Saria tumble from view, down into an irrigation ditch they passed maybe twenty metres back, and she realises she has paused to watch this. She sets herself to slithering again, to focusing only on motion, and eventually hands are grasping roughly at hers, yanking her forward, down into the ditch, into a bed of weeds, reeds and dry mud. Gill, red-faced and panting, is tearing off his coat. Saria stares glassy eyed at Pardue.

Seule is laughing bitterly, shaking his head. 'I knew he didn't like me, but …' He trails away into more sinister cackling.

Gill has cast aside his coat and is now tearing at his sweater.

'Are you okay?' she asks him.

'Hot.'

'What was that?'

'Warning shots.' He throws down his jumper, slumps against the trench wall and begins to regulate his breath. 'Warning shots or shit shots.'

The ditch is waist deep – just deep enough. It runs almost parallel to the airfield, a slight curve taking it away into uncleared brush.

'We should head that way,' Pardue says. 'Stay low, get to cover. Then we can …' She has, without thinking, allowed her head to drift over the parapet, and she has seen something: a forklift truck bouncing out from the base, along the track towards the main gate, towards them. Tiny wheels whirring, tall head bobbing and rocking dangerously as battery threatens to outperform suspension. She tries to speak, but all that comes is a gurgle. It is enough: the other three peek over the edge.

'We should run,' says Gill.

'It's too late to run,' asserts Saria, and she is right.

The truck is halfway towards them. On the forks is a pallet, and on the pallet is a man, his rifle trained on their position.

'Shit, shit, shit.' Gill falls on his rucksack, begins tearing out clothes and packs and plastic tubs, digging deeper and deeper.

Seule, frantic, cries out, 'We should run, I want to run.'

Gill pulls his coat back around his shoulders. No one else moves.

The truck rumbles to a halt near the gate. The gunman, masked and in black from tip to toe, drops to a crouch beside the fence, weapon locked on them. The driver, in jeans and mucky red T-shirt, steps from his cab, strolls languidly to the gate and begins working the bolts. When it is open, the gunman bursts through, eyeing them along the barrel until he reaches the end of their ditch. The driver, hands in pockets, breaks into a trot behind him.

'Up – hands up, up, up,' the gunman says, showing the way with a jerk of his rifle. He blinks hard and shuffles on his feet. On his shoulder is a printed patch: KI Defence.

The driver arrives, scratching at his gut, rubbing at his scalp through red, receding hair. He looks them over blankly, then addresses Seule. 'You must be his lordship.' A smirk. 'Sorry about the gunfire – screw-up on our end. So … chop-chop, mate. Don't make it difficult.'

'Alone,' murmurs Seule. It sounds like resignation, but the man seems to take it as a question.

'Alone, yes. Daddy wants his boy. Not his boy and his

buddies.'

'Don't do it,' Saria whispers.

'Let's not make a scene. Come quiet, then your pals can walk away.'

Seule shuffles silently forward, dumb complicity. The driver nods approvingly. He helps the youth clamber from the ditch and leads him away, a hand clamped firmly across one sloped shoulder.

Saria calls out, 'We'll fix it. We'll see you again!'

Seule falters, half-turns. As the driver digs in his palm, forcing him forward, Seule shouts, 'I can't make him see s----'

His voice is weak and cracked, the protest dissolves in the air. The driver pushes Seule onto the pallet and reaches for his pocket, pulls something out. In one smooth movement, he cuffs Seule's wrist to the cab.

Something in that act makes Pardue's gut churn and dip. Gill emits a groan-growl. Saria clasps her hands around Pardue's arm, lets her forehead fall on her shoulder.

Even the gunman seems horrified. 'Now what?!'

The forklift driver waves away something Seule is saying, turns and yells through cupped hands. 'Get rid!'

'What – why?!' The gunman is on the shuffle again, anxiously flicking his head between the forklift and the crew.

The driver seems to mumble something to himself, then calls, 'Pour encourager les autres! We don't want the camp crowd coming here!'

Pardue feels a sharp blow to her side, just below the ribs, enough to double her up, turn her against the trench wall. It is Gill, barging past at pace. There is a roar from him, an animal expulsion of rage and disgust, and by the time Pardue has steadied herself it is over. Gill kneels across the gunman, forearm on windpipe, knee buried in his victim's stomach. The masked man emits a wet wheeze. Thud, thud, thud: three nails.

Saria is away – up, out of the ditch and sprinting along the road. But too late. The driver has the gate shut before she is even halfway, and locked while she is still a length short. He doesn't stay to gloat, simply hops up and begins reversing the truck. Saria's desperate lunge reaches its natural conclusion, feet giving way beneath her, hands grasping for the chain-link to break her fall. She collapses onto her knees, disconsolate before the gateway.

Pardue rushes to her, spine screaming at the effort.

'We have to help.' Saria is sobbing this over and over. 'We have to help. We have to help him, we need him.'

Pardue pulls her from the fence, pushes her against the ground. 'I don't know what we can do.'

Saria wriggles and writhes in her grip, elbows and knees driving into Pardue's flesh. She hisses, 'You don't care.'

Saria doesn't see it, but Pardue does: Seule raises his free hand and gives a single, sorry wave goodbye before the truck stops, whips around 180 degrees and speeds towards the base.

****

They scurry away, Saria succumbing to Pardue's pull. Back into the ditch, on hands and knees until they reach thick briar, through into a well-screened field, down a steep bank, beyond enemy sights and to rest. Gill, appearing almost as drained and distressed as he had on the boat, rips off his boots.

'I need you to patch me up again. Here …' He thrusts his foot at her, another weeping wound on the heel.

Pardue is incredulous. 'What if they come back? You just killed –'

'They're not coming,' he snaps. 'Not for a foot soldier.'

'Oh, man. It was insane, it was …' She sets hurriedly to work, but shaky hands serve only to slow and infuriate. She mutters as she goes, thoughts spilling. 'And that damn crawl … shit! I thought Seule was dead. Thought I would be too. Waiting … the waiting's the worst part. Imagining it. Would you even feel it? In the leg, somewhere on the thigh, fleshy. But no, not in this world. Flesh wound's death, slow. Head shot, like flicking a switch; better to take that –'

'Stop it!' demands Gill. He coughs, heaves, chokes something down.

She finishes up with a series of rough, fierce fumbles, pushes Gill's foot away from her, disgusted with him in this moment. 'Now what!?'

'Let's get gone.'

'We can't leave,' says Saria. She sits apart from the others, head hanging low, eyes to her bootlaces. She sounds unconvinced by her own reasoning.

Gill waits a moment for her to expand on this, then says, 'This is done. It's over. Seule did better out of it than us.'

Pardue asks, 'How far can you walk?'

Gill shrugs, huffs.

She continues. 'The port's out, the airfield's out. The nearest town is probably Currie. And that's, what, twenty kilometres? More?'

'Fine, fine.'

Only when Gill strides out at the head of their diminished

column does Pardue notice he has shouldered the Defence man's gun.

****

They find the road north, and another litter trail. Empty bags and boxes, trampled scraps and material possessions, those unwanted or untenable in the new environment. A Spanish guitar, pairs of shoes and sandals, a rolled-up rug, a child's skateboard. Dead watches abound. Plastic bags and fabric fragments hang tangled from the bushes.

Gill fiddles with the rifle, stopping every now and then to flick switches and snap levers. Finally, he aims at the dirt and fires a single shot. The others, off guard, duck and recoil. Saria lets loose a piercing shriek, and shoots Gill a look of pure anguish, contorting to rage. She lunges at him, unleashing a flurry of slaps and punches before he, dumbfounded, shoves her back, into Pardue's arms. Saria softens there, and that is the end of it. They reset themselves to walking.

The junk trail fans out before them, spreading to the fields. New patterns, dense clusters as far as they can see. The detritus here lacks the human factor: slivers of curved metal; riveted panels of irregular shape and size; plastics that appear to have bubbled and distorted under great heat; sheets of insulation and ribbed tubing; circuit boards and bunches of wire. It makes sense when they see the tail section, fin standing straight and tall on a distant slope, its flag-carrier branding clear. Now they see seats speared into the ground at all angles, and the first bodies, blessedly distant, distinguishable among the wreckage only by their dark auras – flies and feathered scavengers.

Pardue fixates on the road ahead, but it offers no respite. A figure approaches, a shambling silhouette. It limps and veers, picking a route through the scrap. A man, she thinks. His bearing

205

suggests as much. Something else – or is this a trick of the eye? She thinks he is carrying a suitcase, a vanity or some vintage leather piece. He falters now, staggers to a stop, wobbles, then wanders away to his left, feet skittering. He comes to rest against a fence, propped on elbows, as though catching a breather, taking in the roadside scenery.

Pardue slows to a halt. The others stop, too. Saria is frowning, chewing a lip. Gill hugs the gun to his chest. He shrugs. Pardue moves again.

It is a man, and in his hand a small black briefcase. He wears suit pants, crumpled and stained, but mostly intact, a shirt still tucked in. He stares out over the field, shaking his filthy head. He doesn't acknowledge the passing travellers.

Pardue calls, 'What happened here?'

The man doesn't look back, but says, 'Some guys came and killed everyone.' He nods into the grass, but there is no one, nothing beyond airliner parts.

'In the New Port. What happened?'

'My car broke down.'

She approaches, puts a hand on his shoulder, provoking a wild but noiseless flinch that forces her to withdraw. He doesn't turn though, won't meet her eyes. 'Connection dropped out,' he continues in ponderous monotone. 'No sensors, nav. No power. It's just ...'

'It's awful,' she says.

'Oh, beyond! Beyond. It settles on you.'

'We're going to Currie.'

'No, no, no. I'm going home. I'm going home.' Now he turns and meets her eyes; there is a fire in his, clarity too – no sign of the fog that clouds his utterances. 'Heading north?'

She nods.

'Stay off the road then.'

She rejoins the others. Gills whispers, 'I wonder what's in the bag.'

'It's handcuffed to his wrist.'

'It is?'

'His hand is skinned, covered in blood, like he's been trying to remove it.'

'I wonder what's inside.'

'It doesn't matter,' says Pardue. 'I think we'd better get off this road. Find somewhere quiet to bed down.'

October 12: Blackout +22 Days

They rest on a tree-dappled slope, down low behind one of the widest trunks. They have been surveilling the old farmhouse for an hour. The windows are dark, and nothing seems to stir inside or out. Next to the weatherboard home is a tall barn, its double doors chained loosely shut. Piles of indeterminate rusted scrap dot the yard, weeds growing through and around them, adding to the air of abandonment.

It was Gill who spotted the place – tin roof peeking out from a field to their right about halfway through their day's walk through long-vacant farmland. Pardue and Saria had shrunk from the place to begin, but Gill had made his case, albeit without stating the obvious – that while they had been moving nominally north, they were in all likelihood lost, having drifted too far from the road that they had left but aimed to shadow.

'We're not making great pace here. Her back' – he had gestured to Pardue – 'and my feet. I don't think we'll hit Currie within the day.'

So now they watch and wait until they can be confident no one is around, and they try to ignore the growling of stomachs that demand a more reckless advance.

Pardue occupies herself piecing together a dream, the threads of which had held together another fitful night, their first beneath open skies. A dream that felt like awakening: senses firing. Scent first – a land's end brininess – and then the carrier, the frigid air, a rushing over and around, drawing her into a fuggy consciousness. It was night in the dream, and this dismayed her, although she could not say why. She knew that before she was somewhere else and now she was not, but the transition was lost to her. She saw a shaft of light ahead and made towards it, but her first step was false: her foot found purchase a moment later than anticipated, pulling her into a stumble. She grunted, flailing, grasping at the nothingness … and then what? She cannot summon it now.

With only a huff of frustration as notice, Gill makes a move. He scrambles forward, elbows and knees driving him into a low run. Pardue snaps back to the here and now, and she and Saria, muttering curses at his back, watch as he checks the farmhouse door – locked. He halts a moment, as though taken aback; as though this outcome had simply not occurred to him, then raises the rifle, shifts it in his hands to find a comfortable grip and places the butt against the window nearest the door. He pulls back and delivers a sharp blow. The glass shatters, spills from its frame. And he is off again, sprinting back towards the tree line and sliding down next to them. Saria, to Pardue's great relief, holds her tongue.

They watch a while longer, until Gill rises again, slowly this time. 'Nobody home.'

The women exchange doubtful glances before following. As Gill pokes his head through the barn door, Saria and Pardue approach the broken window, peer into the darkness.

'Should I go in?' Saria whispers.

'It looks like a kitchen.'

'Abandoned. Seule said …' She seems to catch herself, as though the name is somehow taboo now. 'Um … no more farmers around here.'

'I guess.'

'There might be food. Should I go in?'

Before Pardue can answer in the negative, Saria grabs onto the upper part of the frame and heaves herself up, knees onto the windowsill – then she is through the gap, down through it, as though she has lost her grip and fallen. All so quick, and with it a flash-bang through Pardue's mind: alarm and some barely recognisable imagery, as though a memory has corrupted in the upload. Inside the house, there is a thud, a clatter, a strangled cry, then a click at the door. Finally a voice – a man's voice, hard and assured, seemingly unfazed by whatever has just transpired.

'You come in too, lady. Door's open.'

Pardue whips around frantically in search of Gill, but he is nowhere. She opens her mouth to hiss his name, but stifles it.

'You speak English, lady? Come in quick. I've got a weapon here.'

Pardue mumbles her assent so softly she doubts it has been heard. She opens the door a crack, sees nothing.

'That's it,' says the man. 'Keep coming.'

Saria is in the corner opposite the door, down in a crouch, hugging the wall. The man stands maybe a metre to her side, pistol pointing languidly but definitely enough at Saria's body. His eyes are locked on the door, on Pardue.

'Close it behind you,' he orders.

He is wearing the black fatigues of a Defence man – they hang from his body, as though a size too large. His face is gaunt, bearded and lined with dirt. Pardue guesses he is not much past thirty.

'You two from the camps?'

Instead of answering, Pardue reproaches Saria. 'My god, why did you –'

'Hey!' The man demands her attention.

'We were working offshore,' Pardue tells him. 'We managed to make it back.'

The soldier eyes her warily for a moment, clicks his tongue. 'Hmm. No shit.' The gun wavers in his hand a little. 'Uh, we're going into the back room.' He nods towards a door in the opposite corner of the empty kitchen. Saria stands slowly and, as Pardue shuffles alongside her, grasps the older woman's hand, a squeeze hard enough to make Pardue grimace. Pardue does not reciprocate.

The soldier circles them as they move, keeping his distance, falling in behind them. 'Okay, good.'

They cross a hallway that is half blocked by piles of rotting boxes, on into the next room, empty save for a single wooden chair and a dirty mattress pushed against the far wall. Decay and desperation hang thick in the air – mould and rot, sweat – and darkness holds sway, fixed in place by French doors of chipped wood and grimy glass.

'You take the bed,' the man says as he settles on the seat opposite, the gun resting on his lap. 'Just you two is it?'

Pardue thinks, This was a family room once, a place for warm meals and cool drinks, open doors as the sun set. Conversation, laughter; hopes and dreams, love – all of that stuff.

She begins piecing it together: Oh, a couch would go there, rug over the hardwood, and a coffee table, vintage stuff maybe, rustic; houseplant in the corner, bookshelves, art on that wall; and sure, a screen up behind me – what's it playing, what's that sound, that drumming? Oh that? That's just your heart pounding, idiot. Because this isn't a home now, it's a safe house, a decrepit shelter from horrors that penetrate anyway. No escaping it inside yourself, and that man has a gun. That man has a gun.

'Hey! Just the two of you?'

'Yes … yes.' Pardue curses inwardly, because the answer – barked, strangled – seems to reveal the lie. But the man appears content to believe her.

'Throw your bags to the side. You got weapons with you?'

Pardue shakes her head.

'Food?'

'No, we ran out.'

'Hmm.'

'We thought this place was empty.'

'I've been here a few days.' The soldier is talking to Pardue, but his hawkish eyes are on Saria, who is staring resolutely at her knees. 'You girls working the rigs were you?'

'We don't want to intrude. We'll leave.'

'Hmm.' Finally, the man breaks from his glare, turns to Pardue. 'She scratched me. So I scratched back.'

'What?' She looks to Saria, who is unmoved. 'I don't –'

'I've got food. In the bag there.' He points to a draw-string beside the mattress.

'No, really, it's fine.'

'In the bag.'

Pardue picks up the bag, peers inside. Tins, a dozen or more, all the same: butter beans. Her nose wrinkles – a reflex, a throwback to less straitened times.

The man doesn't seem to notice. 'Spoon's in there too.'

Pardue peels open a tin, takes a spoonful of the greasy pellets, and offers the rest to Saria, who glances up for the first time in a while, eyes wide, white with fear. Pardue softens at the sight, nods as reassuringly as she can, and places the tin in her hand. 'You should eat,' she says. 'Best to eat.'

'Finish it,' says the man.

Pardue nods her thanks. Saria takes a spoonful, hesitates.

'Go on,' says the soldier. More order than encouragement, it draws Saria's eyes to his. Whatever the soldier sees in her face seems to make him recoil a little. His fingers flex around the gun's handle. 'Eat up,' he says. 'Please.'

Saria swallows, passes the tin back to Pardue, and the process repeats in awful silence until the tin is empty and the soldier, looming over them, is satisfied.

'Thank you,' says Pardue.

'So you were offshore, eh. How far out?'

'About sixty Ks.'

'About sixty Ks, in tranche …?'

'Tranche two.'

'Okay. So you missed the show.'

'We've seen what happened to the New Port.'

'Ah.' The man's eyes shift to the window, as through the smashed cityscape might be seen there. Instead, streaks and smears of filth; veins of blue, the clear sky beyond. He becomes lost in it for a moment. 'I hate this place … this mess.'

'What happened?' asks Pardue.

'Huh?' He snaps back into focus, regrips the pistol. 'Oh … a tactical, I suppose.'

'Tactical?'

'Bomb. I mean, I don't really know. Something very big and very precise. Something new maybe. Some new toy.'

'But who –'

'Antarctic Oil, I guess.' He shifts uncomfortably in his seat. 'We're not talking about that. I'm not in the mood for it.'

'We need to know,' says Saria, her voice hushed.

The man's eyes narrow, but he continues. 'Our hostile takeover failed; their industrial sabotage did not. Desperation time.' The slightest quiver in his voice. He clears his throat and starts again. 'Couple of weeks back – first there was a power-down, bugs in the system. Total. Everything went dark. Every. Thing. Never seen that. Never even heard of it.'

'You were in the New Port?' asks Pardue.

'If I was in the port I wouldn't be sitting here. I was at Alpha. We heard the port cop it. Felt it too. That was it – the residents demanded we release them. No. So the fuckers torched the camp, overran us, took our material – weapons anyway, the older ones; nothing else works any more. Beta went the same way, I heard. Scum. They're out there now, fighting their way up north against what's left of Defence.'

'You're AWOL then.' In Saria now, anger seems to have overpowered fear, and there is a sneer to her words. 'First sign of –'

'Fuck off!' The soldier's mouth hangs agape for a moment. 'Still in uniform, still got my stripes; sidearm.' He whips up the gun to illustrate, drawing a muted gasp from Pardue. He registers this, but does not lower the weapon. 'I'm moving north too.'

Pardue interjects, in search of safer ground. 'What about

Australia?' she asks. 'No one has come to help?'

'Out here?' A shake of the head, and the gun falls to a rest again. 'They aren't about to dirty their hands with this ...' He trails off, another shake of the head.

'Everyone is heading for Currie?'

'Currie, Wickham, all points north. Food's up there: the agri-plants. So we're having a little war ... a nice, civil war.'

'Some of the execs are holed up at an airfield near here.'

'Well, they won't be flying anywhere. But ... I don't know. Aussie might quietly open the sea lanes for some of the fancier-looking escape boats. Not Tassie, of course. But Victoria ... rock up to Geelong in a yacht, you'll get a warmer reception than you would in a dinghy. Maybe.'

'That's your plan?'

'Plenty of boats up Wickham way, north coast. Billionaire's row.' A shrug, a slump of the shoulders. 'They're not paying me enough for this shit. Probably aren't paying me at all. So I'm not beholden ...' The thought is left to hang as the man's eyes fall again on Saria, who has returned to a glassy-eyed contemplation of her knees.

Pardue thinks, This is bad, bad, bad. And then, in panic, Wait, did I say that, did I say that out loud?

'I could give you safe passage,' muses the soldier. 'You know, for a –'

They are interrupted by a thud, then another, on the ceiling, a footfall in the roof space above them. Pardue braces for a flight-or-fight response from the soldier, but – though his eyes rise to the approximate point of impact – he is unruffled.

'Kid's up and about,' he mutters. More steps, tracking away from them, then, from the kitchen, a slap-smack on the floorboards. 'He's been sleeping up there – weird little unit. Hey, kid?! You coming in?!"

No response, but the boy does come, as far as the doorway at least. He looks about 11 or 12. He wears jeans, an oversized T-shirt that exaggerates his skinniness, and, where others would have a watch, a pink plastic wristband. In one hand he holds a roll of papers; in the other a cricket bat, its grip worn away to nothing, maker's mark covered in red welts. The boy takes in the scene, the two strangers, impassive before it all.

'You're fine.' The soldier tells him, with a nod towards the bag of food.

The boy stares at the women, then at the bag beside them, but he does not move.

Saria points to the wristband, says, 'You're from the camps.'

The boy does not respond.

'He can't remember much,' says the soldier. 'Uh, I mean, I took him out with me – and bugger all thanks I get.'

The boy whispers something, barely audible. 'I know these two.'

'Huh?'

A shudder courses through Pardue. These two: What was that, where the hell was that from? From the night-time? From the dream? The false step, the fall, the grasping hand finding something cool and unbending – a wooden post? Maybe. She had wrapped her fingers around the block, grinding her palm into roughened timber. The ground underfoot was uneven, springy, and this had seemed wrong, although she could not say what would constitute right. She had steadied herself there, and then she was moving again, carefully, towards the light – moonlight? Soon she could see three figures there. She had edged as close as she dared, halted in the shadows, hidden. The first figure lay slumped on its side, motionless; another knelt with it, one arm cradling its partner's head. The third figure was standing aside, observing. Porter, his features clearer, his silhouette unmistakable. 'What else could they have done?' he said, with a gesture of the hand towards the fallen figures. 'What else could these two have done?' Pardue, despairing, had let the question go unanswered, and then sights and sounds and scents had faded, and she had woken to sunlight pattering down through breeze-blown leaves.

'Bloody hell.' This time she knows she has given voice to it.

The soldier's eyes flicker between woman and boy.

Saria snatches up the bag and stands, quickly, fluidly. This draws a startled grunt from the soldier, a ripple of shock through his body. The gun falls from his grasp, and he and Pardue watch as it skitters away, coming to rest at a point nearer him, but close enough to Pardue, and better placed for a lunge from the floor than from the chair. His eyes and hers rise from the weapon to each other, and in him she sees a flash of uncertainty, panic, then something more affected – a snarl at his lips, a challenge. Pardue turns from the scowl, from the man and the gun, to watch Saria approach the boy, crouch before him and offer him one of the cans.

Saria asks, 'What's that?' She points to the papers.

The boy's eyes dart to the glowering soldier. He stuffs the sheaf into his back pocket, snatches the proffered tin, and bolts back into the kitchen before Saria can say another word. They hear him scuffing and scrabbling, back up into his safe space. The soldier, meanwhile, has retrieved his weapon. Pardue pointedly ignores this – feigns a greater interest in the interaction between Saria and the child. Saria is staring into the space left by the boy, holding her position by the window.

Pardue looks again to the soldier, to see how he will handle this shift in the dynamic. The gun is back in his lap, and he is glaring at it accusingly.

'So many times I wished we could burn that fucking camp to the ground,' mutters Saria.

Pardue feels her stomach convulse, bile flooding up her throat, to the back of her tongue. Then, as the heave, so close to completion, is somehow subdued, words push past it.

'It's time to leave.' She reels, tilts, clamps her mouth shut, swallows hard, no less stunned than if she had indeed puked onto her chest. 'Huh?'

The man does not look up, but his face darkens, twitches and twists. He punches his thigh, once, twice, harder the third time.

Now, Pardue obeys her own words as though they are orders from another: she stands, scoops up their backpacks. And Saria is moving too, a couple of slow, measured steps through to the next room, as though she is acting on some other, utterly unrelated impulse. Pardue hurries after, fighting the temptation to look again to the man, who utters a single, pleading 'No.' Across the hallway, and she careens into the back of Saria, who is gazing up to the kitchen ceiling, up above the sink: a narrow gap in the plaster, the darkness of the roof space. This collision, and the subsequent righting of feet and bearings, takes a second or less, but it feels fatal in the moment. Exposed, Pardue braces for sounds of admonishment or action from behind her, from the man. But they do not come, and so she pushes Saria roughly through the room, ejecting her into dazzling light, fresh air. Saria grunts something, and now she responds, moving into a stumble, then a dash towards the trees, three or four steps, before she skids to a stop, pulls the bags from the trailing Pardue's grasp, pulls Pardue too, almost sweeping her from her feet as they run.

There are steps to their rear, and Pardue braces again, waits for the bullet again, willing it almost: get it over with. She breaks her run, turns to look, to confront what is coming, but sees nothing, no one. Instead, over her other shoulder, she hears Gill's voice – 'Go, go, go' – and resets in time to see Saria make the relative safety of the gums. There they convene, Gill last, crabbing in with his rifle trained loosely back towards the door from which they fled.

'What happened?!' he hisses.

Pardue snaps at him. 'Where were you?'

'I heard him. The soldier. I heard him with the gun on you.'

'And you just –'

'Did you want me to run in firing?' Gill glances back towards the farmhouse, frowns. 'Should I have?'

'What about the kid?' says Saria.

'Kid?'

'There's a kid in there with him.'

'We've got to move,' insists Gill. 'He'll come after you … how did you –'

'He's a coward, just like the rest of them,' says Saria.

****

Northwards in weary silence. By dusk, they are among woodland, sparse at first, thickening as they advance. They come to a narrow creek and fall upon the water, palming it down their throats, filling bottles and flasks. Only when they are done do they notice the sign, handwritten and taped to a fence post. 'First-class visa zone. Defence patrols in operation.'

'Still with this shit,' spits Gill.

The sun is dropping below the tree line, dragging the

temperature with it. Above the brush to their west they see four neatly spaced spirals of bluish smoke that seem somehow to suggest community amid chaos.

'People from the camps?' muses Gill.

'We just need … someone,' says Pardue. 'Someone sane.'

They make towards the campfires.

****

It all makes sense in the daylight, when she is grounded by sights that can be trusted and sounds that are easy to define. They pass through shafts of light, rays routed and rerouted by the leaf canopy, moments of warmth. Sweet smells swirl around, salt from the west, wood smoke and seared meat from the north, beckoning.

It makes sense. But the darkness falls so fast, plunging them into something formless and free of context, unreal. As the criss-cross beams are snuffed, Pardue begins to see things in the gloaming, and the scents became ominous: meat/flesh. She glimpses shifting shadows, movements on the margins of vision, swaying branches, disturbances. Pulsating orbs and shimmers of fluorescence, the camp coming to life.

Saria snatches her hand, squeezes hard, and whispers, 'Don't let me go.'

Pardue wonders, is there something accusatory in those words?

Gill unslings the rifle, rests it on his hip.

There is a crunch of boots on dead wood, close, and a suggestion of crouched figures dashing away from them under billowing cloaks. She hears a shuffling and snuffling, a sharp inhalation, groans that could be pleasure or pain, or both at once. The crack of branches above, a dead weight descending or

220

something ascending with great thrust, a frantic grasping or forceful flapping overhead that drives her down onto bent knees, then silence, and an impossible absence of form or movement. A child's cry from far away, or a creature's from nearer. A hushed voice, her own: 'Are there devils here?' There is a static crackle away to their left, on the coast-ward side, then an almighty, unmistakably human shriek of anguish, anger and defiance. Another rattle – gunfire, she is sure – another roar, call and response, and the click-scrape of Gill fiddling with his gun. Sharp breaths, her own, suddenly aware of them, of the process itself. Breathe in, breathe out, and a thought: How do we keep this up over a lifetime? There is another crazed shout, closer, more distinct: 'Come on then!' A light away to the right, the hum and snap of grass fire, a face caught in the flickering, a wax mask, wide eyes framed by hood or shawl, the curl of a lip, then gone, melted into the blackness. Everything happens around the edges, never quite reaching them. They stop, convene in whispers. 'There are people all around us.' 'We should find a camp, a base, someone in charge.' 'I don't know how much further I can walk.' 'Who could be in charge of this shitshow?' 'Maybe we should stop, wait for dawn.' 'What about Defence?' 'The gunfire's getting closer.' 'They're not on our side.' 'We should keep moving, we have to.'

Off again, hugging the nothingness, deviating course only to avoid the small fires that had initially drawn them in – friendly in the day, menacing in its absence – and the dim lanterns and swinging torches, fluoro sticks, even candles. They shuffle along in stop-start fashion for what seems like hours. Maybe it is minutes.

More crouched figures, a train of four, darting and weaving between the lowest bows, alongside them, away from them, doubling back, and Gill waving Pardue and Saria down once more, onto knees, onto stomachs, and him raising his hands in supplication. There is a ripple of plastic, and the metallic clack of a gun being raised, then stillness and silence, before a furious rasp: 'Where the hell have you been!?

'I'm not … I've been lost,' says Gill.

'Defence – they're in the forest now! Come on!'

'I'm not the man you think –'

'We have to push them back. Are you fighting or not?'

She watches Gill half-rise, then half-turn, and half to the stranger and half to his crewmates, he says, 'This is it then.'

The figures are up and away, and Gill with them, broad shoulders filling a space between two trunks, then dissolving into the night, until all that can be seen is the flesh of a single hand, still waving them down, and goodbye.

Pardue and Saria stay there a long while, hands locked.

When Pardue moves again, it is at Saria's urging, a hand on her shoulder, a squeeze, like the flick of a switch, power on. She goes, pulling the younger woman with her, away from dangers unknown, forwards for want of an alternative.

****

She sees more people – one moving, one dead weight, a small body cradled, and the carrier stooping and stumbling under the load, hurrying parallel to her and Saria, briefly mirroring them. A woman, she is keening, repeating a vow to the other. 'My girl, oh, my girl, I'll get you out, I will get you out of here.'

Pardue, on instinct, tries to cut across, to reach out, but the mother is somehow faster and slips from sight, dissolves even as the pledge rings again. 'I'll get you out, I will get you out of here.'

222

'Yes, get her out,' implores Pardue, but there is no response.

There is, though, a new voice, new words – or an old voice and words she has heard before: 'In your country, your home? It won't be safe there. Not forever.'

'Let me help you! Let me … oh!'

She is caught in a beam, a retina-searing glare that stops her, drives her back. When her vision returns, she sees they have come upon a clearing, a ring of immobilised cars pushed in from wherever the road is, arranged like toppled monoliths, their headlights drawing on dying batteries. Strings of fairy lights form spokes overhead, arrowing in from the perimeter to the centre: a red cross on canvas, and a painted sign: SAFE HAVEN.

They stagger into the hospital tent.

'Are you injured?' A voice so toneless it could be automated, triggered by pressure pad or motion sensor. But the woman's pallid features, quarter-lit by candles, speak to her humanity.

'No, not us,' says Pardue.

'Then why are you here?' The woman turns, returning to her work. 'Find a car, bed down. Plenty of room out there now. It's okay around here – should be. Just don't go wandering.'

'There was a girl. A woman and a girl. I saw them coming this way.'

'No girl here.'

'I wanted to help them. I can help. I'm a medic – a doctor.'

'Oh.' No sign of relief, nor gratitude. The woman gestures behind her, a somnolent sweep of one hand across the dozen or so camp beds and cots, only half of them occupied. 'They all need help. There'll be more on the way.'

Saria's shoulders heave and roll, and her hand falls from

Pardue's. For a horrible moment, it seems she is laughing. Pardue clenches her fists, knots of anger that are only partially loosened when she realises Saria is crying.

Pardue says again, 'There was a woman and a girl, an injured girl … my god, what happened?'

'They're clearing out the woods.'

'Why?'

One of the patients begins to groan, low and long, and now Pardue notices another doctor crouched in shadows, tending to someone.

'Why not?' the first doctor says. 'They're still in uniform; we're still illegals. Hard to tell who is winning out there though. It's just noise.'

'There was a woman, and she was carrying a girl. They were coming this way, I'm sure of it.'

'Who knows? It's a bad time, and this is a bad place …' The woman's words trail away, before she continues. 'Every survivor from the port, the camps, they're all out there somewhere. Lots of women, girls.' She shakes her head. 'We are reduced to … ah, it's cruel.'

Saria is tugging at her sleeve, lightly at first, growing in urgency until fingers nip at her flesh. Pardue pulls away, but Saria grabs her elbow, forcing her back.

'What is it?' Pardue hisses.

Saria drags her from the tent, further, back towards the clearing's edge.

'Stop it, Saria!'

'We have to keep moving. Get out of these woods.' The teary spell has ended. Her voice is firm, steady. 'I don't like it here.'

'And where do you like it?'

'We'll die here.'

'I have to help,' Pardue insists. 'I have a duty.'

'A duty?' Saria lays a hand on Pardue's cheek, cool palm, a stroke of the thumb, easing her into the blow to come. 'Duty to what? This place has gone to hell.'

'Exactly.'

'You couldn't stop it, Kathleen. And you can't change it now. This burden, you take it on yourself. But it's not yours to claim.'

Pardue, through grinding molars, spits, 'I forgot, you've seen the way of the world.'

'No, that's not it.' Saria lets her hand fall. 'I need help. So do you. All we have is one another. We're reduced now – that's what she said, the doctor there. There are no roles to fulfil, no duty. It's hopeless, you're hopeless. There was no mother out here, no little girl. We'll die in these woods. And for what?'

Saria is sobbing again and backing away, passing from one light spot to another. Her lips are trembling, or perhaps she is still talking.

Pardue asks, 'Where are you going?'

'I don't know. Right down to the bottom. Back to the vacuum. Maybe I'll swim to Seule's island. Ha!'

'Wait. I just have to find them, the girl –'

'Come with me, or … ah, I feel like I'm losing myself. Piece by piece.'

Pardue opens her mouth to say something, to give Saria pause, to make her stay. But nothing comes, nothing of use, and still she is thinking of the fleeing woman and her child. They were there, she did see them. She heard them.

Saria is gone.

****

She returns to the tent, and to triage by candlelight. The three doctors patch and stitch and heal as best they can, and soon, in the urgency of work, the outside is forgotten – phantom figures and their vows, Saria, Gill, Seule and the rest.

Her first patient is a man, hauled in on a bedsheet by four comrades. He is mewling and writhing, and one of his stretcher-bearers announces he has been shot in the gut. She finds a neat entry point, a mock navel bubbling red about a centimetre above the real thing. The bullet has left through his lower back, and there is nothing cute about that wound.

She asks the male doctor, 'What can we do?'

'Morphine, in the box there,' he says, with a flick of the hand. And he must see something in her eyes, or in the moment's pause before she makes to move – time enough for her to feel that familiar flutter inside, the anticipation of administration, and to recall that blessed grip and release. 'We're running out now. We give them what they need. When it's gone, it's gone.'

'And that's it?'

'That's it. We give them what they need. We do what we can.'

The patient is fumbling limply at his chest, unable to find the strength or dexterity to pop open his pocket. She helps, removes a tall, silvery hip flask and holds it to his lips. He takes two long gulps, draining it dry, then falls still.

A gargled, garbled question: 'Will it pour out my tummy now – like in cartoons? Hehehehe.' His laughter turns to a groan.

Pardue finds herself clasping her stomach, her chest, as though the wound in him can suddenly be felt in her too. But there is nothing there. It is an absence that pains her.

October 13: Blackout +23 Days

The night is done, the dead are dead and the dying are sedated and waiting. She sits against a tree outside the hospital tent and, with quivering red fingers, selects a cigarette from a dead man's packet. Lighting it seems to deplete her last reserves of energy and concentration. She rests her eyes, submits to the headswim, barely registering the thud of a car door somewhere behind her.

'You're back on it then?'

Pardue doesn't stir, doesn't seek to identify or acknowledge the source, but engages nonetheless, as though the voice comes from within. 'He must have been rationing these very carefully. I'll do the same. It's only right. Little gestures …'

'It's so quiet here now.'

'You came back to me.'

'I never left.' A blanket over Pardue's shoulders, Saria sitting beside her and holding her. 'I don't want to be alone,' Saria says. 'I don't want you to be alone.'

'Warm,' Pardue whispers. The cigarette falls from her lips, tumbles to the dirt beside her. 'Warm and light. I haven't felt this since … forever. Light spreading to every corner. A light that grows between us.'

She submits to Saria's pull, responds in kind. Bodies as one, silent, lost in the warmth and the light. Fading now, though, because the moment – the drowsy daydream – is passing, and she is alone.

When Pardue opens her eyes, as she knows she eventually must, she sees the two doctors emerging from their tent, squinting and blinking into the new day. The man puts an arm around the woman, kisses the crown of her head. He lets his lips rest there, and his face seems to crumple in on itself, as though he is about to cry. He doesn't, though. He may be beyond that.

The woman notices Pardue. 'We're going,' she says dreamily. 'You should too, before nightfall. Before the soldiers come back. No safe havens here, I think. Everybody is scattering, it seems.'

'I'll go,' says Pardue. 'But I need to find someone.'

****

She trudges through the woods, beyond the cars, past abandoned bivvies. She finds a young space – the trees slender and thinly spread, yellow flowers sprouting among thick grass. Young but not untainted. There are bodies, ten or so in a line. Men and women, all shapes and ages, hands bound behind backs, slumped forward, cheeks to the earth. No mother and child, though. No Saria, either. The nearest victims lean in to one another, foreheads touching, as though in their last moments they sought comfort in contact. She eyes them until her knees shudder and she grasps for the nearest tree, slides down the trunk, twisting away from the pile as she drops.

She pulls Seule's rucksack from her back and rifles through the contents, pulling out men's underwear, T-shirts, dumping them around her until she finds her flask. She drinks, rests her eyes, draws a series of deep breaths. When she looks again she sees, tangled among the young man's boxer shorts, Daws' mini-tab.

'That's me, it's all in there,' he had told her.

228

Cpl??? Baselli. Hard to remember everything about this one. Fear makes a mess of things but there's enough there to piece it together and tell a story. He was the first one in my unit to cop it but that's not why it sticks with me. What really makes it is the words Baselli said to me – I think we're done for. I didn't disagree not at all …

Pardue stabs a finger at the screen, calls up the next page. She repeats the process, wheeling through several more entries before settling on another at random.

Girl aged seven or eight. I don't know how old she was she was dead when I found her. Still warm but gone or as good as. She was lying on a sand berm outside one of the aid camps. The way she was huddled up curled up I remember thinking she looked like a sleeping cat. Her face was clean, her eyes were closed, and she was a girl …

She skips forward again, noting the names and little more.

Militiaman …

Three in the village just outside …

Capt Holder, Sgt Habib …

Hummels …

Sandrine Daws …

Militiaman …

Villagers …

Sargent, KI exec. Died of shame you could say. No I doubt he could feel shame …

David Broz. What was he in the end …

Ennis Porter. Poor old Porter he was lost from the start and I never even liked him so much but I think he needed me in a way and I hope he found …

Pardue I know it's you. I need it to be you reading this. This is for you because there's not many of us left and you're best suited. One answer comes to me. The girl outside the aid camp I can't forget her. She won't let me sleep! I know why. It's that purity the total innocence that comes with youth and the potential there. Everything she could have done for this world I swear I saw it all in her. I held her as the last of it drained away warm to cold – she could have saved us all. Her and others like her I mean. That's what the world needs – a purity of heart and mind. But it has to be protected from corruption. Love is what it needs what it craves. No one can deny that! You have to do this because I don't think good hearts can survive long alone. You have to be strong. Stronger than …

She flicks back, scrolling through the entries in reverse, searching for the second one she skipped. A red light starts to blink on the corner of the console. She pleads with the machine, 'No, no, no, hold on, hold on,' but the flashing grows more insistent. She lands on the page and begins to read, mouthing the words, as though verbalisation will somehow speed the process, 'Girl aged seven or eight. I don't know how old she was she was dead when I found her. Still warm but gone or as good as. She was lying on a sand berm outside …'

The screen fades, and the red light dies.

****

'Hey.' Here is Saria, solid and real, standing over her.

'Oh! You came back to me.'

A shake of the head. 'I didn't go very far. Hid in one of the cars. You actually walked past me back there. You were heading out? Without trying to find me?'

'You think I would do that?'

'I don't know.'

'I was looking for … oh, I think you were right about last night. Seeing things.'

'Yeah … I'm sorry, Kathleen.' Tears again: one, two. 'I didn't mean the things I said.'

'No, you were right. Mostly right.'

'But you do have your calling,' Saria concedes. 'Maybe I'm just terribly selfish.'

'No, no. There's more than one way –'

'I've been thinking about Gill. I wish he were here now. Not for protection or anything. Just …'

She stands, takes Saria's hand. 'I'm still here.'

Saria smiles weakly, lets her eyes fall. 'I was mad at him. Hated him. But it was different, nothing to do with what went before. I was mad because he was too damn slow. He should have been on that guy quicker, killed him quicker. And then we could have saved Seule. Now he's just upped and left us. What happened?'

'He wanted a fight. He found his place. His calling … I've seen what they did here last night, the soldiers.'

'Everything's a mess. No certainty in anything.'

'No. But there's always … you. What you are, what you believe, Saria. Hold on to that. Don't let it go.'

'I'm not sure this place will allow for it.'

'It's hard. Look what you did for Seule. Our hero: that's what you called him, Saria. You lifted him. And it was just a start, but

... I wish he was still here, too. So you could see, the power that you have.'

'I don't –'

'I've felt it. And I want to help you keep it. Oh, I've done some bad things. I've made mistakes. I always wanted to be a good person. I tried to make a difference. Maybe I did, for a while. I tried to save a girl, one life – Ariman. But I failed, I gave up. Last night, I thought, Here's a chance, another shot. I can help. And I let you walk alone into the dark. Another mistake. Now I know what to do. It's us now. Me and you.' She swats at her cheek, glances towards the leaf canopy. 'So much for the Dry.' She smiles. 'Come on, let's move.'

'Where are we going?'

'North of Currie, near Whistler Point. That's where we start.'

'You know the way?'

'We'll find the coast and keep going. Live by the sea. Like old times. Beautiful.' Pardue allows herself to become momentarily lost in memory. 'Like the orca – so beautiful it hurt. I saw something there worth struggling for. Something too good for ... for the greedy, empty people. That's the fight, them, they're our enemies. And I don't think we're winning. But there are different ways to fight. I think that's the point. For now, it's surviving. So we go to Seule's island.'

'We need to find food.'

'We'll find it around here. Food, clothes, shelter. Then we go.'

'I'm glad we found each other.'

'Come on.'

The merest of twists, the slightest of shifts in weight, one foot to another. That is all it takes. Pardue gasps, strangles a yelp. Her right knee shakes and buckles, and she flaps a hand out towards

Saria, scrambling for a purchase that is beyond her. She crumples into a heap of convulsions.

'Oh! What's wrong?'

'My back,' moans Pardue. 'The disc … ah, hell.'

****

She hobbles from the woods, right arm slung across Saria's shoulders. They emerge into a broad meadow, to a sky of endless slate. The drizzle turns to a downpour that rattles their hoods and stings their hands.

On the far side of the clearing is another screen of trees. Beyond this, the land leans into a gentle climb, and the grass underfoot grows coarse. At the top of the first hillock, she drops to her knees, to all fours, slowly down onto her front. 'I just have to stretch.'

'I can show you,' offers Saria.

'Yes, please.'

Under instruction, Pardue plants her palms, spreads her fingers, tries to push up, to lift her torso and arch her back, marking off each millimetre with grunts and wheezes. She forces ten repetitions, each a little easier than the last, and rises gingerly.

'I see smoke over there,' says Saria.

'Smoke where?'

'There, in the west. Other side of the woods.'

'I don't know how you can see smoke against this sky,' says Pardue.

'I'm not –'

There is a flash, and a vast fireball rolling up behind the tree line. As the flames begin to break and dissipate, the sound reaches them, like faraway thunder.

Saria says, 'It's Currie?'

'Maybe.'

Saria turns from it, and says, 'I hope Seule will be okay.'

'He's safe down south, I think. And maybe he'll leave, get out of there.' Pardue gives Saria's forearm a squeeze. 'He knows where we're going. I mean, I think he'd figure it out.'

'I know we can't help him. Not now. Come on.'

****

As the light fades, they find the remains of some old stable or shelter, its roof long gone, stone walls low and uneven. She collapses in a corner and, over her, Saria erects a tarpaulin lean-to, using gaps in the brickwork to tether and tighten as best she can. They huddle for warmth.

'Tell me a story, Kathleen. A better story. I know Foggy didn't really survive.'

'I told you he did.'

'You were lying, to make me feel better.'

'No. Perhaps I didn't tell the story right. I mean, I told you the bad part and not the good part. Foggy survived. I carried him to the vet, I told you that?'

'Yes.'

'I carried him all that way. I was crying, I imagine. People were veering to avoid us, crossing the road even, turning up their noses. I hated them all. The vets were the first friendly faces I saw. They rushed him away, sedated him, began shaving his fur, treating his burns, and they kept saying, "Don't worry about your pup. Who could do this?" I didn't tell them he wasn't mine. I was enjoying it – pretending he was my pet. Just pretending. It was tar, that black stuff on Foggy. When they were done he was

234

naked but for his head and tail, paws. He looked like a lion. They kept him overnight. "Come back tomorrow with Mum and Dad," they said. "Foggy can go home with you." And I still didn't tell them. One of the nurses drove me home. I wondered what to do: I thought maybe I should just forget about him, leave him to the vets, their problem. But I wasn't sure what they did with abandoned animals. I was … frantic. The anxiety of it all. In the end, I told Mum, blurted it out, and we went back to the vet together. No one was angry. They'd keep Foggy until someone applied to adopt him, and I could help choose where he went. I checked on him every day, and when the bids were in I picked the kindest-looking family. Away he went. And I wasn't sad at all – I was so incredibly proud. Everyone said I ought to be.'

'They were right.'

'But I never asked if I could keep him. I wish I had.'

They drift away to the patter of rain on plastic. When they wake near dawn, the tarp has shaken loose, fallen to rest on their bodies. Wetness pervades everything.

October 14: Blackout +24 Days

The rain is relentless. They are in among the resorts now, marching beside the links, green by green, dodging the sand traps, steering clear of clubhouses still smouldering from the battles that seem to have preceded their every step north; heads bowed, chins tucked into collars, stopping every so often to hitch sodden jeans up over hips and, in Pardue's case, to drop, stretch and reset. Between these times, she dissociates, just as she had on the platform when the storm clouds rolled in. Now, it seems, the process is learnt, the switch located. She leaves her bruised body, retreats to the mind, and projects from there. She becomes an observer from above, a great gull following the progress of the two figures below, two figures merged into one, distinguishable only by the colours of their coats, red and green.

The gull glides serene, effortless despite the tumult of wind and water. No need to work against all that, no need to hurry when the progress below is so slow. Hold fast and watch – that's the role, the remit here. But it wonders, Can I leave them behind? Can I explore, can I roam freely in this place? These wings feel strong, what a tragedy not to use them.

Once the question is posed, an answer must come, and the bird, in its simple way, understands this. It decides to test its limits, the length of its tether. It dips, breaks left into an exhilarating swoop westwards, a deafening rush as it arrows through icy air, out from the land, over beach and waves, white horses charging towards the granite; beyond now to the relative calm of the endless blue. Here, it tilts again, allows the thermals to take it up, up and around, looping back on itself, back from the ocean, back over scrub and shrub, and Red and Green still trudging onwards. Around in a broad sweep, south now, back the way they came, the two walkers. Back to the rewilding, abandoned farmhouses, airfields and quarries, back to the lifeboat, the platform, Melbourne, the desert. But now the wind has changed, tail to head, and the gull's progress is arrested, its wings put to work in a panicked flurry. The saturated sky seems to crack, black fissures opening in the clouds, jagged lines spreading from the outside in, intersecting and merging, widening. And in the blankness, another world is glimpsed. Something stirs there, something vast and unwieldy.

A voice: 'Wait, wait, wait ...'

It is Pardue's voice, and with it the tether is severed – she is back in her body. She glances to the sky, scans the gloom: there is no gull, and no world beyond.

'It's okay,' says Saria.

Pardue feels the warmth of the words, and the warmth of arms, for she is sitting enveloped. They are back among the scrub, the borderland between two resorts. The sea roars beside them, cancelling out everything but the patter of rain on hoods and the younger woman's half-shouted words of reassurance.

'Wait, wait ... I don't want to sleep, I don't think we should sleep here.'

'I think it's okay, Kathleen. Please – I'm just so tired. So tired.'

'But we're close. We must be.'

****

The gull, chastened by its earlier misadventure, returns to its station, to the end of its tether and no further. But its task as

237

overseer has changed. Now, two figures have become four: Red and Green ahead; a darker pair behind them. The shadows are perhaps a kilometre back, but gaining surely.

I know these two, thinks the gull.

It has the air of a race, a long-distance slog, and up ahead a natural finish line. Light, a thin shaft pouring through a crack in the cloud cover. Under it, through wisps of steam-mist, the slopes glow emerald, the sand shimmers like gold.

They'll all stop there, of course, thinks the gull. Anyone would.

When the women reach the light, they collapse into it, like marathon runners finally succumbing to exhaustion in their moment of glory. At this, a signal of some kind is sent to the heavens: the gull's task has changed again. It knows what to do, it always knew. It drops, wheels, diving, swooping onto the pursuers, driving them down under beak, feet and wings, screeching, beseeching them to halt, to turn back from the light.

One attack, then up again, out of the melee to find form and shape, and back again. Two times, three times, before finally a blow is landed in defence, a grasping fist: it is not felt, but its effects are instant – there can be no fourth advance. The gull is brought to the earth, to the mire, to more fists and kicks, slips and trips. When the fighting is done, the bird lies still and watches as the dark pair pick themselves up from the mud and continue on their path, scrambling up a rise and dipping from view on the other side. The gull pursues in an awkward hobble, a broken wing trailing behind, white feathers stained red.

Find the light, it thinks. Just find the light. Keep going. Up here, up here. Up and down, into it. No pain, only warmth … ah! The light, the light. Here. Everything else is gone now – wings, legs, feet, all gone. Stay here. Stay here and watch, witness.

The woman in red lies in a heap. She has a hand clasped to the side of her head. The woman in green is down on her knees. Between them stands a man, and he is pointing at Green. No, not pointing. Aiming. The weapon appears to quiver in the man's grasp, catching the light, glistening. Green is shaking her head.

Red is crawling away now, calling something. She pushes herself up into an unsteady crouch. The man does not notice this; with his free hand, he is unfastening his coat, hurriedly fumbling at buttons and zips.

And now here comes the other dark figure, shorter, slighter – a child. He is moving in from the right, from the edge to the centre, skittering on tiptoes towards Red.

The boy's words – 'Quick, quick, quick … this is it' – are hushed, but Red seems to hear them. She meets his eyes, and her furious gaze is enough to stop him in his tracks. She raises a bloody hand – a halting gesture, then a wave, beckoning fingers, and finally an open palm. The boy seems to understand, takes a few more steps, and lays something long and heavy in Red's hand. Another weapon, of sorts. She plants the blade in the ground, heaves her weight over the handle and pushes herself upright, biting her lip as she rises, drawing a new trickle of blood.

The gunman shifts, half-turns. He sees the boy first, and his features crease into something like confusion, anger and finally shame. In the same instant, the man registers the threat emerging from his blind spot, and he seems to understand, to know his fate. The gun falls from his grasp and his mouth falls open, but no words come. Red is already swinging, an almighty effort that lifts her from her feet, sends her spinning around and down to her knees. The contact-crack echoes around them and the man crumples to the ground.

Green lets loose a piercing howl, buries her head in her hands. 'You killed him. Oh, Kathleen.'

'I did it for you.'

Silence, and all light fading, because the gull's work is done.

****

'I blacked out there.'

Pardue is back again, in part. Sight first, sound too, the roar of blood inside and the waves beyond. Feelings will follow and with them, she knows, will come pain, more even than before.

Blacked out, she said – but that's not quite right, because she knows what happened, she saw it.

Now she is moving, rising, pulled to her feet and ushered towards the beach by Saria. She submits, but turns as she goes, just to be sure – to confirm. Yes, there it is, the body, and the boy standing over it, his head cocked to one side as he takes in the soldier's sunken form – the forehead's somehow bloodless adjustment from convex to concave; the empty stare, eyes open, rolled back to whites. She watches until the boy baulks, steps away and falls in behind them.

They collapse onto sun-bathed sand, a broad crescent of it capped to the south by a rocky outcrop and to the north by something more uniform, man-made: a concrete spit that terminates in a dark cube: a Defence base. The tide is low and, at that northern end, a flock of wading birds populates the shallows, its mass fluctuating at the edges as arrivals and departures occur in clutches.

Tears gather in Saria's eyes, but her expression is firm. She clears her throat and breaks the silence. 'What are you doing here?' she asks the boy.

'We walked here.' The child stands aside from them, eyes on his toes. He shuffles his heels, drives his runners into the sand, forming deep, distorted prints. This seems to preoccupy him for a moment, before he continues, refines his answer. 'We followed you.'

'Where were you heading?'

'Dunno.' A jerk of the thumb. 'He wanted a boat, couldn't get to one. We saw you leaving the bush and … dunno. I just wanted away from him. Shadow Squad.'

'What?'

The boy cringes a little, shrugs. 'The army. Just a stupid name I gave them. The bad guys. He was a bad guy. And he didn't sleep. He uh … just never seemed to sleep. So I couldn't get away.'

'What's your name?'

'Kam.'

'Did he hurt you, Kam?'

'Not really.' The boy glances back towards the corpse. 'Hurt some others though.'

'He wanted to hurt us too.'

'You beat him. Twice. Are you okay?'

'I'll be okay.'

'Her?' He nods towards Pardue.

'Yes. Kathleen was in a war once. The Shadow Squad – it's a good name for them.'

'Look here.' He swings a bag off his shoulder and extracts the roll of papers he had held so tightly in the farmhouse: faded picture pages hanging limply from rusty staples. He unfurls the roll, smooths the pages straight and leafs through them, holding them up for Saria. 'The Shadow Squad. See?' He settles on a single-panel page. Lithe figures in masks and dark fatigues spill from the rooftops either side of a tight alleyway – dozens of them, clones dropping to the cobbles, crouched, poised to strike, their curved blades glinting under the streetlamps. He hands the book to Saria, and is rewarded with a smile.

'Yes, I see. And who's this person, in the red outfit? This is the good guy?'

'The hero. He's not exactly good. Not always.'

'Mm hmm.'

On the page, the hero thinks aloud, weighs his situation: 'Outnumbered! Take flight or fight, that's the choice. But I know something they don't!' The first assailant is dismissed with an almost nonchalant kick to the jaw, an explosion of motion marks and stars. The hero addresses his foes: 'Who's next, boys? One at a time or all together? I don't mind!'

Saria asks, 'How long were you in the camps?'

'All my life. All I can remember.'

'And your family, they're –'

'All gone.'

Saria sighs. 'Do you see over there, past the Defence base, on the horizon? You can just about make it out. That rock. That's where we're going. A safe place, we think.'

'Like a hideout.'

'Yes. Exactly. A secret base where we can hide a while.'

'How will you get there?'

'We're not sure yet. We'll work it out. Would you like to come?'

'Huh?'

'You helped us, Kam. Now maybe we can help you.'

The boy peers warily at Pardue. 'Maybe.'

Saria leans over, whispers, 'Kathleen is our hero.'

'Is she your mum?'

'Nah … although, kind of.'

Pardue lifts a hand to the cut at her temple, screws her eyes shut. When she opens them again, there are tears. The pain is here now, and it rouses her. Without looking, she asks the boy, 'Where did you get this?' She taps the cricket bat where it rests across her thighs.

'I found it. Are you all right, lady? Your head –'

'That's nothing.'

'Kathleen's tough,' Saria tells him. 'And she's a doctor.'

'What do you do?'

'I'm not sure,' concedes Saria.

'You carry her. You carried her all this way. I saw.'

'Sidekick.' Saria smiles and looks again to the distant island. 'And I can swim … a very long way.'

'All the way to that place?'

'Oh, for sure.'

'We'll be on our own there?'

Saria meets his eyes. 'Well, at some point we have to save the world. But we'll start with that little island.'

'Other people will come.'

'That's okay,' says Pardue. 'Let them come.'

'The bad people?'

Pardue runs a hand along the bat. 'Let them come too.'

The boy eyes the soldier's body again, the heap, its odd angles and edges, bulges. He grumbles something to himself, bites at his lip, and steps away towards the corpse. They turn to watch as he crouches beside the soldier and begins ferreting through pockets and pouches, shovelling items out and into his own. A pause for breath, a swallow or something suppressed. Now he grabs a shoulder, pushes, grunts, heaves, and rolls the body up and half over. He finds something underneath and pouches it before the body slams back down on his hand. Apparently satisfied, he stands, hands on hips. Finally, he delivers a swift kick to the fallen soldier's belly, and turns back towards the women.

'I found these.' He hands Saria his haul. Dried fruit and nuts, a hunk of hard bread, chocolate. 'To pay my way.'

'Pay?' Saria looks aghast. 'There's no need for that.' She snaps off a piece of the chocolate, hands it to him. One each, too, for her and Pardue.

'And this,' the boy says, consonants distorted by his slobbering and sucking. He pulls the Defence man's pistol from his waistband.

Saria frowns, is about to speak, but Pardue interrupts her, a long groan as she braces to stand. As before, she uses the cricket bat to drive herself up, until Saria places a steadying hand ready under her arm. When she has her feet, Pardue again presents to the boy an open palm; grime fills each crease in her skin, and blood now too.

The boy stutters, 'Do you … do you know how to use it?'

Pardue nods. 'You just pull the trigger.'

****

It is dusk when they arrive at the Defence base. They skirt the building, held back by the battle scars – the scorched rubble and dust – and the smell: a sharpness, traces of something chemically cleansing, injurious. There are no bodies. Instead, a row of what look like graves, earth piles evenly spaced, an orderly end to whatever occurred there. No one living remains, and the evil smell seems to be dissipating. They decide to take their chances.

A Defence gunboat lies holed and askew on its slipway, bow caught in the wash. They clamber onto the ramp and enter through the exit bay, kicking aside shell casings and shrapnel. Fire has gutted the main hall, but the roof is intact, and the rooms off are untouched. There is an empty armoury, a similarly stripped kitchen, holding cells, living quarters. They find bunks with mattresses, pillows, blankets and even towels. They peel away their sodden clothes, shivering in the transition, no care for who watches or what they see, and cocoon themselves in dry, clean swathes.

October 15: Blackout +25 Days

Pardue lies face down on the floor and instructs the boy to stand on her back, at the base of her spine. He complies in earnest silence. As she wriggles below him, manoeuvring him into position, Kam wobbles and laughs, sharp, quickly suppressed. She repeats the trick, but this time draws no response: he has set to his work, and so she does the same. Saria, sitting cross-legged before them, counts out the presses, marking ten, fifteen, twenty.

'It's better, it's improving,' Pardue snarls.

Kam asks, 'What is it?'

'I think maybe it's a bulged disc. The tissue, it's been swelling, pulsing against the nerve. This seems to help. I think I can manage it like this. Bend against the bulge. Suppress it … for the journey.'

She can't see Kam's reaction to this. Saria, she notes, offers him a reassuring wink.

Breakfast accounts for the last of their rations. Next, they explore the base and find, stuffed away in drawers and lockers, a few useful items: a pair of binoculars; life jackets; waterproofs; boots, big enough for anyone – too big; a wizened sliver of soap; candles; cans of spray paint.

The boy's scavenging skills are at once impressive and depressing. At first Pardue and Saria share wide-eyed smiles at his luck, his ability to strike gold in the most unlikely of places.

He seems to warm to the task, begins talking them through his process, like a commentator or one of his monologue-dropping heroes. But it soon becomes apparent why he is more attuned than them – this is how he has lived, he is a veteran already – and it becomes an altogether more grim exhibition.

In the afternoon they pick cockles, which are found in abundance, and a few small crabs. They bathe in a creek that runs behind the dunes, scrub their dirty clothes. All this under clear blue skies. The Dry, it seems, is upon them.

October 16: Blackout +26 Days

Pardue is awake when the boy comes to through tears and whimpers. She goes to him, but he hurries from her, dragging wet sheets behind him, and she knows better than to pursue. When he returns she takes him to the beach to forage, leaving Saria to prepare for her swim. It is a distraction and they achieve nothing. Kam walks ahead and kicks at the sand, sulking, embarrassed probably. She leaves him to it, following far behind, her focus flitting between the base and the seaward horizon, the dark rock.

The boy, she thinks, seems to run the gamut of ages. In the jerky, straight-armed way he hurls pebbles into the water, she sees a childish awkwardness. In the droop of his shoulders, his stooped gait, is a world-weary adult. She knows now that he is twelve, little older than Ariman in the desert. Could she have guessed that? Unlikely. On stature alone, she would have said younger, closer to Mark's daughter.

That little girl, what was she? Nine maybe? Do they still cry like that at nine? Of course they do. Anyone can cry like that.

Mark's daughter; that night. Pardue recalls seeing the door swing open, light spilling onto the paved driveway, and a figure stepping out, crossing the threshold, planting her feet – white socks, no shoes – with great care. The girl was bawling, snot bubbling under her nose, bursting, streaming down towards open lips. Pardue couldn't hear it, but she could imagine the sound well enough: distraught keening punctuated by sharp intakes of breath, more fuel for the fire. The girl had wobbled along the driveway to the edge of the light. She stopped there. She didn't dare proceed, perhaps, didn't dare push the boundaries further. Just stood there crying. Deeper breaths, throatier roars, and these yells Pardue could hear, even on the far side of the road and through thick glass. From her darkened car, Pardue had watched, transfixed – awestruck, envious even – by this uninhibited display of outrage and anguish. She wondered what could have triggered it. Something simple, inconsequential, a fight with the brother perhaps, a falling-out over some toy or game? Or could it be something more, a loss in the family, a pet or grandparent? Someone immediate? Maybe her pain was more abstract: a bad dream during an afternoon nap, or a child's first thoughts of existential dread – that 'how big is the universe?' moment, taking the mind to places it can't properly navigate.

As she ran through the scenarios, Pardue began to cry too: a single tear to start, the kind of natural leakage that could occur at any time in those days of dope and denial. But more had followed. A breach in the defences, salty streams that no number of sleeve smears and sniffs could stem.

And she thought, Now I've started this, I might not be able to stop; it feels so good.

The light block on the driveway grew wider, longer, then suddenly fractured. She saw Mark, an inky splodge filling the doorway. He hurried out and knelt beside the girl, wrapping her in broad arms, pulling her head towards his shoulder, nestling his nose among golden curls – over and around her, and the child happy to submit. The girl's howls were over, and the only sounds left were Pardue's own hard sobs.

She had thought, Oh, there is more goodness, more power in that gesture than in anything I have done.

Pardue's cries had turned to sour laughter. And Mark was looking straight at her then, peering across the road, brow creased in confusion, mounting concern. He pulled the girl closer, gathering her in, scooping her up and standing, turning slightly to shield her, a kiss to the head, a mouthed reassurance, and eyes locked on Pardue's. How? As he backed slowly away, his concern gave way to dismay, disgust. And still she couldn't understand it, couldn't imagine how he had seen her tucked away there in her dingy corner of the street. It made no sense – because she hadn't heard what he'd heard, or seen what he had seen: the clunk of her car door opening; the slap of a sandal hitting tarmac; the squelch of a wet sock following it; Pardue's shuffling, snuffling, moaning approach.

The light had died, the house was sealed shut. She stood alone in the middle of the road.

All she can remember after that is sirens.

Now she tells herself, It wasn't that I wanted a partner or a child in particular. It was just a connection, I needed. Would it be easier then, to do good?

For so long, she has sought an answer to that question: how can anyone do good in this world? It seems to have dominated her life, dictated – warped at times – her actions. Should you march out, place yourself in the vanguard, try to exert whatever influence fate has bestowed upon you, however puny? Ordinary people forcing change. Sometimes that seems like a fast route to madness, exasperation at the seemingly futile sacrifices required. She can vouch for that. But everything is something, the little acts do add up – that's no ego trip, no retro-rationalisation. The powerful and the malign will take their fill of lives, but everything is something in the battle against them.

She used to believe manning the barricades was the only response. Now she thinks again of Mark comforting his child, stilling her tears, shielding her from the inexplicable terrors that lay beyond the arms of family. She looks to Kam, what he has seen and what he has done, and she wonders where the breaking point is. She remembers Ariman, clinging to her mother until the very end, and she thinks of her own mother's declaration: 'It's okay, Kathleen. It's okay because you're okay.'

Is it okay? she wonders. To pull back, to strive to create some sort of enclave in this world, the horrors put out of sight and mind? Is that enough?

And how to protect these worlds – the wider world or the ones we create for ourselves? With an open palm and an appeal to better natures, a determination to rise above, no matter the consequences? Or should we hit back with amplified fury, meet fire with righteous fire, all for the greater good? Someone probably has to. Gill thought so, and here she is, alive because of it.

Once she would have called herself a pacifist. Now she has killed. And she feels nothing. Empty almost, weightless. Perhaps that's the price: one becomes hollow so others can stay whole. All that remains is this: the knowledge that she did it for Saria, and would do so again.

'Hey!'

Kam is wagging a finger, motioning to something behind her. There is no alarm in the gesture though, nor in his features. It is something more like awe. She turns to see Saria striding down the slipway, clad in silvery neoprene, exuding a cool authority, an otherworldly confidence.

****

They watch Saria leave, smooth strokes slicing through the surf, Pardue's fear receding with every effortless surge, barrelling back in when Saria can no longer be seen.

'She'll be back soon enough,' says Pardue, and the boy nods.

The time till then must be killed, minds occupied. She gives Kam a can of black paint and tells him to write their names on the side of the building – the wall facing inland. 'As big as you can manage.'

She doesn't say why, and he doesn't ask. He hesitates though, fearful maybe – of the task, or of her and her motives. The boy looks over the base, its caged windows, blast doors and rooftop gun emplacements.

Pardue repeats, 'Write it there, as big as you can. Because, you know … fuck these guys.'

That moves him, and once started he seems to relish the exercise, whether as two fingers up to a hated authority or simple delinquency without consequence. Pardue takes some satisfaction in it too, but really it is a message not to foes but to friends. Should they wind up at this bay for want of anywhere else to turn, they will understand.

'What do you think's happening out there?' Kam nods to the sea, the island. Playtime is over, and the weight is on him again.

'She'll find a route up the rocks. A route we can all take; I'm the weakest … but not too weak. If the home's unoccupied, she'll take stock: equipment and supplies, what's there, what's not. Then back to us. If there's food out there, we'll all go tomorrow. Lash ourselves together, wrap up in life-jackets and whatever else floats. It won't be easy. But look what we've come through already.'

'She'll be there by now.'

'She will.'

Pardue chooses to believe that, to indulge in the kind of unshakeable faith that flourishes between friends, and to shun a mother's sense of powerlessness amid the wealth of worst cases.

And she allows herself to dream, to draw the scene as Saria may see it. She imagines her clambering up boulders, scaling the rock wall, cresting the lip, past shell piles, pebbles and scrub, away from salt and onto earth: grass, wildflowers, trees. Natives and then … a garden: apples, lemons and limes. Through these onto a lawn, rabbits scurrying at the sound of her footfalls. The house, whitewashed walls, vines running up them. A greenhouse just visible behind the home, a shed and rows of wooden planter boxes. A rainwater tank, generator. The front door is locked, of course, but Saria forces up a sash window and slides through onto a kitchen counter, white marble. Cupboards hold packets, jars and cans: pasta, passata, preserves, other long-life odds and ends saved for future visits. There are cookbooks and gardening guides, a copper pot over a wood stove. Beside this, a pile of kindling, firelighters. In the corridor Saria finds a glass cabinet, hunting rifles standing tall, polished wood and metal. Now she is through onto carpet, a lounge, couch and armchairs, shelves stacked with antique books. A fireplace and heavy curtains.

Pardue knows she should stop, but it is easier thought than done. She can't help herself, so she doubles down on the fantasy. She imagines a life there, an actual life, months and years passing. Saria and the boy learning to live and grow in their new world, and her manning the defences, scouring their surroundings for friend or foe.

Stop.

Maybe, she thinks, we're making a huge mistake. We should stay on KI and see what happens here. Maybe the detainees will win the day, seize control and make something of this place. Something out of the ashes.

But she knows this is probably fantasy too: the bosses and their soldiers will regroup, or more will arrive, and more violence with them.

So they have to go. Evacuate, get off this rock and onto that one: their enclave. Kam says others will follow them there. Probably they will. Let them come, with good intentions or otherwise, and she will meet them in kind. Out there on the ocean, that will be their world for now. She claims it, a land to save, to shape and protect together. A place of sanity amid the madness. A place of peace and love.

www.ingramcontent.com/pod-product-compliance
Lightning Source LLC
Chambersburg PA
CBHW030619120726
47904CB00006B/1961